Dog Days of Winter

A. Sleeper

ISBN: **978-0991366712**

For my mom. For believing in me.

ACKNOWLEDGMENTS

To anyone who's over-heard me talking about murder in diners, bathrooms, department stores, or proper holiday dinners and didn't know whether or not to call the police.

Thanks for not calling the police.

"'Dog Days' (Latin: diēs caniculārēs) are the hottest, most sultry days of summer. In the northern hemisphere, they usually fall between early July and early September. ... The Romans sacrificed a red dog in April to appease the rage of Sirius, believing that the star was the cause of the hot, sultry weather."

  - Wikipedia.org

Run fast for your mother and fast for your father
Run for your children for your sisters and brothers
Leave all your love and your longing behind you
Can't carry it with you if you want to survive

  - Florence and the Machine, "Dog Days are Over"

PROLOGUE

It was such a silly idea, but he loved it. He was walking her through green trails. The warm spring breeze of May had tumbled her hair about and in the comforting coolness of the forest, sunset dapples played over her sweet blonde locks. She had that smile he'd fallen in love with spread across her face as she followed him, her wrist held in his hand. His other hand brushed over the lump in his front jean pocket just to make sure, for the umpteenth time, that it was still there. That it was real. He was going to do it and he was going to change both of their lives forever.

"Slow down, Trent. Where are we going?"

He didn't answer her. She would find out soon. The woods weren't all that big and he'd known the perfect place for such a long time. Bugs flew up in buzzing clouds as they made their way through the brush. Over roots and rocks and patches of grass. The trail, he knew, would lead right where he wanted to be. It was almost dusk and the forest was becoming dark. The sounds of night were beginning and his eyes would have to soon adjust. They had to get there before the sun went down or he would be doing this by the light of his two flashlights he'd brought along for the walk back.

The light was orange and brilliant colors filled the sky when they came upon the opening to the clearing that he'd been waiting for. A large red tower stood in the center as a solid remnant of some past technology.

He stopped for just a moment to soak in the reality of what he was about to do before he pulled her forward and turned around, walking backward and gripping both of her hands in his.

"Trent?" The question in her eyes had more to it than just the simple, "What are you doing?" that would have been bearable. It was deeper than that. She knew what he was going to do but she wasn't sure if she could handle it. Right now, anyway. Right when he was in the middle of such a nerve-racking case. Right when he was trying to prove himself to the world by capturing more than just someone's errant boyfriend or the next dirty cop. When he was trying to avoid working for an insurance company investigating shady claims as if they were exciting. He couldn't pretend that he was interested in any of that.

It had always been murder that had been on his mind. So when the opportunity presented itself, he took it. When a high school track star had finally lost his goddamn mind, it was Trent Winston on the case.

He hadn't banked on it taking so long. Being so hard. He hadn't thought a teenage kid could be so fucking *tricky*. Not to mention so fucking *insane*. He hadn't thought that anyone could have been human one moment and transformed into a ruthless, disturbed animal—a mad dog—the next.

But all of that was pushed aside when he thought about Grace and the way she moved and the way she held him in the middle of the night. A hard breeze tumbled her honey hair to one side and the question in her gray-blue eyes remained. She squeezed his hands and he looked down at them for a moment before looking back up at her. It seemed to take him forever to get down on one knee, but he did manage it.

A strange feeling overcame him. A nameless dread. He swallowed. Something was wrong. Was it the look in her eyes? Was it the way she held his hands? He brought his hand down to his pocket and pulled out the small black velvet box and held it in three fingers.

He never did get it open.

He felt as though he were getting hit by a truck and it was all in slow motion. The box flew out of his hand and he was suddenly on his back, driven backwards so hard that he was skidding across the grass. It hadn't helped that his center of gravity had been skewed and his balance was off from being on one knee. It hadn't helped that he hadn't actually listened to his gut when it told him something was wrong. It didn't help that there was a one-hundred and eighty pound *rottweiler* on top of him.

There was a loud rending sound and he was suddenly out of his mind, thrashing and struggling with all of his might. He couldn't possibly be so weak, could he? He couldn't possibly be so helpless against some *kid*. Some *smug, punk-ass track star*. He vaguely recognized that he was yelling—screaming more like. There was blood everywhere, splattering and spraying and suddenly he was alone again. He was on his feet in a matter of seconds.

And then he wasn't. He was on his knees. He touched his chest. Blood was pouring out of him. His rear hit his feet and he fell backwards again and there was a ringing in his ears. But not a ringing. A screaming. A constant screaming.

Grace.

CHAPTER 1

THREE YEARS LATER

What was there left to do but dig toes into the cooling North Carolina sand and cross fingers? Tomi put her hands in the pockets of her khaki shorts and took in a deep breath of ocean air through her nose. The sun was setting. The sand was almost cold. The tide was out and a few small patches of darkened driftwood were scattered along the deserted beach. She relished the white noise of the ocean waves as they crashed just off shore. There was an odd discordant note in the blonde's senses, as if it were possible that the waves were somehow *off* in their rhythm. The wind rustled the sea oats behind her on the dunes and blew some of her hair into her face. She didn't bother trying to tuck it behind her ears again. Such actions were useless.

Darkness was gathering over the waves. It was hard to tell the difference between the thunder of the waves and the thunder of the skies. Lightning forked across the dark sky, leaving fading imprints in her eyes. When she turned around toward the dunes it was with purpose. She barely noticed the sting of the sea oats as they whipped across her bare arms on her way back to her seaside home. Her mother and father would be asleep by now but Tomi had no intention of joining them in slumber. There was too much fire in her heart for that. She stomped down the sandy path back to the tall house with too many decks and too many stairs and too many everything. She could see the reflection of light from the flashes behind her on the white paint of the decks. Only the light in her room was on. It was the only light she'd need.

By the time morning had come she had glossed over her nails with two coats of clear polish, picked out exactly the pair of shoes she thought she looked best in, and packed the necessities of life into her bag. With a finger nail against her nose and her bottom lip sucked in, she wondered just how long she'd be gone. Gone. The word was brilliant. The concept was beautiful. She giggled. A box of tampons. Tiny bottles of everything. Shampoo, conditioner, mouthwash, toothpaste, deodorant, body spray. 550 dollars of Daddy's money he'd given her for her birthday instead of a puppy. He hadn't known what breed to buy so he'd just put the money in a card. She rolled up about half of it and put it in a secret compartment in the lining of the bag that she'd sewn herself. She sucked in her lip again.

The words they'd said were ringing in her ears. The scent of the chicken her mother Gina was cooking was fresh in her memory. Her chicken had brought scores of people together. Sometimes Tomi thought that the only reason the neighbors came to the summer shindigs was for the chicken. There were a lot of parties, but not the kind most might think of when the word "party" was implemented. No. They were more like gatherings of snobs so they could bask in the snobbery of the others without feeling like they were amongst the dregs of society. You know, like the way they felt among the "common" people. Tomi nearly gagged at the thought of having to bear one more of Mr. Morack's "accidental" perverted back-of-the-hand brushes against her ass. The words they'd said... She shook her head.

She wouldn't be gone so long. The longest she'd be gone was the summer. Right? Assuming nothing catastrophic happened to her from Point A to Point B. It could happen. Her brows knitted a little while her mind went through all the reasons she shouldn't be leaving. Dad. Mom. Pet-sitting customers. Risks. That was what got her every time. How many times could she stop herself from doing something because she convinced herself of all the risks? How many times could she keep herself miserable? She turned and walked into the bathroom where she

5

applied some "Precious Pink" lipstick before she threw it in her bag.

She packed a t-shirt and shorts as well. Small items that wouldn't take up too much room. She took a deep breath and held it in for a couple seconds before looking out the window and sinking down into a plush chair. When she opened her eyes the sky was orange and the breeze coming in through her window was brisk. Goosebumps rose on her legs and she tossed a razor into her bag. Another thing she'd forgotten. She vowed that it was the last thing she'd be shoving into that bag.

Turned out that at 7:00 in the morning, when the sun was just beginning to warm the pavement under her sling-backed sandal wedges, Tomi was tapping down the shoulder of the road toward the bus stop while sucking on the tiny straw of a juice box. Her bag was slung over her shoulder. It was a bench. Just a singular bench that looked lost on the side of the road without other purpose. It might have splinters and it might be falling apart. The rails and legs might be rusted iron. The flakes might get on her skirt. She didn't care. There was too much to leave for. Too much she needed to do without her parents in the way. When she got there, there were indeed rusted rails and legs. There was also a strange obstacle she hadn't foreseen.

He was sleeping there. His hair was wet from the slight shower that had passed around six o'clock. Just an hour ago. His head was to the side, resting a cheek on his shoulder and his legs were jutting out from the bench with the outward sides of his Chuck Taylors resting on the ground. His hands were resting on either side of him with his palms facing up. His drawstring backpack was beside him. She expected him to snore at any moment.

She sat next to him and pulled her phone out of her bag.

It was very soon that he woke up. He didn't stretch; he just opened his eyes, blinked a few times, and looked over at her. She ignored him. He tilted his head a little bit. She could feel him studying her. His eyes were uncomfortable on her face and body, like little pinpricks over the skin of her cheeks and shoulders. His gaze was only upon her for a few seconds but she felt the bizarre pricks lingering over her while he strained his head the other way, looking for the bus.

He blurted a single phrase after a few moments. The sound of his voice gave her goosebumps. Or maybe it was just the ocean breeze that had blown past them. No. It was most definitely his voice. "Pink lipstick."

"Excuse me?"

"Pink lipstick, it's funny, 'cause it doesn't match anything else you have. You probably should have matched it with your shoes."

Her cheeks might have turned as pink as her lipstick and her brows came together. Did he just insult her? About her lipstick? She looked down at her shoes then back up at him indignantly. "Would you suggest the makeup first and match the shoes or the shoes first and match the makeup?" After she'd said it she couldn't believe she'd fed into this nonsense. If she hadn't said anything, if she'd ignored him, would he have left her alone?

"No need for sass, you don't need makeup anyway."

She was suddenly taken aback. She murmured her reply. "Thank you."

He looked at his hands as if fascinated by them for a few moments before he shrugged and replied, "Well you know. What're you all dressed up for anyway?"

It wasn't part of Tomi's nature to tell half-truths but this one didn't warrant a rant. She sucked down the rest of her juice box before telling him, "I'm going to visit someone."

"Oh, well good. He'll love your mismatched lipstick, it'll be great." There was a tinge of something ugly in his voice. Something like jealousy. It was surprise that rippled through her then.

She ground her teeth together. This stranger had begun yet again to grate on her nerves. Before she could say anything more, he started speaking again. This time there was more acid in his voice.

"Yep, he'll love it. Just wanna kiss it right off, he'll love it so much."

Oh for the love of Pete. She narrowed her eyes. This loser on a bus stop bench with wet black hair (with some other color at the tips but she was too distracted to really comprehend it, as it was dark as well) thought she was going to visit her boyfriend. It was possible that she looked like she would be going to see a boyfriend. Clad in a black pencil skirt, red heels, a black spaghetti strap, and a white blouse. Business dress. Professional. Date worthy? Perhaps.

She ground out, "Are you baiting me?"

His smile vanished, "What?"

She shook her head and anger bubbled up in her throat, "Are you trying to make me slap you? I will slap you, I'm not usually a pretty pretty princess, I *will* slap some stupid ass jerk on a park bench. Who do you think you are that you can just talk to people like that?!" Her cheeks were very vividly pink and her voice shook at the end.

He sat straight up and put his chin up. He looked to be just a bit older than she. Maybe eighteen. Just a boy. He looked haggard and yet still amused. "Slap me."

"What?"

"You heard me. Slap me."

She sputtered, "No."

He shrugged and turned away, "Well you said you would."

"Not if you *want* it."

The bus had impeccable timing. When the hydraulics of the doors hissed open she boarded quickly and sat on one side of the bus while he sat on the other. She gave him a wary glance and he flashed her a sly grin. He was smug, the pretentious ass. When she turned away and looked out the window with her bag clutched against her chest, he was gone from her mind, lost somewhere in the back of it perhaps. Right now she thought about her brother. And the words they'd said...

It was only about thirty minutes later after she'd daydreamed her way into thinking about her lipstick that she looked back at the boy. He was sleeping again with his head against the window and his feet up on the seat. She gently touched her lips with her fingers and wondered exactly what he was getting at.

It wasn't that she hated him or anything. It was just that she was tired of being so ho-hum. She was a boring girl. There was no way to get around that. But maybe once in her life she could do something that wasn't boring at all. Other than running away from home to find her brother of course. Or whatever she was really doing. She wasn't sure quite where she was going. Just a general idea. That wasn't boring at all, was it? So this was her chance to be even more interesting. She liked the idea of being interesting.

She put her feet down off the gray bus seat and straightened her clothes, reaching up and pulling the cord to get the bus to stop. The driver looked over his shoulder at her with a brow raised but didn't question her. She slid quietly over and stood, teetering on her heels when the bus finally made its stop.

"Hey," she smiled as she shook him slightly and patted his head. "Hey, hun, you getting off?"

He groggily stood up and she pulled him up and off the bus, a grin spread across her pretty face. "Where...?" he asked as he looked around, still half asleep.

The bus pulled away and she waved goodbye to it, giggling to herself. "Come on, dear, we'll just be walking this way."

Tomi couldn't recall being this mean before, but revenge seemed to be the only logical course of action. She tapped down the side of deserted road as he looked around behind her, trying to regain his bearings. He was ragged, sleep deprived, and obnoxious. Yet he wasn't homeless. Or at least, he hadn't been. Tomi peeked over her shoulder at him as he rubbed his eyes with the heels of his hands and began walking after her.

When he found himself again he jogged to catch up with her and when he was beside her he blessed her with a small chuckle. "You tricked me."

She sounded amused. "I did trick you, I hope you've accepted it as my revenge for your terrible teasing."

"I accept it," he grinned and they walked together for a small while as he remained blissfully silent. After a small while he looked at her but she chose to ignore him. Without another word he drifted away from her and disappeared into the woods. She looked after him but he had seemingly evaporated into the foliage. Alone, she allowed her mind to wander while she walked.

The words they'd said haunted her again. *What are you talking about, sweetheart?* Like she was stupid. Like she was five. Like she didn't understand what they were doing. She took a deep breath and whispered to herself. "Don't talk to me like that." She could smell her mother's chicken again. She wouldn't miss that smell. It was good, it was really good, but she wouldn't miss it. Her mother's blue eyes were trained on her. She really was the model of a mother. The model mother for the world. Had to be. *No, of course not. You couldn't possibly do that.* Couldn't possibly visit him. Couldn't possibly ever again talk to the only damn person in her life that really understood everything about her. Couldn't possibly talk to the only person who gave a crap about what she wanted. Her father finally put in his two cents. That was the straw, the last one, you know. *No, you don't even have a brother.*

She was holding her breath again. She let it out. She tried to pull her thoughts out of that cold air-conditioned kitchen. Sitting at the kitchen table while the night threatened to break through the windows, the too-bright lights on over her head, the only thing keeping her out of the dark. Her mother wasn't really looking at her while she was talking but her father was paying almost too much attention. His eyes were also blue, but a pale blue. There was no life in them. There was cold hard determination and competition, but no real life.

I just want to see him. I miss him. It wasn't anything too desperate but the feeling in her heart had been just about to burst. The immediate answer was no. No. Always always always no. The image of a politician's daughter was too precious to mar it with being associated with *him.* As if he wasn't her brother. As if he wasn't even human. As if all the years of growing up with him had been nothing but a lie.

She gritted her teeth. Bo wasn't some figment of her imagination. He was her brother. *Her brother.* Tomi could feel hot tears and fought them. *You don't even have a brother.*

Her cell phone rang. The charming jingles wafted up out of her bag and she looked down into it. She almost put her hand in it. Almost. The wind blew her hair in her face and she smoothed it back, tucking it behind her ear while she ignored the jingle.

When she turned her gaze down the road a ways her heart

dropped into her bowels.

Red and blue flashing lights were pulled over. So was the bus. The jingling stopped and she looked around herself. No other cars were coming up from behind her. The woods were dense on both sides of the road.

For a few seconds she just stood on the side of the road, staring at the flashing lights and the stopped bus. Was that for her? Was that to find her? Was the bus speeding? There were too many possibilities. With a quick glance again behind her, she tapped her way across the road and picked through the tall grasses to crouch down in the woods where she could watch the lights and wait for them to leave. The foliage tickled her bare ankles and she crossed her fingers that she wasn't camping out in a batch of poison ivy.

It felt like too long of a wait until the bus pulled away and the lights were shut off but the Crown Vic wasn't leaving. It was just sitting there by the side of the road. Tomi was puzzled. Were they really waiting for her? Had the bus driver told them that she'd gotten off with a very confused young man and started walking in the middle of nowhere?

Her revenge suddenly seemed very foolish, but it had certainly saved her from going back sooner. There was no way she was going to let herself be taken back. A hard determination filled her and reminded herself of her father. Well. It was about time he had a taste of it. After all, the apple couldn't have fallen too far from the tree. It was about time Tomi got exactly what she wanted through her own right. She gritted her teeth.

She almost peed her panties when she was grabbed from behind. She jumped and stifled a scream while the boy laughed at her. Anger bubbled in her throat.

"What in the hell are you doing?" she whispered.

"Maybe I should ask you the same thing." He was clearly still tickled by getting the best of her. He should be, he'd moved around in the woods like a deer, completely silent. That was most certainly something to be proud of, sneaking up on someone like her.

"I'm trying to wait until that cop leaves," she explained. "I would expect that you would do the same."

He gave her an odd stare. "I didn't know you were a runaway."

"Aren't you?"

He shrugged. "In a way." He hunkered down next to where she'd been and peered out at the cruiser that was still parked along the side of the road. "Well good luck getting past that."

"What?"

"Well you can't just wander around a forest in four inch heels can you, miss pretty pretty princess? So good luck waiting for him to leave."

"Who says I can't?" Her cheeks were pink from both the heat and his insensitivity.

"I say." He smirked at her. His hair had mostly dried and she could see the color that had previously been lost to her. It was red. A dark red. The clumps that were still wet looked the color of blood. It hung in front of his eyes a little. He had pronounced collarbones under the straps of his tank-top.

His shoulders were freckled. So was the area across the bridge of his nose. They were the kind of freckles that boys should have grown out of by now. His eyes were blue, but she didn't equate that with any of the blue eyes she'd had experience with. Her blue eyes were clear and pure, her father's cold and distant, her mother's just clueless. His were dark. Almost hard to tell they were blue at first, and sharp. His eyes were serious and experienced. Tomi suddenly felt naive.

"I think I'll be just fine," she said. She didn't really know.

"Well you're running from something, it's about time you made the decision about what you can lose to get away." He turned around and started walking away through the trees.

She stared at him. How bizarre. How could he be so strange? Willing to lose everything? Was it really that simple? Just kick off the heels and start walking down some dirt path through pines and leave all her worrying in the past? Definitely not. She kept them on. He wasn't waiting for her. She'd have to make the decision by herself. Not that making decisions had ever been particularly hard but this one seemed to be just ever so slightly…life-changing. She scraped the dirt with the tip of her shoe.

She looked down at the red sling backs and then up at his back, getting further and further away from her through the green of the trees. She saw him hesitate a little and then stop. He stood that way for some time before he looked over his shoulder at her. The sunlight dappled the ground around him and splayed brilliant light over his face. When she didn't move, he started again to walk away. Tomi finally found herself walking. The shoes were still on. She stumbled a few times but managed to rescue herself several times before she practically fell into his back.

He turned and caught her wrists, pulling her up. It was a wonder she hadn't twisted an ankle or scraped a knee. "You're a tad bit reckless, aren't you?" he asked.

Tomi took a few steps back after he let go of her arms and smiled a little. "Maybe."

"Well good. Let's get to it." One side of his lips stretched to make a fairly lop-sided grin. "Me and Miss Fancy Pants, on the road."

She frowned, "Don't call me that."

"Oh, sorry, forgive me, what was your name again?"

"Tomi," she stuck up her chin.

"Tomi. Tomi, of the Miss Priss class with the mismatched lipstick and shoes. You know red really just isn't your color."

"And what is?"

"I like your lipstick better."

She blew a strand of hair out of her face while they started walking. "Can't you be more poetic or something?"

"I could be a little less blunt." He tilted his head again as if he were listening to someone say something profound. She looked around, there was nothing out of the ordinary, no sounds to even be listening for. His head snapped back up and he chuckled, "*And keep you in the rear of your affection, out of the shot and danger of desire. The chariest maid is prodigal enough, if she unmask her beauty to the moon.*"

She turned from him with a whisk of her hair and walked away, picking her way through the woods again and he followed.

They were silent for quite a while after that. The dapples of sunlight became fewer and the shade of the woods was a relief to the stunning heat that was outside of this sanctuary. Birds twittered overhead and the leaves rustled. She stumbled plenty of times in her heels and each time she did he would give her a disappointed look as if to tell her she just should have taken them off the time before. She was almost a walking disaster with the four inch wedges on but she convinced herself that if the fictional Carrie Bradshaw could walk anywhere with heels on, then so could she. Her companion seemed unimpressed by her determination.

When she tripped again it was worse than a stumble and she reached out her hands to grab anything. She ended up with his arm and then his hand. After she'd pulled herself up again, she was still holding it. She let go as if she'd been shocked by a strong current. He looked at his hand and then back at her before he started walking again, shaking his head.

"What?" she asked him, still standing where she'd recovered.

He turned around and his head made the tilting motion again. His eyes rolled up as if he were looking into the trees. She looked behind her but couldn't see anything. When she turned her head back around he was staring at her, his head straight. Odd. Very odd. He spoke. "Nothing."

"Nothing my butt," she replied. "You shook your head at me."

"And you acted like you'd touched a snake. Are my hands dirty?" He'd said "dirty" with a certain emphasis as if it meant something else to him. Not as if he were thinking of soil but something worse. Tomi wrinkled her nose.

"I don't know." She lifted her head to look down at him. "Are they?"

He put his hands up in a gesture of surrender. "How long are you going to follow me?"

"However long you tolerate me."

His hands flopped to his sides. "Then take those goddamn shoes off before I do it myself."

She took them off without breaking eye contact with him and slipped them into her bag. "Are you quite alright with this now? I don't even know why I did this for you," she spat, "I don't even know your name."

He pulled a pack of cigarettes out of his pocket, the pack bright yellow. He lit it with a pink lighter and took a long drag. After he'd blown out the smoke he responded, "Ren."

"How old are you?" she asked, watching the tip of his cigarette burn.

"Old enough."

"Oh."

"If you please, your majesty," he motioned with his arm for her to get moving. The bright red tips of his hair dangled in front of his eyes and must have tickled the bridge of his nose. He didn't seem to notice.

The whole day was spent walking and it took them a little while to pick through the sometimes very dense foliage. They attempted to stay away from the road but in some cases the trees were much too thick to do anything but go around them. It was nearly dusk when she felt the first prick of a mosquito.

"Ow," she slapped the thing on her arm, her blood seeping from its smashed belly. "Great, bugs. Just wonderful. I need to get to some civilization or I am just going to scream."

"Oi, Miss Priss, I thought you were a runaway. You're not going anywhere close to civilization. Even the dumbest hotel clerk will call a 16 year old in for trying to rent out a room."

"Then where are we going to sleep?" she asked with her lips pursed together.

He gave her a little grin. "There's a factory town a few miles down this road. When the factory closed the homes were foreclosed by the bank. They're all boarded up now. We'll camp out in one of those."

She rolled her eyes, "I can't believe I've been reduced to this."

"How badly would you like to actually make it where you wanted to go?"

Her cell phone started to ring again and his sharp blue eyes flitted toward her bag. She dug it out and looked at the screen. Cayley. No doubt they were trying to get her to tell them where she was going. Not that Cayley knew. They were just hoping that Cayley could find out.

"If you're really serious," he leveled his eyes at her, "You'll get rid of that phone."

She gasped, "What?" She held the jingling device to her chest. "I can't get rid of my phone, what if there's an emergency?"

"There's a global positioning chip in the back of it. It'll give away your location by at least a mile or two. Your parents probably haven't contacted your service provider yet. It hasn't even been long enough to issue any kind of missing persons report."

She stared at her phone, Cayley's name in white letters as a missed call. Her mother had called her earlier. The first missed call. There would be many, she thought as the phone started ringing again.

"Silence it," he casually demanded, and she put it on vibrate. She liked to know that there were people out there who cared about her. At least people who wanted to make sure she was alive. It whirred in her bag for awhile when they walked but the calls died off after about an hour. Was that all it took for them to admit to themselves that she was gone? An hour? She sniffed a little and Ren's cold eyes turned on her. "What's wrong?" His voice was distant and emotionless. It was simple curiosity that drove his inquiry.

"It's nothing," she replied. "Stupid girl things."

"Definitely not my area of expertise," he graced her with a little grin.

She smiled at him. "I don't think anyone really knows what women are all about, so you're probably on the right track." She sighed. "You said you were a runaway."

"Of sorts," he reminded her.

"Of sorts. Okay. Does anyone miss you?"

His smile was the warmest she'd seen from him. "Yes."

"How do you know?"

"I just do." He put a hand through his hair and rustled it. "They were my best friends. They miss me. It wouldn't be natural for them to simply accept my absence without thinking about my health or safety."

She had to think for a few moments before she said in a careful tone, "Is it unnatural to have friends who aren't really your friends?"

He raised an eyebrow. "What do you mean?"

"I don't think my friends really liked me very much. I mean. I suppose sitting at the same lunch table doesn't really mean you're friends.

16

We didn't do much together other than go to the beach every so often. And they would come over and use my pool. But I don't think they were ever my friends. We didn't have secrets that we shared together."

"Maybe if you weren't such a fancy pants you'd have more friends," he shrugged.

"I'm not a fancy pants," she snapped. "I just don't think they liked me very much." She whipped her hair back and lifted her chin again. "Besides, it doesn't matter since I'm leaving."

"Yeah and now you just have to tolerate me," he poked her shoulder to bring her chin down a little. "Don't worry sweetheart, you might be an insufferable bitch but I'll make do."

She slapped his arm and glared at him while he laughed.

It only took them another hour to get to one of the houses he was talking about. The whole neighborhood was desolate. The deteriorating houses stood about in a tree-less environment. She felt almost naked without the forest around them for cover. They were the only living beings in a darkening world as the sun had just barely slipped below the horizon and had cast an unnatural and eerie light over them. It turned the front of one particular house into a yawning monster with the door kicked in. Tomi instinctively sidled closer to her mysterious companion, his warmth and pleasant scent comforting.

"This one looks okay." He took her hand for the first time, his soft palm surprising her a little. His hand was firm and warm and he led her closer to a home that had seen better days. A few toys were strewn around the yard as if it had been vacated in a hurry. The head of a Cabbage Patch doll stared at her from the grass. He turned the handle but found it locked and he looked around before putting his ear to the door.

"What are you doing?" she whispered.

"Trying to find out if there are squatters here. I don't want to break in on someone already here. That, princess, is a very dangerous thing to do."

A panic suddenly gripped her. It was night and she was going to walk into an abandoned house with a stranger she had just met that day. Never mind the squatters that might be in the house, she was going to be spending the night with a boy who could most likely hold her down easily, or knock her out, or drug her. Would he do such a thing? She searched his face for any kind of hint as to his intentions but she could only see his concentration. She took a few steps back and looked out toward the rest of the neighborhood. Nobody lived here. Nobody could hear her scream if he tried to kill her. He had convinced her to follow him here—to a place where he could do dirty things to her. She started breathing a little harder, panic coursing through her.

"I think it's good." He licked his lips before wandering over to one of the windows in the front. There was the sound of glass breaking and he was gone for a few moments. She contemplated sprinting. Her eyes roved over the darkening world around her. A world of vacant old homes. Frightening possibilities. How had she ever gotten herself into this situation? Why did she have to be so dumb? He was staring at her from the dark doorway. "Coming in, my lady?"

Her mouth opened but she tripped on her words. Tears pricked her eyes.

"Afraid of the dark?" He tilted his head and chuckled at himself.

"This is going to sound stupid," she choked out, "but I don't wanna die."

His expression was unreadable, a mixture of confusion and disdain. "Woman, what the shit are you talking about? Did I miss something?"

"I don't think I can go in there with you."

"Why not?"

"What if..."

He took a step onto the porch and she took a step back. He paused and put his hands out, palms up, a surrender. "What if what, darlin'?"

"What if you don't have the best of intentions?"

"And what is it that I would not have the best of intentions about?" He was mocking her now, his cold eyes frightened her. His lips moved backward over his teeth and bared them. Too many teeth for a human

18

being, she thought with horror. Too many teeth for anything alive. Maybe a shark, maybe a human shark.

She closed her eyes against his inhuman grimace and gave a small "eep." The sound that she thought could have been her last. She was sure he was going to open up his mouth and swallow her whole. Is that not what monsters did? Is that not what the boogeyman was meant to do? Surely he could not be human. Surely he had to be something else. She heard a small click and she gave another small "eep" when she flinched away from the sound.

"Tomi," his deep voice said. It was a demand. He took her hand but she ripped it away and stumbled backward off the porch. He laughed. The sound sent a shudder down her spine. "Tomi, open your eyes."

"No," she whispered. Her mind had conjured the most disgusting being she could let it and of course it was complete with a gaping maw poised to rip her apart.

"Please," he said. Again it was not a suggestion.

She cracked open an eye. He was still on the porch. He was still human-looking. He was holding something out to her. Something red.

"Take it. If it'll make you feel better you can even try it out to make sure there's some still in there."

It was mace. She blinked and realized that she had been stiff, her hands at her sides. For a moment all she could do was stare at the small red tube in his hand. It was attached to a black strap that was meant to be a keychain. "What...?"

"So you don't have to worry about me or anyone else." His face was relaxed, normal-looking. "That shit will clear a room so if you want to try it out be sure to do it out here, away from my eyeballs please."

She reached out and took it, curiously touching it and examining it. Pointing it away from the house she gave it a tentative squirt before locking it and unlocking it a few times to make sure she knew how. When she turned back around she found him still on the porch with a flashlight in his hand. "Thank you," she mumbled.

"You really didn't think about that until we got here?" The side of his mouth was tilted upward and she shivered when she saw his teeth.

She wanted to say something mean or witty or just plain explanatory but she found that no matter how hard she might have tried, words would not come. She was too fixated on his teeth. Would mace even stop him?

"Come on, sweetheart, it's gonna get cold you know."

This brought her forward and she passed him into the house. He clicked on his flashlight behind her and the door squeaked closed. The mace was tight in her hand and she had it unlocked. Just in case he might pounce from behind. Instead he moved away from her into the kitchen area where he put down his backpack on one of the dusty countertops. From it he extracted a thin sweatshirt which he put on, about three fat candles which he promptly lit with a small book of matches, and two Slim Jims, one of which he passed to her.

"How many times have you done this?" she asked, her eyes narrowing on him.

He seemed to contemplate the question a little before answering, "I plead the fifth. Now," he took two of the candles and turned to move toward a doorway that led to the living room, or what could have been a living room if there had been any furniture. As it was there was just a dirty little dresser in the corner which he put the candles on. He then grabbed his pack and sat down on the floor. She hesitantly followed, her eyes studying his features in the candle light.

"Come on, princess, do you know how to play Canasta?"

She shook her head and he patted the floor.

After just over an hour she was soundly beating him in their odd two-player card game and he had her perfectly giggling. His real and true smile was spread across his face and made him look even charming in the soft flickering yellow light.

His smile was gone in an instant when his head picked up and he put a finger up to stop her giggles. With fluid movements he blew out the two candles by them and he got up to do the same with the one in the kitchen. She was suddenly plunged into darkness. She could hear the rats chewing inside the walls.

"Ren?" she whispered. She couldn't hear him in the room with her but she could hear the sound of a car. No headlights came through the window and her heart started pounding. She crept to the window and peeked out of it. An old Honda Accord was creeping through the neighborhood with its lights off, the only way to see being the light of the half moon that shined through a cloudless sky. "Ren?" she whispered louder.

"Yes," he whispered back, "I'm here. I don't think they saw us."

"What do they want?"

"They're probably just vandals. I locked the door. Most times they won't bother with a locked door. They're looking for an easy break." He gathered up the decks of cards from the floor and put them back inside two paper cases, not bothering to sort out the two mixed decks. It was just as he was putting everything into his pack that there was a loud bang from the front door.

Tomi's heart suddenly jammed itself into her throat and Ren stood stock still, his head facing the front of the house. Another loud bang and he flung his pack onto his back and took her hand roughly in his. "They're trying to break down the door, come on." He didn't have to ask twice. Her bare feet slapped against linoleum as they bolted across the kitchen and he ripped open a door. With a click of his flashlight she found herself facing the darkest set of basement stairs she thought she'd ever seen. It seemed to swallow up the feeble light of his small flashlight but he urged her down the stairs anyway. He closed the door behind them as another loud bang sounded and Tomi gave a frightened jump.

"Come here, sweets," he said at the bottom of the stairs when her feet hit cold concrete. He picked her up in remarkably strong arms and took her across the basement to a small hiding place behind the water heater. Once there he put her down and pressed her into the corner, turning his back toward her and peeping around toward the blackness of the basement.

She could barely see him even though he was right in front of her. His outline was only apparent when her eyes could adjust and the scarce light from the small windows at the top of the basement could provide her with his form. He was trying to protect her, her brain supplied. Her fingers found the mace that was clipped to the side of her skirt and she held its heaviness in her hand. She unlocked it and took a deep breath.

Another bang from the front door. It was sharper, like they were using an object. Ren never flinched. Even when the door was obviously busted open he remained a solid rock in his place with his arms out on the walls enclosing them. He was immovable.

The sounds of aggressive vandalism echoed through the empty house. Cabinets being smashed in, the wooden countertop ravaged, the loud shush of spray paint. Tomi trembled behind him. Was there reason for them to look in the basement?

"Do you need the mace?" she whispered to him. He didn't move.
"No."

His voice gave her a deep and profound shudder. He didn't need the mace. Of course he didn't. Her mind flitted back to his teeth, that horrifying grimace that had made her sure he wasn't human. He was a predator.

Time seemed to move in slow motion as they heard them move from one side of the house to the other, busting down walls and spray painting everything in their path. Finally it became relatively quiet and Tomi started to breathe a little easier. She'd relaxed too soon, she realized as the door to the basement squealed open. Ren's body tightened like a bow string. Steps came down the stairs and she heard someone whisper, "Fuck it's dark down here."

That was his element. She watched Ren slowly crouch down like a panther, using the dark to his own advantage. For a few moments she was afraid for the vandals. It was irrational, she knew. But it didn't stop her from fearing for them. They were about to be eaten after all. By this creature she had somehow found herself with. She watched his body move with a speed she could never have matched. There were scuffles and a strangled yell. A voice called down from the stairs.

"Darrell, what the hell man? That's not funny."

Ren had backed up again into the crevice she was in, his body thrumming with energy. Her trembling increased. Another? Dear God when would it stop? She put the mace in her bag and her hands over her eyes.

"Darrell what the fuck!? Stop messing around and let's get out of here. The cops are gonna get your ass if we leave without you." There was a pause. "Darrell for serious man, *not cool*." She could hear the fear in his voice. He wouldn't come down. Not until tomorrow. Not until the light of day. "Darrell! Fine you fucking asshole, I'm not falling for your bullshit. Meet us at my place." He slammed the door shut.

They waited for the car to leave and until it did, Ren was still poised to strike. When he was sure that they had left he turned toward her. "C'mere darlin'," he bent over and took her trembling form in his arms. "You got your eyes closed?"

"Yes," she breathed.

"Good." He carried her to the stairs and climbed them easily. When they were upstairs again she opened her eyes. "There's broken glass everywhere, sweets, I think we'll have to find another place for tonight."

"Okay," she squeaked. She pulled her bag close to her stomach and held it tight. What she wouldn't give for a Valium.

In full dark the vacated neighborhood was even creepier. He crept through the tall grasses and they came upon an old shed out in the back of one of the more beat down houses. One that looked like it had been vandalized at least a couple times. He put her down on the hardwood floor, looking about with his flashlight and killing any spiders the light happened to come across. When he was satisfied, he sat down next to her and pulled out one of his candles and lit it. The yellow light revealed blood on the edge of his shirt.

"Oh my god," Tomi put her hands to her lips.

"Whoa, whoa, calm down," he smiled. It was his sane smile. It was grounded and polite and even charming. A smile the devil could give freely. "It's just a little blood. The fucker hit me in the nose."

Sure enough there was plenty of blood smearing his face under his nose and he sniffed a few times.

"You killed him," she gasped. "You killed him and I was in the corner."

He blinked.

Tears started to pour down her cheeks. "You killed him."

"He could have been anyone," Ren stated blankly. "He had a

hammer, Tomi. A hammer. You know what a hammer does to your head?"

"You killed him," she repeated.

"He could have killed me."

"No." She shook her head at him and slowly shuffled away from him on her butt. "No he couldn't have."

Ren tilted his head and his eyebrow shot up. "I'm not following your logic, miss. A hammer will kill me just about as well as it would kill anyone else."

"No," she repeated, shaking her head.

"Fine then," he was smirking a little, "He could have killed *you*."

She nodded. This was more likely. Her. Bumbling little Tomi who had nothing but a pathetic little can of mace that was now probably in the bottom of her bag. She would have dropped it if it had come down to it anyway.

"I think it's time to sleep, sweets," he gave her a warm look and laid down on the hard floor of the shed, his bundled sweatshirt under his head as a pillow.

Her phone was ringing. The periodic buzzing woke her and she was aware of light shining in through the cracks of the shed. Ren was sitting with his back to the door, his hands laced and resting on his flat stomach. He was looking at her.

She sat up immediately.

"Are you going to answer that?" he asked in a low voice.

"I don't know," she replied, digging in her bag to find it. She was surprised it even had a battery charge left. The white letters that spelled "DAD" flashed on the screen and she bit her lip. She had twenty text messages. At least they hadn't forgotten her as she'd thought before.

"Don't press 'ignore.'" He didn't move but eyed her with a cold stare. "If you're going to answer it, answer it, if you're not, don't do anything."

She bit her lip and stared at him. Not a single trace of blood could be found on him. Not even a stain on his shirt near the hem. Had she dreamed it all? No. She was in this shed. They'd been in a house. The buzzing of her phone ceased and she pressed the screen to her forehead. They would call again. They wouldn't stop calling. They wouldn't stop calling until her battery was dead.

She poked the screen until she came to the text messages. Cayley's name in black letters then a pleading, "Where are you, girl? Your parents are worried." Tomi bet they were. What a scandal she'd cause. Her father would be so angry. Her blue eyes found Ren again, carefully watching her. Cayley again, "Hey girl hey! Where you at?" If that wasn't enough the brunette had sent her at least ten more. Another girl had texted her. One from outside her friend group. One from the ranks of the unpretty. "Hey Tomi, I was wondering if you had Mr. Gregg for math last year and if you could tell me if he was a good teacher." An interesting ploy. Her light brows arched.

Ren shifted where he sat, obviously impatient with her.

The callings from her life were tempting her too much. She set down the phone, which had started buzzing again, and straightened her rumpled and dirty clothes. "Okay," she tried to smile at her companion but failed. "Let's go."

He was silent in getting to his feet. "Alright." He flashed her a small but frightening grin. "Are you going to be taking that?" He pointed to her phone face down on the floor.

She got up and with the side of her foot she kicked it to the corner of the structure.

His grin was wider when he opened the door and flooded the shed with light. The creepy neighborhood was easier to navigate with the full brightness of day revealing its every nook and cranny. Tomi imagined the basements of these places filled with creatures. She eyed Ren. At least she knew he wasn't a vampire. Her mind wandered into the dark places where such creatures could thrive. Her mother came into her mind saying what she would always say when Tomi had a nightmare. *There ain't such things as monsters, child, but there is such a thing as the Devil.* Ren was walking in front of her, the bottoms of his Converse scraping against gravel.

"Hey Tomi." He glanced behind himself.

"Yes?"

"How about some Burger King?"

She put a hand to her stomach. She was starving. "Sure."

He didn't respond but his direction changed. She wondered how he knew where he was going but didn't bother to ask. He probably just had his own ways. She could smell civilization. It seemed like an odd thing to smell but she could swear it. It was a hard scent of car exhaust and pavement and perhaps a hint of those little colored rubber bits that surrounded playgrounds. He paused for a moment and pulled a beanie onto his head and tucked his hair into it, effectively hiding his dyed red halo.

"Could you do me a solid, sweets?" he smiled at her. It was charming and careful.

"Perhaps." Her blue eyes narrowed toward him. She should probably do him a favor no matter what it was considering he had protected her so well last night. *But he killed him.* Killed. End. Done. Never going to walk up those basement stairs ever again. Tomi swallowed hard. The finality of death was sucking at her like a leech. Had it hurt? "Umm..." she tried again, her vocal cords stuck.

"I was just wondering if you could take this ten bucks and get us some burgers." He was holding out a Hamilton and his expression was warm. There was nothing in his eyes that betrayed his inhumanity of the night before.

"How's your nose?" she blurted.

His head dipped to the side and his eyebrows furrowed. "What?"

Her face was expressionless as she stared at him but she took the ten dollar bill anyway, making sure their fingers didn't touch in the exchange.

He shrugged and looked away from her but if she wasn't mistaken she could have sworn she'd seen a flash of a grin on his handsome face.

He waited at the edge of the parking lot under a tall pine and watched her as she went in. The restaurant was so cold it was as if she had dove into a bathtub filled with ice. She shivered a little and went into the bathroom to relieve herself and to smooth out her hair and the wrinkles in her clothes before ordering. The large cavernous bathroom was empty, smelling of lilac soap and a hint of bleach. She examined her blue eyes in the mirror.

How mad was he? The image of her father flashed in her mind. He'd never been mad at her before. Perhaps exasperated, but never angry. It seemed like a strange thing to think about when considering parents but hadn't it been true? He had never looked at her the way he had looked at her brother. He had never yelled at her. Her mother had probably never even raised her voice toward her in her whole life. All she knew how to do was speak down to people and her kids were no exception. Tomi pulled down her lower eyelids. She took her looks from her father.

The night Bo came back under the influence of some kind of drug rippled through the surface of her memories.

Her whispers outside the house. *Bo, where have you been? Come up the outside stairs, they're waiting for you in the kitchen. They can't stop you if they don't hear you.*

His trembling hand in hers. *I'm leaving, Mi, I'm leaving. I can't live here anymore.*

The yelling. *Go. All ties of yours are severed. I won't have a son like you.*

She took a deep breath. Could he let her go as well? Could he allow her to be gone? She was the last of them. The last of their children. Their only child. She sniffed. How angry could he be at her? How badly could a politician's daughter fuck things up?

She shivered again and left the bathroom. Her shoes tapped merrily on the cold tile floor. She looked at all the people around her. They had not known fear as she knew it. They had not been carried by the devil through darkness. They had not bought burgers for a creature who had killed a man with his teeth.

She stopped breathing.

His teeth.

It hadn't truly hit her until that moment. That the demon she walked alongside had opened his mouth and killed a man with nothing but his *teeth*. Of course the question could be raised: *how could she know that?* After all, they had been in complete darkness, she didn't *see* it happen...but she felt it in her gut. All that blood didn't come from his nose—as he hadn't even remembered having told her that lie. It must have been. It must have been his *teeth*. The very thought was horrifying.

She swallowed hard and gripped the bill he'd given her in her fist. Could she go back to him? She bit her lip but approached the counter. It would be so easy to simply tell the clerk to dial 911. That she had been kidnapped by a murderous maniac. Then nobody could be mad. Then nobody could tell her that she'd done something wrong. She put the crumpled ten on the counter and stared at the girl behind the counter. *Say it*. She opened her mouth. *I've been kidnapped. Please call 911. He's outside. Be careful though because I'm about 90% certain he's Satan himself.*

"Could I have two double cheeseburgers, one with no pickles?"

"Anything to drink?"

"Two milks?"

Curse it all. She stood around like a stick until the bag was ready and then she faced the door. She felt as though she was in a choose your own adventure book. Definitely one of the Goosebumps ones she'd read as a kid. Except the murder was real and so was her monster. Turn to page 81 if you walk out the door and accept your fate. If you chicken out and call 911, turn to page 42. She tapped the toe of her shoe before scurrying toward the door.

It was more muggy outside than she remembered but she welcomed the heat of July wholeheartedly. He was still standing next to the pine tree, his hands in his pockets. His backpack sagged off of him like a baggy leech, and a shock of bright red hair jutted out from the front of his beanie, having escaped its prison. He seemed unamused, his cold dark eyes watching everyone in the parking lot.

"Burgers," she held up the bag. "And I hope you like milk."

"I very much like milk," he smiled. "Let's go somewhere to be in peace, sweets."

That somewhere happened to be a small park. They were still standing next to one of the picnic tables when Tomi decided to get to the bottom of her fear.

"Where did you come from?" Her heart felt like it was in her throat.

"Avon," was his short reply.

"So you were born on the Banks?"

"Yep."

She leaned against the picnic table. Her heart was suddenly in her stomach. "You killed that man."

"I did." He was eyeing her with curiosity while he lit a cigarette.

"With your teeth."

He didn't reply but picked up the bag and picked out one of the sandwiches.

"Hey! That's mine!"

With a playful smile, Ren held it above her head and laughing when she jumped. "How do you really know? Aren't they the same?"

"No! I get mine without pickles!"

"Oh so you just put pickles on mine because you couldn't fathom that I might not like pickles as well?"

"You can just take the pickles off of yours if you hate them so much!"

"But by then the whole sandwich is tainted. I'm sure you'd agree with that statement, so considering I'm the tallest, if that has anything to do with anything, I'm going to eat the one without the pickles." His cigarette bounced up and down on his lip with every word.

Her robin's egg eyes narrowed on him and her lips pursed delightfully into a pout. Her pink lipstick had worn off. In a brisk manner, she whirled around and crossed her arms in front of her. "If you don't give me that sandwich, I'll be the most insufferable woman you've ever dealt with. I will also never get you any food ever again."

This time it was Ren's eyes that narrowed.

"Untainted sandwich or your wellbeing? Which is it? Are you going to be a petty asshole or are you going to give me the sandwich I specially ordered for myself?"

Ren set his jaw, stared at the wrapped burger, then glanced up at her. She still had her back turned. With a determined gaze he opened the wrapper. Just as fast as she'd whirled around before, she did it again, and this time she was an angry wolf. Her brows had knitted together and the rush of adrenaline was too much.

He licked it.

"How *dare* you?!" she shrilled.

"Do you still want it?" he grinned.

Tomi hesitated but when she said it, she said it with clear conviction and spite. "Yes! Yes I do, Mr. Licky McLickers! No wonder the police are probably after you, you're a jerk off!"

There was a silence between them, cut only by the rustle of the paper wrapping on her sandwich when he dropped it into her outstretched palm. She almost felt bad when a twinge passed over his face, his eyes holding a shine of something she might have related to pain. The next feeling that overtook her was a deep panic. She slammed her butt down on the table's bench and unwrapped her sandwich the whole way. She could still feel his eyes on her. A harsh image of her body stuffed into a culvert made her put down her burger and stare at it. She would look like she'd gotten in a fight with a great white.

"I'm sorry," she added in a soft voice. "I was frustrated. I didn't get enough sleep."

"Don't talk like that," he spat. She cringed from his tone.

"Like what?" she whimpered.

He sat down on the other bench hard and leaned toward her, his teeth bared. "Like you're afraid of me."

"I *am* afraid of you." Tears gathered in her eyes. The burger in front of her swam in her vision.

He threw his cigarette away with a harsh jerking motion and his voice raised, the flutter in her heart at a pace which seemed impossible. "How badly do you want to get where you're going? Huh?" His eyes blazed. "How badly, sweets, how *fucking* badly?"

She hid her face. "You killed him with your *teeth*."

"And I'd do it again." The silence after his words was so intense that not even the birds in the trees could alter it. Everything around them was quiet, or so Tomi thought. It could have just been the ringing in her ears. "He knew there was something down there. An animal maybe, who knows? But he brought a hammer with him. In the dark he would have swung that at anyone or anything. You know why, Tomi?"

She shook her head but still didn't take her hands from her face.

"Because that's what people do when they're scared." She felt his warm hand on the top of her head. "I understand that you're upset. Anyone would be. But you're alive, aren't you?"

"Yes."

He slowly pulled her hands from her face and wiped at her cheeks with his thumbs. It was the most human gesture he'd made toward her so far. His face was close to hers, his hard dark eyes a little softer in the morning light. He whispered while holding her hands away from her face, "You're gonna get tougher, peach. I know you are."

"Are the police really after you?" she asked.

He was quiet but his eyes searched her face, his expression unreadable. After a small time he let go of her hands and reached into the bag for the second sandwich. He shook his head to dismiss her question and started eating.

Tomi didn't know if she was even hungry anymore.

They were back in the woods when night fell, having walked a good way that day. She felt grimy and tired and took a little bit of time with her toiletries in her bag to try to freshen up. She also changed her clothes, gently folding her skirt and blouse and placing them back in her bag. Shorts and a t-shirt seemed more fitting for gallivanting all through nature.

When she approached him he was leaning against a tree, a fresh cigarette perched behind one ear. The orange light of dusk tainted his features with an eerie glow. The wind started picking up and he looked around at the tops of the trees, studying them intently.

"What?" she asked, adjusting the strap of her bag on her shoulder.

He shook his head. Twilight was cooler, the humidity of the day fading into a comfortable warmth. By the time they were going to sleep, she was laid out on top of his sweatshirt in a small clearing. He was beside her on the ground, his backpack serving as his pillow. The lights of a town were visible in the distance, blinking through the whispering leaves of the forest.

Sleep was easy and it came to her without fail. Her dreams were pleasant and harkened back to a time in her life when the biggest worry she had was passing the next History test. She wasn't sure what woke her up. Later she would think it was his warmth leaving her.

She looked around through the dark and finally saw the soft orange glow from the tip of his cigarette. He was just about ten feet away, probably leaning against a tree, the crickets chirping merrily around him. She felt cold and shivered a little. With a voice full of sleep she asked, "What's up?"

"Go back to sleep." It was a shallow command.

She got up and wrapped his sweatshirt around herself, approaching him. "I can't. You made me nervous."

He didn't reply so she simply stood there with him, the planes of his face visible only from the dim light of the town. A small speck of orange glowed in his eyes. His expression was pensive as he looked out. When he glanced at her it was only for a moment as if to make sure she was still standing there. To make sure that she was not just a figment of his own imagination. He tilted his head again as if listening to someone speaking to him and then jerked it back up.

"What did you do?" Tomi asked him suddenly. A knot had developed in her throat. Should she even be asking? The thought crossed her mind that she might not even have any right to know. "You don't have to tell me," she added curtly, trying to sway the conversation so she wouldn't sound too nosy.

Ren took a deep breath in through his nose and let it out with a low hum, still staring away from her at the lights of a distant town through the trees. He contemplated her question for a little bit before he spoke. "It's not a complex thing to say in words. I could explain it in four words but four words don't really do it justice. You know how words just seem to make everything smaller?"

She nodded.

He nodded back, "It's like that. If I tried to tell you what I did it makes it seem so simple when it's not really. In here," he tapped his chest, "It was something gigantic. It is something gigantic. I would need you to understand that if I were to try to tell you because you'd have to know that the four words I would say aren't really the four words that I mean."

Tomi wasn't sure she understood but she nodded anyway. The curiosity was killing her. All the tiny bits of floating sleep that had been left in her mind were now gone.

He bit his lip and blurted it out while staring off into the dark. "I killed my father."

Tomi looked away, down at the ground, at the canopy above them, then at the distant lights. She cleared her throat.

"It's not just that. Do you understand? It's not just killing him. It's a whole 'nother thing. It's a complex set of emotion and..." he swallowed, "and hurt."

Tomi nodded, still looking off toward the lights. She shivered despite the warmth of the night. "I think I know what you mean, that words diminish things. Whenever things are really important I never really know how to articulate how important they are." She paused but he was silent. "The reason I ran away was because of my brother. He's my best friend. My parents wouldn't let me visit him because to them...he's nothing to them. I couldn't get how I feel out through words. So I ran away." She wiped her tears from her face and sniffled a little, glad he couldn't see her cry. "Why did you kill your father?"

Ren took another cigarette in his mouth and in the glow of his lighter Tomi could see coldness in his eyes. After he'd taken a drag and blown it all out he said softly, "You ever had a dog?"

She shook her head. The money for her puppy was safely tucked away in her bag.

"A dog is a good-natured animal in general. They're called man's best friend for a reason. When properly trained they can be companions, listen to direction, and take a few waps over the head with a newspaper."

Tomi nodded to let him know she understood his train of thought.

"But any dog will bite you if you kick it one too many times. They get scared. They get irrational. They get unstable. He took another long drag of the cigarette. His voice was hard. "And I'm just a dog in the end."

Tomi wrapped her arms around herself, taking in the scent of his sweatshirt. She sidled up to him, pushing her head against his arm. His comforting energy surprised her. That she could be so frightened of a being and yet so drawn to him was fascinating. He confused her. "How did you get away?" she murmured.

"I just ran." He shrugged. "I'll never really get away from it. It'll always be part of me. But I can't help but feel that it was destiny. That I was always meant to kill him. As if I was just denying my destiny for my whole life thinking that I could ever possibly survive alongside him."

"How many people have you killed?"

He gave a sigh and shook his head. She'd overstepped her bounds. He turned toward her and with one hand he adjusted the hood around her neck. "Look sweets, I think it's time you went back home."

"No!" she nearly yelled. "I won't. I won't, I won't, I won't!"

"You're not cut out for this kind of life, Little Miss." He sounded like he was scolding her.

Tears started to prick her eyes. "You don't understand. You don't get it. I can't go back there." She gripped his shirt in her fists.

"You're not safe here, Tomi. You're not safe here with me."

"Are you going to hurt me?" she glared at him, the challenge set in front of him in her scowl.

He was clearly taken aback. "I would never..."

"Then how am I in any danger? If you tell me to go home now I will promise you one thing. I will never make it there. I'll never go home. Not in this lifetime." Tears spilled over her cheeks. "I'll run from them forever. With or without you."

He faced her now, fully. The trees rustled around them, whispering their despicable secrets, their disapproval, their loathing. "You'll never make it alone."

Her voice was filled with a venom her etiquette class had never taught her. "What are you going to do about it then?"

She wasn't prepared for his reaction and she squealed when he picked her up like a sack of potatoes and carried her back to where they had slept. When he put her down she was on her back and he was over her. Fear gripped her heart but he simply stared at her.

"What are you doing?" she whispered.

He took in a deep breath and replied, "You're going to do what I say, when I say it. Is that understood?"

A sob was stuck in her throat. Her thighs were pressed tight together. It wasn't as if he wouldn't be able to pry them apart but she thought she might try to give him a run for his money anyway.

"Understood?" he calmly repeated.

"Yes."

"Good. Now I said for you to go back to sleep about ten minutes ago so you're ten minutes late. You think you can manage to go back to sleep now?"

"Yes."

"Thank Jesus." He rolled away from her.

She lay awake for some time, pondering him. She had set the challenge before him that he would not hurt her and indeed he had said he would not but yet she had still shied from him. She watched him sitting with his head in his hand and suddenly thought of him as a man.

Her sexual experiences were very few and the most intense to date she knew had yet to brush the surface of the possibilities. She had been at a party when she was 14, having slipped out of her beach home to meet Cayley at the end of the drive. She had slipped into the backyard and seen Greg Harner sipping from a red plastic cup. He acted like he owned the house, strutting about with a casual air. His warm brown eyes were the color of caramel and his hair a rich chestnut.

He had approached her easily and kissed her on the back patio. Then he'd nibbled her ear. The adrenaline rush from just that one simple act had been enough to allow him nearly anything he wanted from her. They were behind a tree when he'd kissed her again and used his tongue. She had been woefully naïve about anything such as French kissing but he seemed patient enough. He had tasted like mint gum. His hand had played with the lacy edge of her skirt, tickling the delicate flesh of her thigh.

She glanced at Ren. His animal strength and prowess came back to her memory. His willingness to protect her. Certainly he had not killed *for* her. It was as much for him, was it not? If he could even be killed, she reminded herself. He had touched her with gentleness in wiping away her tears. Was he capable of more? Her legs squeezed together again but this time not out of fear.

He lay down after a time. He was faced away from her but she was still comforted by his warmth and presence. She turned to face him and closed her eyes.

When Tomi opened them again he was facing her, watching her sleep with a drowsy but content expression. She rubbed her eyes with the back of her hand and asked, "What?"

"Nothing," he whispered back. He looked her straight in the eyes. "I was just memorizing you."

"What do you have to do that for?"

He lifted his head in a gesture of uncertainty and then sat up. "C'mon, pretty miss, we got a bit of walking to do."

CHAPTER 2

It was about two weeks after Tomi Balekowski had disappeared when Trent Winston, P.I., poked the screen of his Droid and said "hallo" with a huge bite of turkey sandwich stuffed in his cheek. He chewed while listening and then swallowed before taking a gulp of Dasani and replying.

"Naddy, please. You know I have other cases here." He made a small gesture toward the rest of his sandwich which was sitting on top of about three manila folders. It didn't occur to him that since she was on the phone (all the way in the Banks even) that she couldn't see his small gesture. "Are you sure they're telling the truth?" He took another bite of his sandwich while he listened to her. She had a pleasant voice so he didn't mind her chatty nature much. "So essentially you need a professional tracker." He nodded a few times to himself. He didn't even glance upward when his partner walked into his office and leaned against the doorframe. "Well I'm sure Avery could do it. Is she on her own?" He grabbed a pen and began jotting things down. "How could one little girl give you dingles the slip? She shouldn't be *that* hard to catch. Unless she's been completely avoiding all human contact." He looked up at Avery whose dark eyebrows rose in question. "Look Sis, I'll see what I can do to slip this in but I'm very busy so it'll probably take a little bit of a back seat. She's not exactly high on the priority list right now. Not unless she's suddenly killed five people and eaten half their face." He chuckled along with Avery. "Alright, I love you too, say hi to Dave for me, the fucker. See ya." He clicked down the receiver and leaned forward with his arms on his desk.

"So Nadine needs my help?" Avery smiled. His small smile could put anyone on edge but for Winston it was a normal occurence. The man could make the Pope himself confess to murder.

"She's got this case down there where some politician's daughter ran away and the assholes at the bus company told her they have no idea who she's even talking about. She can't find a single person in twenty miles that can honestly say they've seen her."

"Think she's even still alive? Has she considered murder?" Avery's eyes always shined when they talked murder. It might have been because the two of them were the go-to guys that clients called in when they had a particularly dangerous job. They'd first started as independent P.I.s down in the Banks, finding cheating boyfriends and the like. But that had gotten old and when the first call came in looking for a murderer, they'd jumped at it. Even after their first and last serial killer nearly made lunch out of Winston and then got away, they were still chasing down killers (and the occasional corrupt politician)--but now in Washington D.C. Eight solved murder cases in D.C. and they were beginning to become well-known for it. A trip to look for some runaway girl would be something of a favor if they did it at all.

"She considered the parents as suspects but all those leads have dried up too. She's fairly convinced that the girl ran away but she's vanished. Now she did say that a bus driver said that there was a girl who matched the description but he couldn't say for sure and he couldn't remember what day or what time."

"So we've got a possible witness who may or may not have driven her to the main land. Well that's useful." Avery rolled his dark eyes then examined his purple tie. "Do we even have time to go on some wild goose chase after some little girl?"

Winston shrugged. "Maybe we can go down there and kill two birds with one stone. I seem to recall that we've had some interesting adventures down there and this would give us an excuse to sniff around the ol' homestead and see what the parents know and what Naddy knows." His hand moved to his chest and he rubbed where he itched—a six inch scar that rather resembled a shooting star if one had an open mind. All he had left to show of his last adventure back home. "Also, if I'm not mistaken I believe Rayne just dropped this one on my desk." He held up one of the envelopes that had been under his sandwich. "There's a good chunk of change in it for us if we can find Collie Landall's killer. Serial. Killed a few others and he's around the same area. Could make it worth it to take a gander."

Avery grinned. The sight could chill the blood in any man. "Let's get to it."

He was meandering his way over to the fax machine a few minutes later after having sent a text to his sister for the details of Miss Balekowski's disappearance. The reports from the police department could prove crucial in finding the girl. The agency was a small gray setting with a few offices connected to a larger room that one might call a bullpen. There were maps spread out over tables and lunches on plates from the nearest delis and chinese food restaurants. The agency had quite a few detectives working in collaboration. A collection of some of the better private investigators in D.C.. In the opinion of most of them working there. But they had been there for a long time. Some since the agency started.

"Winston," came a voice to his left. He looked over slowly, recognizing it as Greg Freeman. 35 years old, Greg was the son of Ned Freeman who'd started the agency years ago and who was currently its administrator. "What're you up to? Heard Rayne left you with a doozy of a case." Greg was wearing a gray suit with a boring blue and white striped tie and a white shirt. He was careful to match his black belt with shiny black shoes. "You just do it all, don'tcha Winston? None of these cheatin' assholes for you."

He didn't say anything. What was there to say? Nothing he'd said required a response and his question sounded rhetorical. So he just stared at the younger Freeman.

Predictably Greg simply continued on. Winston had tuned him out even as he stood there looking at him. His short brown hair that constantly reminded him that Greg was three years older than him and had more color to his hair. It was all those cushy politician cases. There was no stress in his life. There was no excitement. He also imagined that Greg was so vapid that there might not even be any internal struggle. For a few seconds he entertained the idea of just plucking out one of the little bastard's eyes. Maybe just to see what would happen. Would he scream like a little pussy girl? Winston's mind suddenly flashed back to the dream he'd had the night before. A balloon made of a woman's organ. He'd filled it with the helium himself.

He blinked. The vapid victim of nepotism had stopped talking and was staring back at him with his brows knitted. "Winston, did you just hear anything I said?"

He didn't bother responding to that either. His fax had come in so he snatched it from the fax machine and turned around, heading back to Office 19 which he shared with Avery. He could hear Greg's grumble to whomever would listen as he left.

To think when they came I thought Avery was the fucked up one.

She was hot, sore, and had blisters on her feet. Her hair was a knotted mess despite several combings throughout the day and her skin felt as though it had grown its own thin film of grime that might just be protecting her from viruses for all she knew. It was about four in the afternoon when they were sitting by a stream. She was washing her face with a bar of soap she kept handily in a small water-proof container.

He was brushing his teeth with bottled water, spitting the foam into the stream. It seemed that the boy had everything he needed in his backpack. Ren sighed a little after wiping off his face. "You're a trooper, aren't you Little Miss?"

"I'd better be," she said quietly. "I don't know if I can walk with these blisters." She examined her sore feet, poking at the little bubbles. "I think they need to heal a little."

He licked his lips and his cold eyes watched her. "You're right. We've gotta find a place to hunker down and collect ourselves."

"What I wouldn't give for a bath," she breathed. "A hot bath with bubbles and little duckies."

"Dream on," he replied. He didn't react to her glare because he didn't notice it. He was looking out at the water and scratching his head.

She watched him and her glare lessened and then melted away. He was just wearing his jeans and his tank top. Whenever he wasn't looking at her and she had a free moment she had been taking to watching his muscles move. He was a sleek creature, his body always posed in such a way that his movement was never restricted. As if he might have to kill at any moment and he had yet to know from which direction his foe came. His skin was perfectly molded over his body and if she was lucky enough to see him sans shirt her cheeks were flushed completely pink. He was tanned and beautiful. His inherent danger simply made him nearly irresistible and fascinating. It was irrational. She tried to shake it many times but kept finding herself staring. Drinking him in.

"Stop it," he said without looking at her.

She blinked and looked away. "Stop what?"

"Looking at me."

Flustered, she shook her head. "Sorry." She could feel herself blush. Her heart was pounding. She was silly for ever creating some kind of attachment to him in her mind. He was obviously less interested. Although the way he'd watched her sleep was still in the back of her mind. Memorizing her. As if he willed himself to never forget her. She glanced at him and then quickly looked away. He was smoking again.

"Has it turned out the way you thought it might, sweets?"

She frowned. "Nothing's turned out yet. But I suppose this is what I signed up for and it's a little bit harder than I expected."

"We're not caught yet."

"You must be good luck." She shrugged and looked back down at her foot.

He started to laugh.

She stared at him. The sound of his laughter had made her heart feel like it was shrinking into itself and she swallowed. Tears started to flood her eyes despite there being no reasoning for it. She was suddenly struck with the impulse to run from him but there she sat, like a rock.

When he stopped laughing he was looking at her incredulously. "Are you kidding me, sweets?"

"I..." she tried.

"Good *luck*? *Luck*? Is that what you think it is?" He laughed again and she shrank back. "It's a little more than just luck."

They had a small moment where they retained full eye contact. She was on the defensive of this bout, clearly searching for some kind of joke in his eyes.

"I've kept you out of trouble as much as I could, sweets. If they get a whiff of you they'll be on you. On *us*. You're not the only one being searched for. Your stealth is my stealth. Your ass is my ass. That's why I help you, Little Miss. That's why you're not caught yet. That's why you're still on your little yellow brick road."

"And I..." she paused to take a breath and collect herself. "I appreciate your help."

"Of course you do," he mumbled as he turned away, inhaling from his cigarette and leaning against his tree.

Anger bubbled in her chest. "What in the hell are you so angry about? Why are you so angry all the time?"

He shook his head.

"Tell me, damn it," she raised her voice, just a shade higher. Her tears spilled. "You can't stay angry your whole fucking life, can you?"

His reply was so quiet she almost lost it in the whispers of the trees. "Maybe."

"I'm going to stare at you however I want. I'm going to talk to you however I want too. Like I like you. Like I'm afraid of you. Like you're a—"

"Stop." He was looking at her, his cig shaking in his hand. His dark brows were knitted together and his dark eyes stabbed her with anger.

She gasped before she leaned forward toward him with the darkest glare she could muster. "No."

His lip twitched. She could see it from where she sat. His eyes narrowed into slits before he disappeared. It was so quick she could hardly remember if he had ever existed at all. But he was gone. Off into the sanctuary of the woods she supposed. For a few moments she was shaking with her anxiety and her rage. The tremors subsided but her anger did not. He could have left her so much earlier and saved himself all the trouble of these past two weeks. The trouble of sneaking into outside bathrooms in the middle of the night at dubious-looking gas stations with suspicious looking truckers and sleazy teenaged cashiers. The trouble of sharing his two-for-one ice cream sandwiches. The trouble of letting her borrow his sweatshirt when it was too cold at night. The list went on and on.

Tomi Balekowski was a sack of pure trouble. She sat with her blistered feet and pondered what in the world she was going to do now. Now that he was gone. Now that she wasn't sure he was ever coming back for her. She tried to compose herself as best she could before getting up and limping off with her bag on her shoulder. She wasn't sure how much more her bare feet could take. And all this to find that rascal brother of hers somewhere up north. At least they were going in the correct direction despite all the twisting and winding they seemed to do through towns and woods and fields.

Around six she found a structure in the middle of the woods. The roof was bowed in but the walls were made of brick and it looked as though it had been a small bathroom at some point. Perhaps for a park or a playground. Ivy grew up the dark stained walls and as she approached she noted the deep silence around her. She paused and stared at the two doors to the structure. One for women, one for men. Would anything be living in there? Would any*one*? She remembered Ren with his ear pressed hard against the door to that abandoned house. He had been hesitant to barge in on squatters and rightly so considering what Ren could do to any trespasser.

She reached into her bag and pulled out the small red tube Ren had given her. She unlocked it and held it poised while she pushed open one of the doors with her other hand.

The tiles were falling off the walls and the thick scent of rotting leaves came to her nose. The window was broken and a tree branch had grown into it, twisting its bony arm as if trying to reach something inside. Perhaps the leaves it had dropped to the floor. The bathroom was not cramped but not the Taj Mahal by any means either. The floor would

43

need a little sweeping off before she could sleep there but for the most part the place looked as if it could keep water out. She looked in each of the stalls, expecting at least a rat or even a snake but she was met with empty cracked toilets and more leaves. There were a few spiders and strange enough looking bugs but they didn't bother her too badly. She'd seen worse spiders in her two weeks with Ren.

With careful strokes she loosened the leaves off the floor and swept them all away into a corner, leaving a relatively clean area in which she could lay down. When she looked back up from her work she screamed. The sound was shrill in the small area and her back was flat against the door before her mind had any sense.

He was chuckling at her from the window, his head surrounded by the leaves of the invading tree branch.

"You *bastard.*"

He simply continued to chuckle.

"I didn't think you were going to come back." She slid down the door, her butt landing hard on the tiles. It felt good to be off her feet.

"You'll never make it by yourself. Look at this mess you made."

"I was trying to make it so I could sleep on it." His chuckles infuriated her. "What's wrong with it?"

"Any tracker worth his spit is going to find this and think it's a treasure trove of information."

"So let them." She frowned. "Let them find it. I need to sit my skinny white ass down and sleep for a few *days.*"

He was smiling at that. It was a sane smile. Nonfrightening. "Come on, sweets, I got a place that will do us just fine and it's much better than this crummy little toilet." His head withdrew and the door opened behind her back. With a small squeak she was lifted easily by him, her bag dangling from one of her arms. He carried her the whole way to an abandoned gas station that had to have been at least a mile from her small rest area. With the amount of abandoned buildings they seemed to find she was beginning to wonder if they weren't trapped in some postapocalyptic world and nobody yet had the decency to tell her.

It was cozy inside and miraculously dry. Soft beams of early evening sun trickled in through holes in the roof and the floor was covered in dust but no dirt. Stale candies and chips littered the place and Ren promptly dug his hand deep into the back of the cigarette shelves and pulled out one or two dusty old packs of Camels.

"Make yourself at home," he told her, gesturing to a pile of old work shirts and a tarp. "It's not a waterbed but it'll do. There's also a plastic garbage can out back that's been collecting rain water."

"Oh fabulous," she sighed, digging through her bag to find some of her toiletries. After having brushed her teeth and hair, and having washed her face, she felt much better about her situation. She felt clean and fresh and eager to explore the new location. They were settled along a muddy dirt road, the painted sign for the business so faded and chipped it was unrecognizable. Ren was lounging in his little makeshift nest, examining the cigarette packs he'd managed to fish out from behind the shelving.

She made her way around the counter and poked around at things while sticking her tongue out and touching it very delicately to her nose. It was a skill she still didn't know how she could manage but she did and did it well. She could see him out of the corner of her eye, watching her with an odd expression. It was probably her tongue on her nose, she thought. It was a shocking little talent for sure. She almost blushed with the feel of his bold eyes on her and she pretended not to notice his staring, even when he made that odd little head tilt as though listening to his favorite part of Bach or Mozart.

Underneath a small bit of cardboard she uncovered a little nest of shavings and fabric that held five tiny baby mice. Their cuddled sleeping forms pulled at her heart strings and she eeped in delight. "Oh my goodness. Ren, come look." She beckoned him over and he complied, examining the little mice with a cold glance. She was giddy with both the excitement from the mice and his closeness. "Aren't they just the cutest thing you've ever seen?"

He seemed to consider this question for a small moment before he gave a very decisive "No."

Her eyes widened and she quickly turned in order to criticize him for his blatantly icy manner but she found herself lacking words or even the means to speak them as he had swooped in very quickly and claimed her mouth in a kiss. It didn't last for very long at all, just a short little thing but very powerful, his energy behind it a forceful entity that easily claimed her as his own. The moment directly after his mouth had taken leave of hers was the most interesting as he continued to stare into her eyes. He had taken on a rather intriguing look, an expression that just hinted at a willingness to let her win an argument or a casual interest in her hobbies and passions. She of course was shocked and allowed her face to betray her. Her mouth hung slack and a deep scarlet filled her face. All words had left her and she was outrightly befuddled. It was up to him to make the second move since he had left her speechless. She almost leaned in for another kiss—hopefully deeper and more heartfelt— but couldn't seem to make her body work.

With a carelessness that was rather unlike him he said, "I need a smoke," and was promptly out the door.

Tomi's soft fingers touched her mouth when she closed it. Her eyes lingered on the door he had just exited and her ears had a slight ringing in them. The mice were forgotten and she drifted over to one of the aisles of candy, her eyes still on the door. He had kissed her. Just a simple kiss. Her little high school heart was beating faster every minute. What had he meant by doing it? What did this mean? Did he like her? Did she like him? Could she like him? Wasn't he the devil?

She blinked. *Did she care if he was?* She sank to the floor. His deep cold eyes flooded her memory and she shivered and lurched forward as though she had been pounded by a strong ocean wave. She stared at her toes, unthinking, all the questions in her mind had suddenly fled. She was left with whiteness and the ringing in her ears.

She barely heard the door click open when he came back but she looked up at him, standing at the end of the aisle contemplating her. His face was blank, his eyes dead as usual. She found herself looking at his lips. The same lips that had just kissed her, shared their warmth with her, also hid behind them the terror that was his teeth. His too many teeth. His murderous, bloody, awfully white rows of teeth. She couldn't stop her shuddering.

"I didn't know you could touch your tongue to your nose," he told her in a flat voice.

Tomi didn't know how to reply so she didn't, just staring up at him with wide blue eyes. She could feel them start to water.

"My apologies," he added. He then ambled over to the canned aisle and picked out a rather dusty can of peaches. He looked at the date, seemed to be okay with it, and pulled the tab to pop the lid. She watched him drink them as if they were Coke, gulping them with ease. When he licked his lips she had to turn away. She couldn't risk getting a glimpse of those teeth or her heart would simply burst. What fear she had in her heart.

Her stomach growled. In his cold voice he said, "Eat something."

Nathan Balekowski was a charming man with a strong chin and almost pure white hair. He was almost too charming. A man who, in Winston's eyes, could not have possibly gotten where he was without some kind of odd dealings in the background. He wondered to himself if the Balekowski family might not have some kind of business dealing with the Rizzoli family—and what a family.

Mr. Balekowski's eyebrows furrowed slightly and he leaned forward, "I suppose since you're now involved, a private detective agency, it's a little bit less hopeful."

"We're going to do everything we can," Winston assured him. "I owe a favor to this department and we've got a better tracker." He grinned at his partner. "The guys down here are pretty sure your daughter caught a ride to the main land and has managed to slip herself out of correspondence. We're going to track her cell phone's GPS system and see what that can tell us. It's possibly the easiest way to track her at this point."

Mr. Balekowski nodded with his carefully preserved concern etched into his features. "She was very attached to that phone. It could get the internet, you know. One of those smart phones."

He nodded and his eyes flicked to Avery who had been watching the scene from the doorway.

They stood in the driveway for a little while, Winston smoking and Avery examining the ground in a casual way.

"I think he's got nothing he can tell us," Winston said around his cigarette. "He didn't even know her. She's his daughter and he didn't even know her."

"The wife was worse," Avery mumbled.

"Fucking parents," Winston shook his head. "No wonder she ran away." It wasn't a sentiment he'd had to voice. The two of them were almost always on the same page. He looked at his partner and asked, "See anything useful?"

Avery shook his head. "We can puzzle it out from here I suppose."

They drove slowly down the only road until they came to the bus stop bench where Avery got out and quietly looked at it. Without a word he got back in the car and they drove away again, crossing the bridge. They stopped at a small motel and set up their little portable HQ, Winston calling in for the GPS coordinates for the girl's phone took at least an hour and Avery was lightly napping through the lot of it.

When Winston sat heavily down on the bed, Avery's one eye opened and he reminded the other very much like a cat. Avery mewled, "What's wrong, bud?"

"Nothing's wrong I suppose. I'm just having flashbacks. This place isn't very different."

"What about the girl?"

Winston's phone jingled and he picked it up. He said nothing but listened intently and then poked the screen to hang up. With a strange expression, halfway between serious and puzzled, he looked at his partner. "We've gotta take a trip to the morgue."

Tomi's eyes were glazed as she stared upward at the ceiling. He was asleep next to her, his even breathing making her even more nervous. Even more uncomfortable. How could he be so calm and yet so angry? How could there be such a wolf under his skin? How could the man she slept next to with the careful even breaths be the boogeyman?

He turned over toward her and she stiffened. Out of the corner of her eye she watched his face, eased by sleep. His face held the guise of innocence, there was no anger hidden in his brows nor unease in the tension of his upper lip. Everything that she could find to be evil about him had gone. There was no coldness about him. Only warmth. His mouth was slightly open and she could see just a bit of his teeth but they held no terror for her. She turned to face him fully, her eyes scanning over him easily while he slept unguarded. The freckles that dusted the bridge of his nose made him look even younger than he had, just a boy as she was just a girl. *Just a dog* he had said. No. Just a boy. Just lawless and wild.

She moved closer to him until she could feel his breath on her throat. He stirred a little and stretched, reaching out. His wrist touched her and she closed her eyes and pretended to sleep. She could feel him stiffen a little as he awoke and considered her. His hand, warm and soft, settled on her side and he again relaxed.

In this way she fell asleep, safer in the thought of his hand there.

Winston looked around the sterile halls and wished to god he could smoke in here. What happened to the days when one could smoke in a hospital? His fingers pattered over the top of his cowboy killers in his pocket. Avery came out of the double doors in front of him with the coroner, their faces grim. Winston gritted his teeth, "Looks like one of ours," he stated and there was a small nod of agreement. "Feeling nostalgic yet?"

"It's been a long time," Avery said very softly, studying Winston's face.

A case long gone. A failed attempt at tracking. A careful investigation that had been made obsolete. Gone cold. *Cold.* A killer who had simply disappeared. Evaporated. And yet here this body was. Evidence of this particular killer. The one that got away. Winston rubbed his chest again. "This has to be a coincidence. We come back to the Banks and he goes back to killing? This was weeks ago."

"Are you suggesting this is unrelated?"

"I am."

Avery shrugged, "Then let's treat it that way. Until we get confirmation otherwise."

Nadine was the one to interrupt them when she passed around the corner. "I've been looking for you guys, I heard you were out on my wild goose chase. Anything on her?"

Winston's mouth softened from the hard line it was. "I've gotta call them to get the coordinates but that'll have to wait, we've got this body here..."

Nadine's brows furrowed. "Your guy's long gone if that moldy thing is one of yours. As I recall, he tends to get the hell out of Dodge quite quickly after he's done with...you know. Whatever he does."

Avery gave Winston a strange look. "We might as well GPS the girl's phone, your sister's right."

He gave a sigh and at the tail end of it he breathed, "Fuck it."

Their coordinates led them, metal detectors in hand, to the suburban wasteland that was once a housing development for a factory. Crickets chirped in the high wet grasses and the wind rustled everything around them, pulling loose shingles off of the decrepit houses and making flat "plunk" sounds when they hit the ground. Winston rubbed a butt with his heel into the gravel of an overgrown street and gave a sly gaze toward Avery. His partner's stance didn't betray how worrying this situation was. The two of them were standing within sixty feet of this girl's phone and the place was frightening. Even more so to them.

They meandered about until Avery emerged from a shed with the girl's phone in a plastic baggie.

"Anything else in there?" Winston asked, already knowing the answer.

"No. Just that. Not even scratched."

There was a long pause before Winston said it. "Think she's alive?"

Avery shrugged, moving the grasses around with his toe. "There's only really one way to find out." He glanced toward the other crime scene, marked off with tape. "Still think these are unrelated?"

Winston bit his bottom lip while he gave a shrug and the two of them walked off into the forest, Avery in the lead. It took Avery a little while to get his bearings as it must have rained several times and the wind in such a place was bound to do much to hamper a tracker's work. Winston had smoked nearly half his pack before Avery whistled for him.

"Yeah?"

Avery's fingers were pinched together and out of them sprang one blonde hair. He pointed into the woods and proceeded to make his way through in that direction. Winston followed. Avery's dark voice reached him. "If she's dead we should find what's left of her soon." He looked around himself and at the ground. "There's no trace of a hurry or a rush. Whoever came through here was calm and careful." He knelt down to the forest floor and examined the mud there. "There's too much wash-out. Damn it." He still kneeled there for a long time, looking at the ground with careful dark eyes. "Fuck it all, Winston."

Winston left the trail and eased his way through the trees, using his nose to try to sniff the air for any signs of decay. When he came back to Avery he asked seriously, "Body dogs?"

"No," Avery's lip twitched. "Bloodhounds. I think she's alive and I'm sticking with that until I see her dead."

"Alright," Winston grinned. "But let's wait on the bloodhounds until we check this town that's about a mile up. She had to have eaten sometime."

They had checked at least a dozen restaurants, the host or hostesses completely useless. The cashiers at the Wendy's, McDonald's, and Arby's were even worse. They walked into the Burger King with weary eyes and even wearier feet.

They dropped their photo of her onto the counter. "Have you seen this girl come by here in the last couple weeks?" Winston stared at the cashier, expecting nothing. He looked very much like the type of teenager of whom nothing is expected. His eyes drooped like an old dog's and his shoulders were slumped forward. He looked at the photo with disinterest.

"Uhhh." He started his statement off well, thought Winston. "Sure. Yeah. She came in here. I think she got a burger."

Avery looked around them at the eating establishment and gave a short snort and rolled his eyes.

"No shit, sherlock," Winston growled, "You saw this girl, not some other blonde girl with her friends but *this girl*."

The cashier shrugged. "Yeah. It was her. She looked kinda...you

51

know."

"No I don't know." Winston's ire was rising.

"Kinda like she was on a walk of shame or something." His doofy face curled into an ugly smile.

Winston turned around and slipped the picture back in his pocket. "Well that's that. She's alive. Great. Wonderful. I'm exuberant." The cold air inside the restaurant was putting him further on edge so the two of them headed back outside to the mild breeze off the ocean. "I'm running out of cigarettes," he stated in a bland tone. "This girl is gone and I'm running out of fucking cigarettes."

Avery nodded. "She probably passed through this town and just stopped there. She must be sticking to the woods. Quite clever of her to do so..." He was thinking. Winston could see the gears turning in his dark head.

"But where did she go after this?" Winston turned around in a circle in the parking lot. "She obviously didn't go the direction she came but what if she's not moving in a straight line? How are we going to track her through here if the cashier is the only person she talked to? Carl's bloodhounds don't do well in an urban environment.

Avery tapped his lips with his finger. "We'll send out an alert, give her picture to all the locals in a two hundred mile radius and if they see her they pick her up. It's really that simple at this point. Now of course there's no telling whether or not a local is ever going to see her. You and I both know, better than anyone even, that some people are missing and they stay missing."

"Speaking of..." Winston spat angrily in the dirt. "I think it's time to see about the real case."

Mr. and Mrs. Landall were a thin couple, aged in many more ways than just one. Mr. Landall had sunken dark eyes that were set back into his skull and his clothes hung off his body. Mrs. Landall stared somewhere over Winston's left shoulder when she spoke, her mouth barely moving and her expression blank.

"She was a wonderful daughter," she stated breathily, "We may not have always agreed but she was my baby. She was everything I ever had. In my whole life." Her tone was lilting and she wavered a bit before Mr. Landall steadied her with a hand on her shoulder. "Please, sit down, Detectives. Sit down." She held out a limp hand toward their couch and the partners did as they were asked. The Landalls shuffled over and sat in two overstuffed recliners, their backs rigid and their expressions dull.

Mr. Landall's voice had a tinge of hope in it when he asked, "Will you take the case? Is it something you'd like to do?"

Winston looked at Avery and when the other didn't speak, he opted for it. "Well to be honest, Mr. Landall, we've already been looking around. We're here on another case, a runaway. Your daughter's killer has been claiming lives for quite a bit of time now and we're worried about the safety of the girl we're looking for. We'd like to ask you a few questions about your daughter and the night she disappeared."

"Another girl?" Mrs. Landall's eyes became even more glassy and fell to the carpet, her head tilting a little in a complete resignment. "If there is anything we could tell you that could save her. Anything at all."

"Do you remember anything off-kilter about the way you and your daughter interacted the last night you saw her?"

The mother shook her head, "She was obstinate as usual. That wasn't a strange thing for her. She was always hard-headed. She was always off getting into trouble. You know at that age you think you're invincible."

Winston's lips thinned. It was the very thing that Ted Bundy had looked for in his victims. Youth. For that very same reason.

Avery asked the next question in a soft inquisitive tone, "Do you remember her saying anything about where she might have been going?"

"No, she didn't say anything but we knew. We always knew where she would go. A few times we went out and found her but lately we just let her go. She would come back later strung out or hung over. She spent a lot of time out there. In the woods. She'd go out there and explore. Sometimes she'd bring her friends. Sometimes she'd go alone."

"Did she ever tell you about her experiences in the woods?"

Mr. Landall shook his head and moved to take his wife's hand. "She didn't talk about that kind of stuff with us. We didn't listen enough to her. Maybe if we had kept an open mind she would have told us more. What the heck was so bad about a little weed now and then anyway?"

Mrs. Landall sniffed.

Winston tapped his knee with a finger and wondered why exactly he and Avery were even wasting their time. "Who could we talk to about what she did in the woods? A friend? Boyfriend? Lover?"

Mrs. Landall replied, "George Jalinski. He lives up the road a little way. He would know. And before you go, Detectives, I want you to accept a check. Right now. It's part of the payment we offered and of course your standard fee."

The road was dusty, the wind kicking it up and forcing it to swirl around the two of them as they walked. "Should have taken the car," Winston groaned in the heat of summer. His hair was whisked around by the invading breeze and he put his hands in his pockets while he walked. He didn't expect a response from Avery and of course he didn't get one. The dry wind had cracked his lips and he'd left his chapstick in the car. He opted for a cigarette instead, having to shield the lighter and attempting at least three times before his Marlboro could take the flame. A simple knock on the door and it was opened by a squinting adolescent from a dark interior. The cool artificial light of a TV shined in the background and Winston recognized the videogame readily. *Dead Rising.*

"Are you George Jalinski?" Winston asked finishing his cigarette in just three long drags before stomping it out on the sidewalk.

"Maybe. Are you the cops?"

"Nope, not cops."

"Then I am. What do you want?" He still hadn't opened the door all the way. Winston could smell the faint skunky smell of pot and grinned, remembering his younger days.

"We're private investigators. We've been hired by the Landall family to look into Collie's death a little bit further. We're not here to get you into any kind of trouble. We're looking for answers, plain and simple."

He narrowed his already squinting eyes then opened the door further and stepped out onto the porch. His hair was long and stringy, reaching his shoulders as limp tendrils of black. His face was pocked with acne and he was almost deathly skinny. He reeked of marijuana and B.O. He shut the door behind him and pulled up his plaid pajama bottoms, revealing sickly fishbelly white feet underneath. "What did you wanna know about Collie?"

Avery snuck his way in, earning himself a suspicious look from Little Greasy. "We need to know about the woods. When Collie went into the woods, what did she do there? Where did she go?"

He shrugged, "We'd go everywhere. We'd just kinda explore. We found some cool buildings before. Some trees. Made forts."

"Was there anything that you can remember that was weird? Anything in particular that you might have noticed?"

"What do you mean?"

Winston chimed in, "He's trying to ask if you were ever wigged out while you were in the forest or if Collie ever mentioned being creeped out. Ever meet anyone in there?"

Little Greasy wiped his nose with the back of his hand and sniffed. "I dunno. I mean the woods were kinda creepy at night I guess. She wasn't ever freaked out though. But we were usually really high and I get paranoid when I'm high." He frowned down at the ground, "You sure you're not cops?"

Winston allowed himself to smile, "I'm one hundred percent certain that I am not a police officer. We're private detectives. We don't give two shits about you smoking it up."

He nodded, satisfied, "Sometimes when I would get high I'd like look up into the trees. And a couple-a times I thought I saw someone. You know? But I didn't wanna say anything 'cause I wasn't sure and I thought I'd ruin the mood and you know. It was stupid. Someone in the trees? And sometimes I could swear we were being followed. Thought it was the cops but nothing ever happened. Just heard noises. I didn't tell the cops 'cause it woulda sounded dumb. And we was high most of the time. Can't tell the cops that." He was staring at Winston's crushed Marlboro on the ground.

The detective reached into his pocket and pulled out another cigarette, offering it to the kid while the wind rustled the leaves in a giant maple in the yard.

"I'm only seventeen."

"I'm not a cop," Winston shrugged.

The kid took it and he lit it for him, sliding the Bic back into his pocket and watching the kid smoke. Little Greasy looked at the burning tip as he held it in his hand before grinning at the two of them. "You guys is alright. Are you gonna find who killed Collie? I miss her bad, you know. She was good people."

"We're gonna try," Winston nodded, "Do you remember at all what the person looked like who was in the trees? Or do you remember what you heard when you heard things?"

He shrugged again, "I don't remember. I was so blazed I just remember thinking, 'that's a person' and being kinda creeped by it. As for the noises, just like branches snappin' and stuff. Like footsteps and shufflin'. Like them cops was after us."

They thanked the little greaseball and turned to walk back to their car. They were silent. Winston was listening to the trees rustling and watching little dust devils spinning across the road as they walked. The heels of his shoes scraped the cement of the sidewalk, grating on his ears. He couldn't think hard enough. Avery was always quiet. He was thinking too. A killer. Stalking his victims in the forest. Seeing them out doing their thing—smoking weed, exploring places, whatever. Snatching them up out of the darkness. Pressing his thumbs down into their throats. Feeling the rush of life fading.

He rubbed his eyes with his fingers, watching the brilliant light play that came from the act before opening them wide to the blue sky above them and the fluffed white clouds that moved away from the ocean.

They had dealt with eight successful cases. They'd only dealt with one serial killer before. He wasn't one of the eight. They either were murderers who had significant motives or mysteries that were almost too easy to solve. Agatha Christie type murders with a set number of people involved and a logical motive for murder. Money was usually the case. Infidelity another. The investigators were always hired by family. This one was no exception. The only difference was that there was no shortage of suspects, no set amount of people to look at, and no discernable motive.

It seemed like a long time ago. It had been winter. An awful deep January that had a distinctly cruel chill that seeped into one's very bones. He could remember standing on the porch of a Healy Martin. The father of a victim. A victim that had been *chewed* to death. He could see his breath and it lingered above him in a steamy ethereal cloud illuminated by a yellowed porch light with a cover that was filled with the carcasses of flies and spiders. He could remember taking the case. Cocky and full of himself. He could handle it. He could track down a serial killer. No problem.

He rubbed at his chest again. He had tracked down a serial killer. No. That was wrong. He *had been tracked down* by a serial killer. Yeah. That was better. The corner of his lip twitched downward when he got in the car. Avery started it up and they drove away, Winston with nothing but a distant pain to ease the silence.

His hand was flat on her belly when she woke up, her sleep-fogged eyes fluttered open and settled on his face. His eyes. Dark blue and full of the same fog. He blinked a few times but it failed to repel the warmth she saw, the sleep in his mind. His hand felt hot through the fabric of her T-shirt. He inched forward and eased his lips onto hers, slipping his hand to her side and pulling her gently toward him. She obeyed and rolled into him, her arms tucked between them awkwardly.

He continued to kiss her. Light kisses, delicate and hesitant. His full lips played across hers with finesse and grace and the hand that had been on her side moved to gently stroke her jaw.

How many girls has he kissed like this? Her mind roiled as it came fully awake. Her eyes focused on his face. His lashes resting against his freckled cheeks. He must have become aware of her sudden tension and his small feather kisses stopped. He appeared sheepish when he examined her expression.

His voice was husky, whether from lust, sleep, or cigarettes she couldn't be certain. "Mornin' sweets."

"Mornin'," she murmured. Her eyes fluttered and she opened them as wide as she could in order to dispel any floaters in her vision. She watched him staring at her. "What?"

The curtain of coldness had yet to descend on him still but the hints of his surly demeanor had started to push together his brows. "I'm sorry."

Without thinking she pressed her mouth to his again in a short but well-aimed peck. "Don't be sorry."

His expression was that of mild shock. With a strong grasp he pulled her closer to him, their bodies pressed together in a rather intimate way.

"Ren?" Tomi asked in a hesitant manner, "What?" Her cheeks flushed a deep dusky pink when she realized just what was nestled against her thigh.

"I'm not sorry," he breathed into her ear, the warmth giving her goosebumps and sending little shocks through her body. He ran his hand up and down her back, once at least fluttering over her hip. "Forgive me."

She was trembling. The early morning light filtering in through the small window above them shined in the tiny dust motes that floated around them. She closed her eyes and tried to even her breathing. "Forgive you for what?"

Ren paused for a few moments before replying, "I'm not the gentleman you deserve."

Tomi frowned and opened her eyes again. His mouth had a downward turn to the edges; he was sad. Sad! It was a new emotion from him; she was impressed. "Ren," she stated blandly, putting her hand on the side of his face. "Deserve and desire are two wholly separate entities. Can't a good girl just enjoy her bad boy?"

"You don't know what you're getting into."

"Do I ever?" She giggled at herself. "That seems to be a common theme in my life recently. I have yet to regret it."

"You will."

"Probably. But that's what teen years are for, right?"

He sighed but his arousal still pressed insistently against her thigh. "You don't know what you're saying."

She tucked her face into his neck and nibbled him a little, relishing the small gasp she managed to elicit. She nibbled his fingers when he tried to push her away and he started to laugh. It was just a chuckle and it was warm and friendly. She laughed with him. "Look, boy, I know how this works. I'm not some silly little girl who's never kissed someone. Just because I'm a virgin doesn't mean I haven't had a guy's hand up my skirt."

Ren continued to laugh, harder this time and his face was turning a delightful shade of pink. She wasn't sure if it was because of her honesty or because of his laughter at it. When he finally settled he tickled her brow with a kiss and said with humor, "I suppose I'd never thought of you at some party playing eight minutes in heaven."

"I wasn't," her cheeks must have been ten shades of red. "I was out behind a shed at a party where Cayley and I must have been the youngest. He was some star football player and I was just some stupid kid."

His hand tickled its way down to her hip and settled there. The heat of it was incredible. His eyes were suddenly warmer, any hint of his normal coldness lost in some dark recess of his mind. He whispered, "What'd he do to you?"

"He..." she tried, but she couldn't bring herself to describe the lusty teenage fumbles that marked her sexual life. She shook her head and giggled instead.

Ren, however, remained perfectly serious as he pushed his lips to the side of her mouth and whispered gently, "Did he do this?" He pushed her slowly to her back and nibbled her ear, "Or this?" His lips found their way to her throat and in an even softer whisper he repeated, "Or this?" One of his hands was gripping her shoulder and the other fluttering somewhere near the hem of her T-shirt.

Her heart was pounding hard in her chest, her breaths coming in short pants while he hovered above her, his presence unlike anything she had felt before from him. She tried to ease her arms to her sides but when his fingers slipped under her shirt, she found herself gripping the sides of his so hard her knuckles were white. The tension in her body mounted.

He nipped at her collarbone through the fabric and breathed, "Don't be afraid of me. Please don't be afraid of me."

She forced her fingers to let go, her hands stiff and claw-like in their leaving. "Ah," she vocalized, "I'm trying." That's what it was. It wasn't simply unease at the idea of sexual interaction. It wasn't arousal tightening her body like this.

It was fear. She started to shake, the realization putting tears into her blue eyes.

Ren stopped. He cuddled her, his cheek mashed against the bare skin of her belly and her T-shirt bunched up under her breasts. "Just breathe," he told her. He followed his own advice along with her, taking deep breaths. After a time he lay beside her again, his eyes toward the ceiling.

"I'm sorry," she choked. "It was...sudden."

"You have nothing to be sorry for," he told her, the chill in his voice the unmistakable mark of the return of his frosty demeanor.

She let out a harsh sob, her mourning for the loss of his warmth.

His eyes flashed to her and she met them with hers, wide and red-rimmed. "It's just as well when you come down to it," he snapped.

She let out another sob and turned away from him, unable to stand his wintery gaze.

He rolled toward her and molded his body to hers, slipping his arm under hers and gripping her shoulder to push her further against him. He murmured against her shoulder, "I don't mean to be scary."

"What does it feel like?"

He whispered his question, "What does what feel like?"

She seemed to contemplate her question a little before asking it. As if she were afraid of getting in trouble. "When you become cold."

"Hot."

She blurted, "How did you kill your father?"

He took a long time to answer her question, laying behind her with even breathing. "Hmm," he finally started. "Uh...I..." He swallowed a few times. "I had washed the dishes after supper. It was dark out already. I went to my room to read a little. I never did finish that book." He pressed his forehead against the back of her neck before continuing.

"He...He called me upstairs to the kitchen again. I went. I was...confused. He usually just reads his paper and goes to bed." His arms tightened around her body. "I had barely walked into the kitchen and...I was on the floor. He broke a plate across my face. A plate. A thick porcelain plate." He spoke as if disbelieving himself. "I just laid there. I guess I was pretending to be knocked out. He left me there.

"The next morning, before anybody else was awake, I went down to the shed and I got a crowbar. I came into his room and I killed him. It only took one downward stroke. I sat on the floor afterward. I didn't have any strength in my legs. My..." He shifted and took in a shuddering breath. "My mother told me to run. So I did and...and I have been ever since."

They breathed together for a while. Tomi put her hand on top of his that was on her shoulder. She could hear the rustling of the trees outside and the scent of dust and old things helped her calm down. "Thank you for telling me," she said. Her reflections on his tale had soothed her wild heart. He'd been beaten. *Just a dog* he'd said. He simply bit back. And of course bit others, she reminded herself. He was in many ways just like a dog. A big dog, she thought, with a lot of teeth. A rottweiler.

They sat around the large table as if they were knights of Camelot. Their cheeks were in their hands and they were all staring down at the large black and white map in front of them. A map of the coast and parts of the main land. Large red dots had been poked in a few places.

"I don't get it, Avery," Winston grumbled. "There's no real pattern here." There were murmurs of agreement from the other detectives and even the intern. They'd come back to D.C., back to the agency if only to get ideas from their other partners. It had proved a futile attempt at best. A wasted trip.

Avery blinked a few times. "I'm sorry Trent, I wasn't even thinking about that."

Winston lifted one brow and drummed his fingers on the surface of the table.

"I was just..." Avery drew a line with his finger from the bridge connecting the islands to the main land to the small town they had visited. His dark gaze shifted one way and then another before he dragged his finger harder into the closest and longest patch of forest. "I was just thinking about where she might have gone. I'd search these woods first. Hounds of course," he mused.

"I made copies of her picture and gave the cops a description of what she was wearing." His voice held a barely concealed edge.

"I think we're dealing with a rather intelligent girl, Winston. Despite all you might think of her and her family I think we're dealing with a girl who's got a gift."

Winston grunted and frowned, scratching the back of his head in a sudden fit of unease. He told the others they were dismissed and they filed out of the room. None of them had any useful ideas anyway. He put a finger to his upper lip and tapped a few times. "I shouldn't feel as if some little girl is going to be harder to find than a real case."

"I think," Avery smiled, "You'll find that eventually she might just become a real case of yours. She's a worthy opponent, is she not?"

"Until she tears out a man's intestines and writes on the wall with his blood she's not going to be any kind of opponent to me," Winston stated darkly.

Avery was not deterred by his sentiment. He stared at where his finger had been and smiled his creepy little smile. "She's certainly intrigued *me*, that's for certain." He tapped his finger on the map again and gave Winston a knowing stare. "She may not be a threat to anyone, Trent, but he's out there. If he finds her..."

Winston gritted his teeth. "Dogs. Dogs now."

Carl was of a likeable sort. He was an independent dog trainer who specialized in the training of tracking dogs such as bloodhounds. Their lonely howls could be heard from their luxury kennel and Winston smoked a cigarette while the two trackers spoke to one another. Carl's reserved personality fit well with quiet and confident Avery. His comfortable clothes and baseball cap betrayed his willingness to remain an independent entity that happened to be highly respected by Winston,

Avery, and the local authorities.

"So you need the best is what you're saying," Carl flashed them all his rare grin. Much like Avery, tracking was what floated Carl Tanner's boat. "How long are we talkin'?" Winston could already see the man calculating his price.

Avery was smooth. "She's just a girl. I couldn't see it having to be more than just one day or two." He blinked once and his eyes shifted to Winston. "I'd like to get this matter settled as soon as possible, you understand of course."

Carl's grin grew wider. "Butt-hurt you couldn't find her, eh?"

Avery's dark eyebrow lifted in a playful manner. "I merely believe that a dog may be able to track her faster." He shrugged lightly. "I'm sure that if I were set to the task it would become complete, however as time is of concern in this matter I must delegate responsibility to a being who is able to smell her."

Carl nodded but was still amused. Winston chuckled as he watched the two of them. "Come on, kids," he said with humor, "Let's find our girl so Avery and I can go home."

The dogs took matters very quickly into their paws. Her scent was taken from some dirty laundry her mother had provided and the dogs soon began to sniff around the edges of the forest Avery had fingered on the map. The first few hours were boring for the young agent, his fingers fussing about with his lighter in his pocket or his shoes digging into the loose sandy soil at his feet. The wind whipped his hair and raked invisible fingers through it. He wondered how in the heavens such an animal was to be expected to sniff for one girl's scent when thousands wafted from the sea begging for attention.

The dogs were not to be diverted. Their noses meticulously moved through the brush and at last one of the handlers called out. They ran to him, Avery in the lead. His dark haired companion followed closely behind the animal, searching for any traces of human contact with the ground or the branches around them.

It was dusk and the dog was still following the trail when Avery looked over at Winston and sighed, discreetly telling his partner what he'd been dreading all day. "This is going to take longer than we thought. She's traveled fast and carefully. There's something about this girl, Winston. There's something about this whole situation I don't like at all." Something caught his eye. He frowned.

"What is it, bud?" Winston asked.

"There's something not quite right." He was staring off into the forest, away from the trail the dog had been making through the brush. He took a step away through the leaves on the forest floor. With hawk eyes the man put his fingers behind a leaf and examined it carefully.

"Avery?"

"It's...it's nothing. I think."

"If you're sure."

"I am." Avery didn't look sure. In fact he looked a little out of sorts.

CHAPTER 3

"Ren?" she asked with fear fluttering in her heart.

"Yes?" came his reply from inside the structure.

She continued to bathe herself but cast wary glances around into the woods. "I was just making sure you were in there."

"I'm not spying on you, Little Miss," he chuckled. "I'm sure you're very lovely but I have a little more respect for women than that."

She smiled but her wariness did not fade and she quickly dried herself and pulled on the rest of her clothes. The warm breeze that filtered through the woods rustled the leaves of the dense foliage and the whispers of the wilderness around her made her shiver. She felt eyes on her. Perhaps it was just some woodland creature. A doe maybe. Nevertheless her body felt a gaze. Tomi felt better when she had reentered the crumbling gas station. Having neglected to put her bra back on she blushed when his eyes flitted very swiftly over her breasts, outlined by her T-shirt. Respect for women her butt. He had said a *little,* her mind conceded.

He cleared his throat when he looked away from her. She had started to think of him in terms of seasons. Most times he was winter. But early in the morning he was autumn and late at night he was spring. Summer she had yet to see from him. The true extent of his warmth was still a mystery to her.

"You should have some supper," he told her, offering her a small plastic plate with a slice of spam and a pile of canned peas with a few chips on the side.

She smiled at him but he didn't look at her. "Thank you," she told him, leaning forward in a blatant attempt to catch his eyes. When she couldn't she just sighed. She had been trying to appeal to his wintery side for a while but her efforts met with a stone wall. He was approachable only in the morning and the evening when sleep fogged his mind and his attentions could be swerved toward his desire for her. And yet she did not feel complete. She could not. It was her resolution that she would never feel at ease with him until one of two things occurred. Either she had to dispel all of his chill entirely or she had to make even the cold parts of him fond of her. She chewed her spam when she sat down in their little nest with determination set in her features.

"You thought I would spy on you?" he asked. He didn't seem offended. Just a simple question.

She felt foolish about thinking that she had felt someone watching her bathe. It was probably just normal to feel that way when one was mostly naked in the wilderness. She brushed it off. "Maybe I was hoping you would."

"Liar," he teased. She was glad for his humor, however deadpan it was.

"You can't deny I'm pretty."

"No. I can't."

"You also can't deny that you would like to touch me." She swallowed. What was she saying? She set down her plate, her food half eaten. "I'd like to touch you too, Ren."

"Tomi, please. Eat your food."

"No."

The frost in his expression should have cooled her but it didn't. They were at a stalemate. Either he would get up and leave to eat his supper in peace or he would let her have her way. Her mind raced for any way she could get him to sway one way rather than the other.

Action, not words, was her choice. She took his hand and pressed it to her breast, nothing but the thin fabric of her T-shirt separating their flesh. His palm was warm and he watched his own hand on her as if he were unsure of what his next action should be.

Good, she thought. Let him suffer. Let him decide whether or not he would squeeze or pull away. It felt like such a long time she was waiting for him to make his decision.

When he finally did she squeaked with surprise. He had her on her back before she knew it, his hand cupping her fully and his mouth covering hers in a kiss that was very much unlike those she had experienced from his warmer seasons. It was harsher, deeper, less controlled. His movements over her were fast and hard, his mouth nipping over the side of her thoat and then her neck, his teeth closing lightly on her shoulder. She gasped at the feel of his bared teeth on her flesh through her shirt, the light pressure and the danger of him shooting a strange desire mixed with her sudden fear through her body. His crotch ground into her hip, the force of his pushing revealing his rigid erection through his jeans. He made a deep gutteral sound in his throat as he breathed and his hips thrust against her.

She wasn't quite sure what to think of the situation until he forced her out of thinking. He had pulled her shirt up over her breasts and his bare palm was feeling her, his warm skin rasping over her nipple in a way that made her gasp out of shock and pleasure. The pleasure was soon replaced by panic when he ripped her shirt completely off and his fierce gaze roved over her. His mouth spread back to reveal his vicious rows of white teeth and he came down upon her as though he were an animal, his hard member being pushed against her thigh as he came over her. His teeth closed around her shoulder as his forehead touched the floor under her.

He bit her.

She screamed.

His whole body was shaking. A soft tremble that had not left him for hours. He had not said a word. He simply stared past her and smoked, his hands shaking almost too hard to bring the filter to his lips. The cool night air was rustling through his hair and he still was staring off into the forest when she came out again. He had disappeared for a long time, retreating into the forest as it served as his sanctuary. She had patiently awaited his return and had been relieved to find him washing his face in the rain barrel in the dark. He hadn't been able to meet her eyes so he had just sat out front and smoked.

"Ren," she murmured, "You need to sleep. It must be close to midnight."

He didn't reply. He took another drag from his cigarette.

"Ren, please," she begged. She sat down next to him with her back against the crumbling wall and took his free hand. He did not look at her. "Ren, you need to sleep."

It was a long time before he said anything and still he did not look at her. "No."

"I won't take no for an answer, I will take 'yes Little Miss' or 'okay' but I will not take 'no.'"

He blinked. "I can't."

"Why?"

His voice lowered to a whisper. "Every time I close my eyes, I hear you scream."

She bit her bottom lip and put her head down on his shoulder. "I know you didn't mean it."

"It doesn't matter if I meant it. It matters that I did it. I...I hurt you."

"I'm not bleeding."

"You'll bruise."

Tomi squeezed his hand in hers. "I'm a trooper. You said it yourself. I think I can handle a little bruise. Plus I think we can both agree that I was completely asking for it. Literally."

"You didn't ask for what I did," he corrected her. "You were not expecting what happened. It should not have happened. No woman asks for that. I lost my composure...and I'm sorry."

She took in a shuddering breath. "I'm sorry too. For goading you. I shouldn't have been so pushy." She bent toward his ear and smiled when her breath made goosebumps rise on the bare skin of his arms. "I like being intimate with you."

"I don't want to hurt you."

"You won't," she whispered when she leaned toward him and

flattened her hand on his stomach. "When it comes right down to it, you won't." She got him to go inside with her after a tender little kiss and in minutes they were asleep, cuddled together under his sweatshirt, Tomi contentedly drooling on his chest and his hand softly covering the bitemark he'd given her.

Nadine was furious. She stomped through the long grass toward him with rage sparking out of her very eyeballs. "What do you mean you've stopped using the dogs?"

He'd have to use a silver-tongue to get through this one. "My dearest sister." He tried to bat his eyelashes but she was having none of it. "Your boss doesn't want to make the expense and they weren't as useful as we thought they were going to be anyway. Our agency certainly isn't going to foot the bill so we're left with you, me, and our lovable hound, Avery. Now have you heard anything else from the family?"

"Yes. Mr. Balekowski is relatively certain that she may be attempting to find her brother, Bo. They had had an argument about Bo and Tomi had gotten rather upset. Apparently she was forbidden from seeing him. That didn't really sit well with her."

"He didn't tell us this sooner...because?"

Nadine shrugged. "The man is a born liar. I wouldn't be surprised if it was some kind of half-truth. If you ask me, I'm surprised there's even a trail to follow. If I didn't know better I'd think this *was* a wild goose chase and that girl is buried in the backyard of that stupid beach mansion." She rolled her eyes. "There's no way that family doesn't have some kind of connection with the mob."

"Agreed," Winston grinned. "But I have a feeling the mob isn't what we'll be dealing with in the end."

Nadine frowned and her arms crossed. She turned her eyes towards the woods. Avery was nowhere to be seen but he was busily tracking, setting down bright yellow markers at every movement he could find. A step here, a step there, a broken branch, a turned stone. Soon even Winston, whose only skill was his hard ass and his charm, would be able to pick his way through the trail.

"You see, Sis," Winston grinned, "we'll find her. Whether she's alive or not, we'll find her."

"What's that supposed to mean?" she snapped, "She's coming all this way, she'd better still be alive."

Avery popped out of the brush. "Did she have any friends who might have gone with her?"

Winston shook his head.

Avery frowned, "We have a problem then, Trent."

Nadine leaned forward and Winston's shoulders tensed.

"She was being followed."

The three of them stood there contemplating what had just spilled from the rather disheveled agent's mouth. He wiped his sweat off his forehead with the heel of his hand and tried to read the others' faces.

Nadine was the first to speak, swallowing hard before she did. "So you're saying she was being followed--but by *whom* exactly?"

"If I could guess I'd say he wears around a size thirteen but he walks on his toes and balls of his feet. The tread is almost completely worn away so there's no telling what kind of shoe. He's left no other trace."

Winston looked down at the ground and let out a large breath. "What of her?"

"She's barefoot. She has tiny feet." The side of his mouth eased upward for a small appreciative grin. He was the type to be affectionate to small women.

"How old are the tracks?" Nadine pried.

"About a week I'd say. She moves fast. She might have known she was being followed."

Nadine's eyes filled with horror. "Oh no. What if...what if he caught up with her?"

Winston picked his teeth with one fingernail and flicked away the offending piece of pepper he found. He swiped his tongue over his top teeth. "We'll just have to hope that didn't happen yet, won't we?"

With that he followed Avery back into the woods. It was nightfall again before they stopped at the nearest rented motel room. Winston had just gotten out of the shower and was walking about with his cheap motel towel wrapped around his waist when Avery cracked open an eye.

"Trent, there's something I didn't tell you."

"What's that, bud?"

Avery took in a deep breath. "I think there's something wrong with this whole Balekowski business."

"Think she isn't really running?"

"No, that's not it. She's really out there somewhere. Alive or dead, she's out there. But there *is* someone following her. And there are bad men out in this world. You and I know that more than any. But my question is...how in the hell did she make it so far and why is she making the choices she's making?"

Winston sat on the edge of the bed. "I don't know, buddy. But you're right. She's clever. Not the type of clever you'd usually see from some teenaged brat of a politician. She's more than that."

"Not to mention that it's actually a little disconcerting. I'll see the tracks of the follower and then they'll disappear. Just...gone. As if he weren't there at all. I can't even follow them off into the woods. It's like he swung away into the branches like some kind of chimp."

"Maybe he did." The younger detective laid down on the bed, his bare damp back scratched by the cheap bedspread.

Avery rolled over onto his stomach, losing some of his poise. "I just can't help but wonder how long it'll be until we won't be searching for a girl anymore."

"We still have another case," Winston reminded him.

"Please, Winston," Avery chided, "that one's depressing. The girl is easier and she's much more exciting. I'd just rather find her...and not her body. She's challenging and the case makes me hopeful to find her. Not to mention that it would probably be best to find her before *he* does."

Winston turned his head toward his partner. "Stop staring at her picture when I'm not looking, you've fallen in love with her."

Avery laughed heartily. "In love with her..." he chuckled to himself. "Do you think that's it, Trent? A boy who's in love with her?"

"I'll ask Nadine to poke around for possible love interests. I can't believe we're spending so much of our time to look for some errant little girl. I just hope we can catch up to her."

"She's a wily one," Avery agreed.

Winston chewed his lip a little and murmured, "Not quite as wily as our others though."

Avery softly agreed.

"Well..." Avery grinned when his eyes flashed toward the small structure.

Winston placed his shades on top of his head and put his hands on his hips. Two days ago he had decided he wasn't at the office so he might as well forgo the suit. Avery had followed his example and they gallivanted around the countryside in their more comfortable T-shirts and jeans. He examined the structure with unease in his features.

"She was traveling alone at this point. Of course I say alone but we both know he wasn't too far behind...just...somewhere else." His eyes shifted through the trees.

"Was she running?"

"No, same steady pace. A little slower though I think. I think her feet hurt."

Winston made a small "tch" sound and he picked at the bark of a tree. "Can I look in the bathrooms now?"

"Yes, Winston, you can look in the bathrooms now."

He trudged on over to the small decrepit brick building. He nudged open the mens room door first and with a small peek inside saw nothing out of the ordinary. She wouldn't have been in there anyway, he told himself, she's a lady, she would have gone to the ladies room. When he moved over to the other side of the place he put his ear to the ladies room door. There was a faint rustling inside but with a small glance around the corner he realized that there was a whole tree branch that had grown into the room. No wonder there was rustling.

He eased open the door and announced himself as Detective Winston. There was no reply. "Avery," he called out. "I think your girl slept here."

His dark haired partner loomed behind him like a specter. "I think you're right," he agreed in his soft voice. He moved around Winston with movements like a big cat and he frowned at the floor, looking and taking in everything. All the different movements she made to clear out a space for her to sleep. "Mmmf..." Avery made the small noise of disappointment and Winston tilted his head in question, knowing Avery would elaborate whether he saw it or not. "She didn't sleep here. There would be less small debris on the floor. It would have been picked up on her clothes. She didn't sleep here but she thought she was going to."

"Odd."

"Very." With that his partner left the room and started to walk around the building to the right. "There are tracks over here. Around the outside. The one following her was out here, I think." He paused for a minute and Winston used that time to follow him. "Do you..." Avery started and paused to smell the air.

"Smell something?" Winston finished for him and sniffed as well. A very faint odor met his nose. It was not pleasant. "Yeah. I smell something." He started walking around the back of the building, taking in deep breaths through his nose as he went. He looked around him at the ground. The smell grew in intensity as he and Avery stepped further away from the back of the bathrooms.

"It's decomp," Avery said in a grave tone. He was disappointed.

"Yeah, now if we could find where it's coming from..." Winston's eyes continued to scan the forest floor. There was a downed tree just a few yards away from them and he decided to investigate it. The smell grew worse. "Over here, Avery, I think I got this." It was the kind of smell that a normal person only ever encounters on the highway when someone's mashed up a deer and didn't call the cops. So it sits there bloating and rotting for days before some kind of scavenger decides to pick it up and drag it off. The smell that you remember the very next time you drive through so you put up your windows and put the air on "recirc." Winston didn't even put his hand over his nose. He'd smelled it so many times it was just annoying. Like finding spoiled meat in the back of your fridge after a power outage.

When he moved around the log he was hoping for an animal. But he knew it wouldn't be. The blueish tinted flesh of an arm was enough to figure that out. "I found something, Avery." He could feel his lip twitching.

"Fuck." His partner kicked at some leaves hard.

"I'm gonna call it in."

"Is it her?"

"I can't see her face, I don't want to disturb any evidence."

If there had been a wall to punch, Avery looked like he could have punched it. As it was there were only trees and Avery had to be satisfied with putting his hands in his pockets and slumping his shoulders in a mope.

When she woke up Autumn was staring at her. Memorizing her. She cuddled into his chest.

"I've done terrible things," he stated.

"I know," was her reply.

He wrapped his arms around her. "You don't know the half of it."

"Tell me then," she whispered before giving him a small kiss on his lips.

He looked pained for a few moments before he sat up and looked down at her. He didn't say a word, he simply packed a few things in his bag and stood.

"Are we going?" she asked.

"Yes. We're going."

She got up as well, ruffling her hair around her face before putting it up in a messy bun. "My feet feel better."

"Mmm." Winter had come.

They traveled for a long time. When she got tired, he carried her on his back. They didn't speak much, only enough for them to figure out what they were going to eat and where they were going to get it. She had learned how to be resourceful. Ren was very good at making food simply appear. She had the thought that it may or may not have come out of a dumpster but if he could make it look appetizing then she would eat it. It was in this way that she managed to keep much of her money.

When the sun started to sink in the sky, Ren found them a very small grassy spot under a tree in the middle of a corn field. Cut off from eyes by the tall corn, Tomi felt safe and secluded with him. A warm summer rain came down just before sunset but the tree was a haven from it and it cleared just before the sky turned orange and pink. She watched him, awaiting Spring with an eager heart.

"I managed to swipe us some chocolates," he grinned as he reached into his bag.

"From a store?"

"Nah. Their sell by date is today. You don't mind, do you?" His head tilt showed her that he was perfectly serious in his question.

"Of course not, silly."

He was digging in her bag when she heard it. A small rustle in the corn. Her eyes tried to find the source of the sound, looking for an animal. Maybe a chipmunk or a rat. Her sharp intake of breath was enough to alert Ren.

"What?" he asked, the chocolates in his hand. He examined her and then moved his gaze to where hers was affixed to the corn. "Tomi, I don't see anything."

"I thought I saw someone. In the corn."

"Someone?" Ren dropped the candy and stood up, casually walking toward the crop wall with easy steps. "I'll be right back."

"Ren, don't," she put her back against the tree.

"I said I'll be right back." He didn't look at her before he stepped off into the maize.

She trained her ears to follow his movements through the field but soon she lost him in the rustle of the wind. She moved her eyes to the sky and tried to take her mind off of him and whomever he was stalking. She had just barely been able to make out a duckling in the shapes above her before she was startled to her feet by the cries of a flock of cowbirds who rose steeply from the stalks of corn into the sky.

She trembled with her fingers to her lips for what seemed like an eternity before crying out sharply when a figure slunk from the wall.

"It's just me," Ren was grinning.

"Was there...?"

"I saw some tracks but they could have been from an animal. Calm down, sweets. You're getting a little paranoid out here, aren't you?"

"Maybe," she sighed. "I was probably just seeing things. I'm sorry if I upset you."

He sat her down under the tree again and handed her the bag of chocolates. "Don't be sorry. It's okay to be scared sometimes."

She could hear Spring's blooms in his voice and her heart fluttered in her chest. She opened the bag and started to munch while she gazed at him, his eyes watching the corn with just a slight bit of concern in his features.

She whispered, "Is something wrong?"

He didn't look at her when he replied, "Yes. There is something wrong." Ren's shoulders were stiff as if he were poised to attack. "I think we'll be all right here tonight. But something doesn't feel right. Something's a little..."

CHAPTER 4

"Off. Something's off," Winston was again standing outside the morgue. "This is just getting weirder and weirder."

Avery was tracing his finger over the grout between the bricks in the basement wall. They'd been sitting in the county police station for a few hours, discussing with the assigned detectives their involvement with Tomi Balekowski. They were trying to explain why they had been the first to find the body. Winston had done a very decent job in also explaining their involvement in an independent investigation into the murder of Collie Landall and had handled being told to stay the hell away from the police investigation with finesse and, as he saw it, poise. But here they were, with their hands on the cause of death and a simple peek at most of the evidence. This one was no doubt related to Collie. But the fact remained that she wasn't Tomi Balekowski. Tomi, being alive, took precedence.

"First we can't find our girl. Then we think we found our girl. But it's not our girl. How do we know we haven't been completely wrong this whole time?"

"The dogs," Avery scratched his head. "We were on the right track. We didn't make a mistake. Tomi Balekowski was there. I'm not wrong. This girl isn't even blonde. But she's definitely one of ours."

"How the fuck did she get there?" Winston gently kicked the wall. "God. What the fuck is going *on*, Avery?"

"The M.O. is right, Winston. She's one of ours. You know exactly how she got there."

"And yet I don't know enough. He's too stealthy. We know nothing about him aside from just the most basic of details. Where are we supposed to go with this? Assume that Tomi figured something was amiss and got the hell out of there?"

Avery put the heel of his palm to his forehead. "Honestly Winston I have just a little bit of a problem with that theory."

It was just then that Nadine once again interrupted their meeting. Her chesnut hair swayed in its long pony down her back when she ran down toward them. Breathless she asked, "I heard you found a girl."

"Not yours."

The look of relief washed over her face and made Winston just a little jealous. "Oh thank God," she breathed. "Have you figured out who she is?"

"Not yet."

"Is she one of yours then?" Her lip curled up in distaste. Nadine didn't have much of a liking for any of Winston's cases. They had too much mystery for her. Plus they were just a little more morbid than she was willing to work with. Her career was more for the quick in-and-out. Winston and Avery were in it for the long haul. They worked the cases with the freaks.

Avery answered her with a small nod.

She visibly shivered. "How old?"

"Doc said she was around eighteen," Avery murmured. "God knows where he found her."

Nadine shook her head. "When I heard that you guys had found a girl...god I must have just nearly died right then and there. Are you keeping this in mind? That he's out there? That Tomi's out there too? She must look like a fish in a barrel out there."

Winston picked a cigarette out of his pack and put it behind his ear to smoke as soon as he could. "We're aware, Naddy. We're trying. You know this."

"I know." She rubbed her eyes with her fingers. "I definitely know."

When Naddy had left and the two of them stood outside in the too-bright summer sun and the cool ocean breeze, Winston turned to Avery and sighed. "Maybe we should have told her that someone's following her. And we might have a good idea who that may be at this point."

"Speaking of," Avery looked at the ground. "I was about to tell you something before Nadine got there."

"Right," Winston took a drag and let it out. "You have a problem."

"Yes, with the theory that Tomi sensed something fishy and blew the Popsicle stand."

"What's the problem?"

Avery took a breath and let it out before he dropped the bomb. "She didn't leave by herself."

There was a pause in which only the wind spoke, rushing past Winston's ears like a hurried lover. When he spoke he took his cigarette out of his mouth and held it in his fingers too tightly. "What do you mean?"

"I mean that I did a little snooping before we left the scene. There are no footprints from her leaving that structure. The prints are from her follower. I'm fairly certain he caught up with her, Trent. He still walked on his toes but the impressions are deeper. He was probably carrying her."

"Fucking God. We're too late."

Avery was silent for a small time before he said quietly, "He wouldn't kill her so easily. He'd take her somewhere else first and then dump her. Wouldn't he?"

Winston shook his head, "I don't even know. I don't even care. But we've got his tracks. That's a start at least. Besides, there's been something wrong with this business from the start. Maybe this is no different. Maybe there's something wrong with this too."

Autumn was holding her tight when she awoke, his arms surrounding her in a protective manner as if he were holding some kind of golden idol Indiana Jones wished to put in a museum. She watched his face while he slept, his lashes gently resting on his freckled cheeks and all cold seemingly gone from his visage. Birds chirped in the trees above them, their twittering a reminder that despite her odd surroundings and the strangeness that had suddenly filled her life, the world moved on. Her mother was probably folding laundry around this time. Her father might be in his study, going over some of his papers. Or whatever he did in there, she thought with a roll of her eyes. They wouldn't stop everything just because she was gone. It wasn't as though she had been the first of their children to leave. Laundry still had to be folded and papers still needed to be looked over.

What would they have thought of her lying in a clearing in the arms of a boy? Not just a boy. She closed her eyes and swallowed hard. If only he had been simply a boy. Not a killer. Not some kind of demon on Earth to tempt her. If only he had been more innocent than that. Even then they would not have approved. But nobody could approve of Ren. Wild, lawless, untamed Ren. Destructive, morbid, ruthless Ren.

She stared at his full lips and started to cry. The shaking of her shoulders woke him. He didn't say anything. He merely sat up and held her to him and rocked her back and forth very slowly, petting her hair. He didn't seem bothered by the tears and snot on his tank top and shoulder. He didn't say a word when she gave unladylike snorts and harsh intakes of air that made a strange choking sound. She couldn't see him through her tears. She couldn't smell him through her snot. All she could have of him was the feel of his warmth and his arms around her and the steady rocking.

He would never ask why. He knew why, she thought. He knew that it was the sudden horror and sadness of a death too soon. To the rest of the world, she knew, he was dead. He held no more worth to society. Not only could she shed tears for those he had cut down, she could shed tears for him. No wonder he was so cold. He was dead inside. The only warmth within him was the warmth that came from an escape from this world. His dreams. His sleep.

Enough time went by that she could feel her tears cooling and drying on her cheeks, making salty snail trails down to her chin. She laid her head against his chest and he stilled, his hand buried in her hair while she stared out through her blurry vison toward the line where the corn met the sky. She could still hear the birds in the trees as they were unimpressed by her sobs.

She felt a few more warm tears slip down her cheeks when she thought of her next words which she whispered out toward the morning breeze. "I don't know where home is anymore."

He didn't say anything. He didn't have to. He pressed his lips to the top of her head and breathed with her. This man. Autumn. This boy could be her home. Surely she loved him though his time with her was fleeting. His fading warmth comforted her. He would die. Like he died every morning when Winter snuffed out the rest of his compassion. She couldn't keep him there. There weren't enough tears in the world to keep him with her forever.

Tomi took in shaky breaths before she moved so she could look him in the eyes. He did not shy away from her stare. "I want..." her eyes flitted to the ground and then back up at him again. Did she? Her heart felt like it was going to burst. "I want to have sex with you."

Ren made a small movement away from her so she caught him with a hand on the back of his neck. His eyes shifted one way and then another.

"Don't go away," she pleaded, one fresh tear sliding from the corner of her eye. "Don't go away, please. I don't know how to say it any other way." She put her head down and pressed the top of it into his chest.

His hands brought her chin up and his thumbs wiped away her tears. "You don't know what you're asking for," he murmured.

"I know goddamn well what I'm asking for."

He seemed to think for a moment, the bottom lids of his eyes shaking a little as he made his internal decision. When he kissed her it felt as though everything in the world was right. As if something had clicked into place. Like a key fitting perfectly into a lock. There was a sudden intake of breath on his part as if he couldn't fathom her.

She held him tighter and closed her eyes so hard she could see spots dancing in the dark. There was nothing feverish about their movements. Nothing desperate. Everything they did was deliberate.

It wasn't long before she was naked in his arms. His jeans were still on and her soft flesh rubbed against the rough texture. Their kissing was lighter and sweeter. Autumn was careful with her, his hands moving about her with the lightest of touches. When his fingers found her he was almost reverent in his ministrations. She sighed against him and grasped a handful of his hair, squeaking into his ear when what he did pleased her.

The morning sun kissed her bare flesh and when she opened her eyes and looked at him, he was illuminated by it in a way that made him seem much younger. His eyes were cloudy from lust, his lips swollen from her kisses, and his cheeks rosy with his blushing. She pushed her forehead to his and whispered, "Don't make me wait."

He pushed his jeans and boxers down just far enough and she felt him bare at her backside while she straddled him. Without quite knowing what she was doing, she tried to guide him into her, sliding down over him with hesitancy.

"Wait," he gripped her hips hard, keeping her poised above him, trapped at some barrier she thought could be both mental and physical. "I don't want to hurt you."

"Well that's just inevitable," she pried his hands off her hips and gritted her teeth through the pain. For a few seconds she breathed with him, staring into his eyes while he was buried within her. "That was not so bad, was it?" she joked, chuckling a little at his worried expression. To ease the wrinkles between his eyebrows she kissed him and gently rocked her body against his. It wasn't long before she was able to get him into a rhythm and all worries of his hurting her were gone.

"Wait, sweets," he groaned, putting his hands on her hips, "Wait." He pushed her forward onto her back, the spongey grass comforting her in the shade of their tree. He pushed his knees into the soft soil and breathed hard in her ear.

She wrapped her arms around him, pulling his hair hard with every fervent thrust. His jeans chaffed the delicate flesh of her inner thighs. She gasped and sighed when he kissed her throat and nibbled at her ear but found herself suddenly cold as he pulled from her and fell backward, supported just barely by his elbows behind him.

When she sat up and pushed her mussed hair back from her face she found him breathing hard, his cheeks a dusty pink. Shiny off-white liquid was beading on the damp grass between them. "I'm sorry." He closed his eyes and his breathing began to slow. "I wasn't sure when..."

She crawled to him and kissed him. "Don't go away," she whispered to him. He didn't have to understand. He just had to hear her. Really hear her. Deep in that chasm that was inside him he had to click into place. Something had to happen inside him. Wasn't that the way it worked? Wasn't that how she was supposed to get her way? She had to sacrifice something of value and of course in every fairy tale that was the quiet little mouse of a virgin who was to be married off to the best and the brightest. Here he was. The best and the brightest. "God please don't go away," she whispered again, wrapping her arms around his neck and holding him as tight as she dared.

"What do you mean, darlin'?" He was smiling a little. That little sane grin he'd had when she first met him. "I'm not goin' anywhere."

"You don't understand." She shook her head and kissed his temple with all her might.

"You're right, sweets." He was full-blown smiling now. That normal smile. Cute and innocent. The smile of a boy band hottie on the cover of their lastest album. "I don't quite understand you sometimes."

She realized suddenly that there were tears slipping down her cheeks and she wiped them away with the back of her hand and sniffed. When she sat back on her heels she could feel the stickiness of herself on the inside of her thighs.

When her clothes were back on and they were rightly in order, she looked at him for his signal to leave which was mostly always a simple nod of his head in the direction of his choosing. He adjusted the way things were situated in his napsack before making the small gesture and they were off on their way.

She stared at him with wide blue eyes a little puffy from her crying. She was trying to see if Winter was back. She was trying to see how long Autumn could stay. Her hopes, she knew, were set much too high when she held him and begged him not to go. But when he looked over his shoulder at her and she looked up at him he paused a moment in his walking and put his hand out beside him, his fingers outstretched. An invitation.

She took his hand and walked beside him, his too-warm fingers closing over hers in a firm grip. As if she were the one who was going to disappear.

"Isn't this just a fucking mess and a half," Winston took a deep breath in and out to calm himself. "She left here. He left here. He took her here. He didn't kill her here but he took her here and now she's with him. Great. They were together. Awesome. Now he has her, cool. But what is he *doing* with her?"

Avery had his finger to his bottom lip. His deep eyes were taking in every detail of the scene before him. "She's rather compliant," he mused.

"Fear does odd things to the mind," Winston stated darkly.

Avery gave him a complacent little nod. "Black hair. With some kind of red dye. Probable that it's generic. Maybe a disguise. One that grew out with his natural color. Nothing good enough for DNA testing though. No semen, could have raped her with a condom."

"Not his style," Winston rejected the idea with a careless wave of his hand and side-stepped around one of the lab guys who was dusting the shelves with a careful hand. "Haven't come up with any prints either. Must have been awful careful with what he touched." The scene in *Hannibal* where the doctor uses a cloth to drink his wine came back to him. Was he dealing with someone who was truly that intelligent? "There aren't even prints on these old cans he must have eaten out of. Did he wipe them off when he was finished? What kind of careful fuck are we dealing with?"

Avery smiled at his partner. He had much too much patience with the childlike Winston. "Trent, take a breath and calm yourself. She was alive and he kept her alive. They left together. We'll leave the lab boys here to see if they can find anything and we'll move on ahead on the trail. We can pick through his brains when we've caught him. Literally if your temper gets to you." His dark eyes flitted to Winston's nine millimeter then back up to his face. There was a first time for everything, he told himself not without a little humor.

"There are...extra tracks in places. Like someone stepped over their prints," Avery told a very bored and very hot Winston who had been scuttling behind with a bottle of water.

"Great. What kind of shoes?"

"Sneakers. Like those types you used to wear in high school."

Winston smiled, "Maybe Nike."

"Size around nine I'd say." He scratched the back of his head and then swatted a fly on his arm. "I don't know if they matter. Probably not. We'll just keep them in mind."

They tracked well into the night until it started to rain.

"Son of a bitch," Avery said, whipping his flashlight around while big fat drops of rain poured from the sky. "It'll be so much harder after a rain."

"Nothin' you can do," Winston's voice sounded muffled as if it were only inside Avery's head.

The rain was relentless. It poured down as the sun set, making the whole world take on a strange yellow color. The two of them had wet hair that was spiked upward from their foreheads. They were wearing damp sweatshirts and muddy jeans and Adidas sneakers that squeaked when they walked with the extra moisture. The bull pen was relatively quiet as it was late in the day but they knew the detective working the Holly Marden case would still be there, burning the midnight oil and a little bit of his sanity. His name was Oliver Patten and he was the lead detective for all of this serial killer's work.

Patten peeked out of his office at the far end of the bull pen and recognized the two of them immediately. He made a vague "come hither" motion and then popped back into the office. Winston and Avery complied, squeaking and squelching across the pen until they were inside the warm little office. Patten's desk resembled Winston's more than Avery's spilling over with files and papers and photographs that marked the day's work and stress. Stress was the key factor and apparent in Patten's sullen expression, sunken green eyes, and messy brown hair. He might have lost some weight as well, his suit hanging just a little too baggy on his shoulders.

"Gentlemen," he started, shuffling around the papers on his desk and bringing out a file folder. He motioned toward the two chairs on the other side of the desk and the two of them sat. "You are private investigators who have been hired by the Landalls to investigate the murder of their daughter Collie. That is correct? You've taken the job?"

Winston nodded and stated, "We have accepted the offer."

"And you are aware that the working theory on Collie's murder is that she was killed by a serial murderer."

"We're aware."

"And you were the first on the scene of his latest killing."

The two of them were quiet for a bit before Winston leaned forward with his elbows on his thighs. "We were here that day, we answered the officer's direct questions but we didn't quite go into the details. We were called into a different case. As a favor to my sister. Her department is working a missing persons report on a sixteen year old girl. She moved out of the jurisdiction so my sister asked us to jump in for her and try to track her down. She's turned out to be rather clever."

Patten looked distinctly uninterested. "So you were trying to track down this girl and managed to stumble over mine."

"Yep. Thought she was ours at first."

"Lucky you. But now, since you're investigating Collie's murder, you want to know more about Holly's so you can kill two birds with one stone. Find your girl and find my guy. Lookin' to show me up?"

Avery grinned and responded before Winston could, "If we were trying to do that, we wouldn't have come. Unfortunately we have something of a problem."

"What's that?"

"We have reason to believe that our girl is *with* your guy."

Patten leaned forward, his forearm on top of the papers on his desk, his brow cocked. "Is that so?"

"Their tracks," Avery continued, "They're very telling. It's an interesting story if you'll believe it. She's with someone. And considering the evidence, the nearness to the murder site, I'd be willing to bet she's with him."

Patten tapped his finger on the desk and bit his bottom lip in thought. "Think I remember this girl. You guys faxed out a picture and description of her a little while back. Didn't really think much of it. Just the usual runaway. But of course she didn't know she was running into serial killer turf."

"They never do, do they?" Winston sighed.

Patten's eyes found Winston and he frowned for a moment before his head tilted a little to the side. "Wait. What's your name again?"

"Trent Winston. And this is Martin Avery."

"You're those two P.I.s that got themselves in pretty deep up in D.C., catching killers and solving actual crimes. Got tired of looking up ex-boyfriends and doing background checks on lawyers huh? Small time crap. You guys are the go-to guys for murder now. Ever handle a serial killer?" The detective's brows raised and he had a smug little grin on his face.

Winston wasn't talking, his mind lost somewhere else. Some*when* else.

Avery piped up. "We tangled with one. Once. Awhile back. It was actually around here, back on the banks. We used to live here, you know. Back in the day. Would have been mucho dollars in it for us if it had actually panned out."

Patten shook his head. "Slippery fucks. Never found the guy, huh?"

Avery smiled a wistful smile. "We never found him. *He* found *us.* Put Winston here in the hospital. Scared the shit out of his girlfriend at the time."

Oh Grace. Winston's eyes were out of focus. He could still remember the way she'd screamed. He'd never heard her sound like that before. Shrill and terrified and hopeless. It had filled the room as if it were a scent. The sound of her screaming. The sound of him fighting. The pain and the slickness of his blood. He blinked and tried to bring back some focus to his vision. Sweet, loveable, patient Grace.

"I would bet," Patten nodded, "It's a good thing you two got out of that. And now you're willing to tango with the same type of guy? You're brave."

"Brave," Winston said, "Or stupid. The latter is possibly closer to the truth. Is there anything you can tell us about the victims in terms of similarities?" It was a stretch. The thought that the police would be willing to allow them privileged information on a case. Winston was going out on a limb by even asking. It would be unreasonable to expect cohesion between a P.I. Agency and an official department. But Patten's gaze had softened.

"I'll help you guys out under one condition."

"That is?"

"You take my number and you call me if anything comes up. I mean hints, I mean bodies, I mean the killer, I mean *anything*. And believe me, if I hear of one damn thing you didn't tell me I'll have you for obstruction and interference in two shakes of lamb's tail." His expression was serious. So serious in fact that Winston couldn't help but swallow a tiny part of his nerves. Patten was nobody to be meddling around with. "The two of them were trouble-makers. They used the woods as their personal get-aways. That's how it usually is with these girls. They know they're not supposed to be in the woods, they go there anyway out of some type of teenaged defiance and end up just like the ones they were warned about. Collie Landall was into drugs, alcohol, would get high and drunk and stumble around in the forest unfettered. Holly was a little older but it was the same basic story. She would leave her mother's abusive boyfriend's clutches by going into the woods. At first we were looking at the boyfriend but turns out he's got an alibi so we're working with the idea of the strangler." He leaned back in his swivel chair, the cushioned back of it making a small squeak on its hinge before he continued. "If your girl is in those woods then she's hoofing it right through his turf. We've determined that he's spread out his victims in an area with about a ten mile radius, give or take. There could be more and it could be bigger, we don't know."

"Do you think they were impulse buys?" Winston asked. "Did he stalk them or did he just find them?"

"Most of the victims spent a lot of time in or near the wilderness in this area. So we're going with the idea that he stalked them first."

Avery scratched the underside of his chin. "We can't thank you enough for your aide," he said, "And we'll do everything in our power to keep you in the loop. Handing him over to you is the end goal in all of this, we'll do everything we can for you, detective."

Patten grinned, "We all know you P.I. types are a bunch of little weasels. You can get in and out of places the cops could never hope to find. Having you is going to be an interesting experience. I'll put out an APB on your missing girl and I'll have her in the papers by tomorrow morning. You know. Just in case someone's seen her."

When they were both showered and Avery was typing away on his computer, most likely reports from today's hunt, Winston laid down in his pajamas on his motel bed. This one was nicer than the last but the woman at the front desk had given the two of them a funny look. As if she expected the beds pushed together in the morning. Winston peered over at Avery and tried to think of the last time the dark haired agent had a girlfriend.

"What?" Avery asked without looking up from his screen.

"What do you think he's playing at?" Winston wondered out loud to his partner. "Keeping her alive."

"I don't know. Maybe he's fascinated by her. Maybe he likes her."

Winston snorted. "Won't last long."

"You never know," Avery said. "Some killers have hearts."

"And my mother is a French hooker," Winston replied with a small grimace.

Avery laughed a little. "Maybe I'll just have to start spending a little more time at the Winston homestead then."

"Maybe you will," was his lazy response. He flopped down on the bed. He tried to focus on who Avery's last girlfriend was but the only person he could think of was his own long lost ex girlfriend. The one who'd split with him as soon as his job became more important than she. He could remember sitting up with her in that cold, dreaded silence at three in the morning, looking at her defeated, unable to say what she wanted to hear and unable to bear what the consequences were about to be. The next day she was gone. Her things were picked up by her friends. Her clothes, her CDs, her scarves, and the silly little things that she kept in the bathroom that he would never understand. All the things that added up to Grace. They took them away from him and his apartment. It had left it very Trent. Very Trent Winston. And left it very *not* Grace Thompson. Bare. Naked. Lonely.

He had been alone. He blinked over at Avery. But not quite alone. He'd had Avery. Good old Avery. The one who'd offered him a sympathetic expression, a gentle hand on his shoulder, and a single white can of Molson Canadian. It was the beginning of their real friendship. Before that they had simply been partners. The partners that worked well together under pressure and under the seige of stress and exhaustion. Grace leaving had left Winston with nobody. Nobody except his partner and now his best friend. He knew that Avery was merely trying to tell him something that would give him some hope. That Tomi would come out of this alive.

His thoughts were cascading through memories of photos, experiences, and files about the case when there was a distinct knocking at the door. The two of them stared at each other for a moment before another set of knocks snapped them out of it. Winston opted to get up, rolling off the bed and shuffling in his bare feet across the worn carpet to the metal door. When he opened it just a crack he frowned.

"Mr. Balekowski?"

The rain was making flat slapping sounds on the plastic hood of his bright yellow poncho. Winston ushered him into the motel room. The cold from the rain seeping off of him and into the air around Winston's warm body caused him to shiver. Nathan Balekowski shrugged once and began to take off the dandelion yellow poncho while explaining himself. "I'm sorry. I'm sorry about showing up like this." Winston took the slicker and hung it up on the doorknob. The man was wearing a dark navy hooded sweatshirt and a ratty pair of jeans over what looked to be a brand new pair of New Balance shoes.

"Mr. Balekowski, it's almost ten o'clock. And how did you find us?"

The first time they had seen the man he had worn a confident visage, a carefully placed smile that was clearly as fake as his constituents would have it be. Now he was wet from the cold rain, his

90

smile still present but nervous, twitching at the sides and a little more crooked. His eyes held in something else. Secrets? He was slumped over and seemed lost. Disoriented like he'd just woken up from a long sleep. "I'm sorry it's so late. I-I didn't...I mean. I was driving around and I have people to find things for me and you two weren't so hard to find when it came right down to it. I just was driving around. I couldn't go home. I don't really have all that much to go home to." He laughed but it came out as a harsh sound so he stifled it and then put his palm to his forehead and closed his eyes, breathing deeply. His shoulders trembled and Winston wondered if he'd have to catch him.

"Are you okay, Mr. Balekowski?" Winston looked up helplessly at Avery who had gotten to his knees on the bedspread, ready to assist if necessary.

He sucked in a breath and nodded his head but then quickly shook it. "No. No I'm not okay. I have to sit." Winston helped him move to the edge of his bed and sat him down. With a reassuring hand on his shoulder he waited for the distraught Senator to get a grip. "I've never been emotional. That's my mistake. I've never been the type to have empathy. That's awful. Awful for someone who's supposed to be leading his voters, but it's true. I put my job before my family and I know my wife prefers it that way. She likes having her boys on the side. That's fine but I can't handle that I've lost the only thing in this whole world that can keep me sane."

Winston sat next to the trembling man and marveled at the pure vulnerability that radiated from him. He was a crumpled mess. He looked much older than he had at their first meeting, his eyes dark underneath and his hair unkempt. He had a gritty five o'clock shadow growing in that made him look even more sallow. Pathetic. "I know it's hard. To lose your second child."

His body tensed. "I shouldn't have said what I said." He covered his eyes with a hand and his mouth pulled back in a grimace. His voice was full of grief. "I told her that she didn't even have a brother. I tried to erase him from our lives but she's so stubborn. Of course she couldn't let him go. How could she? He was her brother after all. Practically raised her."

The detective simply nodded despite the man not being able to see him.

"God I was so stupid. How could I have driven her away?"

Winston sat next to him with his hand still resting on his shoulder for support.

"If only I had given them more of my time. Then they wouldn't have left me. They're my only real life. My only true loves. If she isn't alive, detective—I don't know how I'll ever go on living." His body was suddenly racked with sobs and he covered his whole face with both of his hands, curling downward until the backs of his hands on his face were touching his knees.

"We're going to do everything we can," Winston tried. "We know she's out there, sir. We know it. We'll find her somehow."

His shuddering shoulders raised and he took his face from his hands, his palms lying on his knees upward toward the ceiling, shining with his shed tears from the desperate yellow light emanating from the bathroom. He looked up at Winston with red-rimmed eyes and a startlingly clear set of ice blue eyes. "If...If you can make sure that she's alive. If you can bring her back to me." He lost eye contact for just a second before bringing it back. His eyes were clouded over again. Disconnected. "If you can bring my baby girl back. I'll make it worth it. None of this 'favor' crap. This is a job. I want your whole she-bang. I want all the bells and whistles. I just want my girl back. Any expenses they're paid. Anything at all. And you two will be two rich motherfuckers after I'm through with you."

There was a long silence in which the two detectives had their mouths open. The only sounds were the lone bulb in the bathroom buzzing and the hard pounding of the rain on the cheap motel's roof.

Avery was the first to speak, capturing Winston's attention when he stated in a soft voice, "We'll do our very best, sir."

His cold ice blue eyes were still focused on Winston when Balekowski replied, "That's what I'd like to pay for. Your very best. I know you've found more dangerous prey before. I need her home."

Winston nodded. "I understand, Mr. Balekowski."

She had her hands around a cup of coffee. It was cold in the diner so she was wearing Ren's too-big sweatshirt which sagged around her bird-boned shoulders. There was a television mounted on the wall in front of her booth with the news on, the small white captions popping up under the anchors' faces a little off in timing. She knew she had an annoying little tendency to move her lips when she read things. She tried not to, concentrating fully on steadying her mouth.

She had come into the diner in the middle of the newscast. She hoped it wasn't too late to catch something about herself--if there was anything at all to see at this point. The blonde woman anchor was finishing up a story about some girl named Collie. Odd name for a girl, she thought.

There had been a fire. Arson, they thought. The faces of two men came on the screen. They always looked so undignified. As if they thought that criminals could never be handsome. She tapped the side of her mug with her fingernails and watched for more.

Ren had sent her in here. To watch the television. To watch the news. Autumn had stuck around for the entire day, holding her hand and speaking to her in a sweet conversational tone. When night came and they had found the diner he had kissed her again under a tree in the warm rain.

"We need to know what they know," he had told her with serious eyes. "I need you to watch the news. I need you to tell me if they know anything about you. Or about me. I need you to look at anything weird and tell me everything. Everything. Okay?"

She had nodded. He had been nice about it. Nice about everything, his hands on her upper arms had comforted her. "Where will you be?" she had asked in a timid voice. As if this question could have possibly destroyed his warmth.

"I'll be out here. If you don't see me when you come out just wait by that street light right there." He had motioned to one at the far end of the parking lot. Its dim circle of light showed a patch of bushes. She had felt better about being alone.

"What if someone recognizes me?"

He smiled at her, a warm but slightly condescending smile. "Just trust me, sugar."

Just trust me. Those were the words she feared the most.

A robbery. Three suspects. All African American boys under the age of twenty. They had sulky looks about them and fuzzy black hair. They looked tired and worn out. She wondered what her mugshot would look like. Probably equally as tired. Probably equally as disappointed with herself.

Her cheeks suddenly turned pink and she lowered herself in the booth, staring at her own cheerful face on the screen with nothing short of mortification. Her mother had given the police her school I.D. photo. Her hair was down, her smile plastic-looking and frozen. Her eyes were too wide. She looked crazed. Seeing this picture would make anyone sure she was set for the looney bin.

Was she? She read the captions easily but forgot to make her mouth stop moving with the words. Disappeared. Runaway. Might use back roads and wooded land. If seen call 911. She grasped each and every set of words with greedy eyes. No mention of a friend. No mention of a follower. No mention of anyone else at all. She sipped her coffee and watched more of the news, seeking the familiar face of Ren. Maybe a photo of him with a little more weight. Maybe with a different color hair. She wondered how long ago he had dyed his hair. Had it been to escape detection?

Of course it had been. She rubbed her cheek with his sweatshirt. She didn't even know exactly how old he was. Definitely not old enough to drink quite yet. She felt wet tears warm her bottom lids. She wondered if she was going to walk out into the dark parking lot and stand under the dim cold light of the street lamp forever. She imagined herself curling into a tight little ball of agony at the realization that he'd left her there.

She paid the dollar thirteen for her coffee and slung her bag over her shoulder, trying not to look like she was hurrying too much. When she walked out into the cool summer night air she didn't see him. Her heart started to beat a little faster. The wet pavement shined under the circle of light she was supposed to wait under. She looked down at her feet and pursed her lips. She had worn her red heels. Most definitely conspicuous. Would he leave without her?

Why not? She took in a breath with a small hitch in the middle of it. She thought she might cry. The shoes were comical on her feet. Bright red under the earthy tones of her other clothes. They were covered with splotches of dried mud and the ribbons that were twisted over the toes were frayed around the edges. She sniffed and looked off into the bushes.

A drop of rain dripped onto her nose and she wiped it away with Ren's large sleeve. When she pulled her arm away again he was standing there in front of her. As if he'd always been standing there, his shoes covered in dirt, oil, and grass. He cleared his throat and tried to summon a smile but it was almost like the corners of his mouth were being pulled by invisible strings that he fought and failed against. Winter was coming back and there was nothing she could do about it.

"Hey sweets." He put out an arm and she came to him, allowing him to wrap it around her shoulders and lead her away. He led her to a park. A small open air structure over about three picnic tables was hidden off in the trees. He sat on the top of one and put his feet on the bench part, lighting up. While he smoked Tomi rooted through her bag for a spare NutriGrain bar he had filched. She was taking off her shoes and putting them back in her bag when Ren spoke to her gently, as if he knew she would be upset with him for failing to ward off the cold. "Did you see anything?"

She nodded when she nibbled her snack. "Mhm. Just a god-awful picture of me. Nothing about a friend or a follower. Just me. Just how long I've been missing. Just your basic run-of-the-mill stuff about runaway girls who are blonde and pretty."

He chuckled but the smile didn't stay. He seemed nervous and fidgety. Tomi chewed the fruity bar and watched his body movements. He was looking around his shoulders as if he were expecting someone.

"Do you want a bite?"

"Uh...uh sure." There was a silence when she held up the bar and he took a small bite.

His legs were spread open a little while he sat in front of her. She narrowed her eyes and put her knee on the bench in front of him, her hands steadying herself on his thighs. He took the cigarette out of his mouth and let her kiss him. For a few wild seconds she had thought he would taste coppery and metallic. Like blood. But he didn't. He merely tasted of tobacco and beyond that—Ren. Just Ren. He seemed pensive when she backed away from him, her hands still on his thighs.

"What are you thinking?" she murmured her question, trying to give it an inflection of indifference.

He shook his head. "I'm afraid you've just erased my thoughts, sweets."

She could see his lie in his eyes. She didn't press the subject. "Have you ever regretted killing someone?"

He took a long drag and let it out before saying casually, "Of course." He seemed more calm after he'd finished smoking. He eyed her. "Do you think I'm heartless?"

"No," she frowned. The question had somehow offended her. As if she had any right to be offended. Wasn't Winter heartless? Wasn't the cold part of him too cold to have any real feelings? And yet hadn't she hurt him once? Hadn't she hurt him enough for him to leave her for a time? "I'm just curious about you. I don't know anything about you."

He had humor in his eyes. "I like the color red."

"You know that's not what I mean."

Ren shrugged. "I don't know what to tell you, darlin'. I'm a simple guy. I eat, sleep and survive."

"You kill people, Ren."

"Is that all that defines me?" A touch of anger laced his calm voice.

"That's all I know of you." She'd said it out of spite and she could see his heart hardening against her again.

"Tell me something Little Miss." His eyes were cold steel. Any trace of warmth was gone despite it being night. Despite it being time for Spring. He leaned forward and put his warm palm against the side of her neck, his thumb settling lightly over her throat. "If all I am is a killer to you, why'd you go to the trouble of fucking me?"

"I..." she trembled before him, his hand on her neck hot and too real. *He said he'd never hurt me.* For all the times tears had come too readily, none came now. She was too angry with herself. "Maybe..." Her voice was stuck. When she finally got the words out they were sticky and sounded dumb. "Maybe I just...wanted you to like me."

His expression was blank for a moment and then pained the next, his thumb pushing a little against the middle of her throat and his other hand sweeping around to the back of her head, gripping her messy bun tight enough that she gasped. She was caught by him. At his mercy. He whispered to her while staring into her soul with his cold dark eyes. "I don't think you're telling me the truth, Little Miss." His thumb tightened against her again, the pressure hurting her a little. "I don't know what the truth is and frankly, that frustrates me." His lips pulled back and she closed her eyes to avoid looking at his teeth. He shook her a little by her hair and she squeaked in fear and pain, forced to open her eyes again. One of her hands found his wrist and tightened. The other reached desperately into her bag still dangling at her side. His voice raised to a growl. "At least I know who and what I am, Princess. You can't even settle on your own identity." Her fingers found the cool plastic tube at the bottom and she gripped it hard. "Tell me, sweets, are you a good little girl? Or are you a whore?"

She didn't know she could move as fast as she did. But she hit him square in the eyes.

He pushed her away from him as hard as he could, her butt landing on the concrete floor of the pavilion. His whole body was shaking and he made an odd roaring sound with his rage and pain. He scrambled backward with one arm covering his eyes over the top off the picnic table, falling awkwardly over to the other side.

In her terror she stood and ran, her bare feet slapping against the concrete and almost slipping when she reached the grass. She ran through the trees, ignoring any stings of pain on the bottoms of her feet. She stopped only when she was sure he wasn't following her. She was panting hard, her back against the prickly side of a pine tree. She was still wearing his sweatshirt. Finally tears came and she curled into a tiny ball against the tree and wept into the large sleeves, the small red tube of mace still clutched in her hand. To think she had imagined this moment just half an hour before. Just a half-hour before and she'd been crying over *him* leaving *her*.

How naïve.

She awoke to brilliant morning sunlight coming down as dapples through the treetops, sprinkling her with their fluttering sparkles. She was still against the pine tree, huddled against it and cuddled into Ren's sweatshirt. The tube of mace was warm from her palm. She blinked at the world around her but froze immediately. The tension in her shoulders and back mounted and she stiffened considerably. Sitting innocuously in front of her were about five daisies in a dirty Solo cup filled with muddy-looking water. She stared at them as if Cthulu himself were to rise from that very small portal.

Tomi's head whipped around and she scanned the area. She couldn't see him. She eased herself around to see behind her pine. Other than the birds chirping in the trees there was silence. Silence and a cup of daisies. She picked it up and held it to her chest, the mace in her other hand. On shaking legs she stood, her bag thumping against her hip as if to remind her that it had survived her run through the forest.

It didn't take her long to find the pavilion. He wasn't under any of the picnic tables so she moved her gaze over the surrounding area. She spotted him under a pine whose branches were low to the ground, making a small cavernous area in which he had settled himself. She slowly walked toward it, her legs still trembling and her knees still weak. The flowers she held were still tight against her chest as if they would protect her from his more violent moods.

He was curled like some kind of animal. The sound of his soft breathing did nothing to soothe her. She sat with her legs crossed outside the little "door" to the natural pine tree cavern and waited.

Ren stirred very slowly and when he came fully awake he lifted himself up, pine needles stuck to his tank top. He did not open his eyes. He was frowning, unaware of her, blind to the world. She swallowed as she waited for him to notice her. He put his palms to his forehead and took a few deep breaths through his nose as if waiting for some kind of sleepy rage to leave his body. When he did open his eyes, they were squinted and narrow. He moved slowly when he saw her and studied her for a few moments. From her position she could see the skin around his

98

eyes and the bridge of his nose was an irritated shade of pink, the rims of his eyes a dark angry red. Her heart shriveled. He must have been terribly angry.

Her fingers were so tight around the cup that she was amazed it hadn't crumpled under the pressure of them. He looked at them. Then he looked at her other hand, still holding the little plastic tube. He blinked. And blinked again. And looked her straight in the face.

"Hey sweets," he said, his voice filled with gravel and sleep.

She couldn't find the words to respond.

He nodded a little and then closed his irritated eyes again. "I deserved what I got."

She remained silent.

"Probably deserve a lot more." He took in a deep breath. "I'm sorry for scaring you, Tomi. It was stupid and I don't know why I did it."

Her voice was weak, "You were--"

"Don't." He cut her off with a strong tone that sent a few roosting birds fluttering out of the tree above him. She withered back and he continued. "Don't make up excuses for me. I know what you're trying to do, sweets, and while I appreciate your need to rid me of my inhumanity with excuses, there's nothing you can say here." He opened his red-rimmed eyes again and sighed. "I was...out of control. And I hate that about myself. You don't have to forgive me. I'll never ask you to forgive me."

Yet in her heart she knew she already had. Was this what love felt like? Crazy, stupid love? She bit her bottom lip and pulled the flowers closer to her face to smell them before putting them down on the grass beside her. She pulled off her bag and put down the mace. He watched her with casual interest. "If you won't ask me to forgive you," she murmured, "what would you ever ask me to do?"

He beckoned for her and she crawled forward into the circle of his arms, breathing him in when he enveloped her in warmth. Her jaw dropped open a little when he shook very slightly and she felt warm tears on her neck. His arms tightened around her and he said very softly, "I would ask that you never forget me."

"Never," she promised.

CHAPTER 5

It was about five o'clock in the morning. Still dark outside. Puddles in the parking lot of the cheap motel reflected the solitary glow from a street lamp and rippled in the breeze. The two detectives lay silent and still in their beds. Winston could hear Avery's breathing. He knew he was awake. Staring up at the ceiling just like him. He looked over at this partner but couldn't see him perfectly. Just a dim silhouette.

"Martin." It was the first time in a very long time that he had used Avery's first name. His partner looked over, the shine of his eyes reflecting the light that came in through the blinds. "We need to bring her home."

"I know," was Avery's reply. "I just don't know what that's going to cost us."

"Are you worried about the money?" Winston licked his lips and wondered where he'd put his chapstick. That was the perfect thing to worry about in the middle of the night.

"A little. I don't know what that would do to me, Winston. I don't know how I could ever really go on with that kind of thing just floating around me all the time. Too much hassle is what it sounds like." There was a pause in which it started raining again, tapping the roof above them angrily. "Where would that money come from anyway? Is he pulling it from his personal stash or is he getting a loan from the mob? The Rizzolis? I don't like the idea of being tied to dirty money."

"I'm with you, bud." He nodded and closed his eyes. "But think about it, Avery. We have to bring her home. Her father is nothing short of distraught. His last child. His youngest. His only girl. How traumatic."

"How come he wasn't so traumatized the first time we talked to him?" Avery had brought up a good point. The man had been fairly icy the first time they had spoken to him about his runaway girl. Perhaps he had been confident of her return. Perhaps he had never thought of her as independent?

"Well maybe he just didn't think of himself as a loser until now. I mean. He lost his son. He lost his wife to her boyfriends and now he's lost the last thing there was to lose. His daughter. That or he needs her for something else and we're getting duped."

"I don't think that's the case."

"Me neither."

"The Rizzolis don't work with marriage deals." Avery sniffed back a little laugh and Winston chuckled.

The two of them fell into a comfortable silence despite the roiling anxieties that plagued them. The rain tapped the roof with a little less gusto and the harsh red numbers on the bedside clock read a depressing 5:15. It was 5:25 before he said anything more. Avery was still awake. He knew that at least. "What do you think the odds are?"

"Of us bringing her home?"

"Yeah."

Avery sighed before he made his response. "Interested in being rich, Winston?"

"Not particularly." He wasn't sure if that was a lie.

"Slim."

Winston nodded. "Thought you'd say that."

It wasn't as hard as Avery had thought to pick up the trail again. In fact they made a decent amount of headway right at the beginning of their trek. Winston's dark haired companion was happily bouncing down the trail putting small markers every few feet and stopped once with his eyebrow lifted to meander a few feet to the right and place a small piece of light green gum into an evidence baggie.

"Oh Tomi," Avery smiled, "You are just one clever little girl, aren't you?"

"Leaving us bread crumbs?" Winston pushed his sunglasses up the bridge of his nose a little more.

"And yet not conspicuously. Almost carelessly. Like she doesn't quite mean to."

It was at that moment that Winston's pocket jingled and he reached for his cell. "Yeah?" was his easy salutation. "What?"

The tone made Avery stand straight and rigid, looking over his shoulder at Winston with a hard stare.

"No no no, we'll be right there. No, right there. Don't...don't lose anything she's said. Record it or something. But tell her not to say any more until we get there. Damn it, I know. But if we're in then we're in, you can't just pick and choose." He shoved the phone back into his pocket. "Play time in the sandbox is over, buddy, we're goin' into town."

The side of Avery's mouth stretched up into a pleasured grin. It stayed that way until the two of them were walking through the doorway to a nice suburban home that smelled like honeysuckle. They were led into a sitting room with a fake Persian rug and god awful floral wallpaper. Patten was standing in the middle of the room with his arms crossed, his sunken green eyes filled with obvious impatience. He motioned to the couch that was across from a nervous teenager who was sitting straight-backed in a wooden chair that looked as if it belonged in a dining room. An awful arrangement at best but what else did he expect from the police?

Winston's notebook was poised in his lap and the plain teenaged girl in front of him had her ankles crossed and closed body language. It would have been worse in a police station interrogation room so he silently blessed Patten for having the decency to keep her in a familiar environment.

Avery was the one to speak, crooning easily in the face of this nervous girl. "Now love," he started with a complimentary pet name to ease the foreboding sense of formality that had pervaded the room. The girl's mother was standing at the mouth of the room, staring in with acute parental awareness. "Could you go over what you went over with that detective?"

She nodded a little and her hands clenched together. "That girl. Tomi, the politician's daughter. Blonde. Freckles. Saw her on the TV. Last night. She was in the diner where I work."

"Was anyone with her?"

"No."

"Are you absolutely certain that nobody was with her? Was there anyone standing outside?"

"No...I mean...I don't know. I don't smoke so I don't go outside." She fidgeted uncomfortably and her eyes kept shifting to the police detective.

"Was she barefoot?"

"No, but I didn't really look at what kind of shoes she was wearing. Something like heels." She shrugged and looked toward her mother.

Avery shifted a little in his seat and allowed for a little silence. The scratching of Winston's pen was slight enough that it did not distract her. When he chose to break that carefully placed silence he did so in a very soft tone. "Did Tomi seem distressed?"

She shook her head. "No. Not very much anyways. She left in kind of a hurry."

Winston's eyebrows were raised. He leaned forward and posed his own questions, careful to keep the mood that Avery had suggested by his voice. "Holly do you remember what she was wearing?" She tilted her head.

"A sweatshirt. It was too big. It looked like it was out of a trashcan kinda. Dirty."

The rest of their questioning had not been very fruitful in the least and they stood out in the driveway with tense shoulders and furrowed brows. Patten standing with them with his knees locked, staring at the cracked pavement.

"I don't understand." He puffed quickly from his cigarette.

"She was drinking coffee. In a diner," Avery mused. "In a diner...how...strange. Why would he let her do that?"

Patten sighed. "What if he didn't? What if she escaped?"

"Still doesn't make sense," Winston murmured, "If she escaped a vicious killer then nothing should be worth being tracked down again. She would have asked for help. She's not asking for death. And the girl said that she was wearing shoes. That doesn't *fit*. A baggy sweatshirt and shoes. They must have been his. Meaning he coerced her into that diner. He has something of hers. Collateral or something."

Patten tapped the toe of his shoe on the ground. "This isn't like our killer. Our killer takes and then kills. He doesn't hold. What does he have to gain by holding her?"

Avery flashed Winston a knowing glance. He'd been right. This killer was doing something out of the ordinary. And for a killer to do something out of the ordinary... Winston cleared his throat. "This is absurd. There is a rational explanation for this."

Patten grunted and crossed his arms, leaning against Avery's black Ford Fusion with a scowl firmly set in his features. Winston offered him a cigarette and he took it, examining it for a second before popping it in his mouth and allowing the P.I. to light it for him. He coughed a few times and Avery grinned at him. In a raspy voice he replied, "If there's a rational explanation for why this killer is doing what he's doing then we're going to need one when the shit hits the fan. Either this girl is mistaken or our guy has your girl and she's suddenly become my girl too. Frankly I'm not sure if I care that he's doing something that his profiler says he shouldn't be doing. As long as that girl is alive I'm not sure I mind at all."

A young officer approached Patten with his hands clasped in front of him, nervous. "Detective Patten, we're ready to form a search patrol."

"Good." The detective blew out some smoke away from the officer and turned back to him. "Take these P.I.s here with you, they know this girl and the way she moves and they've been tracking pretty well so far. All final actions are approved by me, got it? Any evidence is undisturbed."

"Understood."

Winston and Avery nodded in compliance.

Winston had never been as good as Avery when it had come to finding trails and hints. His eyes weren't sharp enough. He wasn't observant enough. But this day he was determined. He set off from where Avery told him with several volunteers from the police department with him to go off in different directions in the woods and grassy areas to the North of the diner. He was lucky for their presence. It was their down time. They were strictly civilian. But they carried their guns. If Tomi and her companion, whomever he was, were here, someone would find them. His fingers brushed the top of his firearm and he was calmed. It wasn't long before he was entirely alone. The rest of his group of officers had headed off in other directions and were entirely out of his sight.

He set out looking for the clues that Avery always seemed keen to find. Human hairs, human foot prints, broken twigs, disturbed brush. The other agent seemed to be the office's golden boy. And yet he had Winston as a partner. His abilities were sorely lacking in comparison to the other more seasoned detective. He could never possibly even pretend to match up with the calm, composed Avery. His tendency to be easily ruffled, impatient, and angry had led them into so many different problems during their partnership. He tried not to think about the cases of his past and tried to clear his mind. He supposed that's what Avery did when he looked for those needles in the haystack. Maybe that's all it would take. A little focus. He could do that. He did it every time he worked writing up reports. It was just a state of mind. He took another deep breath and then another.

He was focused. That would end up his downfall. His ability to focus intently on the smaller things tended to subtract from his larger observational skills. Many times he would spend hours at his table writing reports and barely notice that the sun was setting until he couldn't see the papers in front of him. When his eyes finally lifted from the forest floor his heart shriveled in his chest and his throat closed.

Those were eyes he knew. Eyes he knew all too well. And for fuck's sake those goddamn *teeth*.

"Detective Winston," the killer hissed, "Back again? For me?"

"It's been awhile," he managed to respond through a suddenly dry mouth and a throat that was fighting him. He thought he might vomit.

"It has, hasn't it?" He had a smug little grin pulling his lips away from those teeth. Those many *many* teeth. Winston had experienced them before. Tearing. A sensation unlike a clean cut. He managed to suppress the urge to touch his chest. The memory of ripping pain made his hands shake a little in nervousness.

"Didn't quite expect you, to be honest," Winston gulped, his hand hovering toward his side. He noticed the killer's eyes flitting to that hand and he stopped, easing it forward again. He'd never even get a round off if he tried. "I'm actually looking for someone else."

"Are you?" his grin sharpened, crinkling the corners of his dark soulless eyes.

"Yes. Little blonde girl. About sixteen, you seen her?" Winston tried to chuckle at his little joke but only managed a stressed little wheeze.

"Seen her?"

Winston's heart flopped around in his bowels.

"I've *tasted* her."

The agent's voice was reduced to a whisper. "You're lying."

"Would you know if I was?" he teased. "What are you doing chasing after pretty little girls anyway? Aren't you a little tougher than that? Isn't there someone more dangerous you should be looking for?"

"You're trying to get me to admit that I was after you. But you're just a coincidence." Was it right and proper to be insulting a serial killer? Winston had the distinct feeling that this forest floor was going to be getting a little taste of his blood one way or another. It wouldn't matter if it would be sooner rather than later. His best bet was to make his enemy a little clumsier. A little less cold. "You're just a rock I happened to stumble over. Have you given any thought to giving up? You've had a while to think about it. It would be very easy."

"You're a silly little detective. I knew I always liked you. But how about we forget about this little interaction, *Clarice?*"

106

Winston's eyes narrowed at the name. "I can't let you leave."

"Oh you and your moral code," he sounded bored but the eyes under his dark gray knit beanie betrayed something else. A playfulness.

"Yes, me and my moral code. I'm sorry my friend, but I am going to have to ask you to put your hands behind your head." His memory flashed again and he swallowed convulsively.

"Do you think that's a good idea, Winston? Do you think it's a good idea to ask me to do that?" His speech was getting a little quicker. He was getting excited.

"Please don't make this hard for us."

"We're an 'us' now, are we? Speak for yourself now Winston, speak for yourself. Say, 'Don't make this hard for *me*.'"

Winston's eyebrow twitched and he shut his mouth, facing his foe with a determined stare.

"Say it," he whispered with a broad smile that showed off what seemed like an infinite number of perfect white teeth.

"No," Winston said and his hand went to his gun.

The killer pounced.

He'd come out on top. That was the most important part. He couldn't remember most of it. Just a flurry of flesh and muscle. At the end of it he felt as though he had been fighting a dog. An insanely strong mass of muscle and weight and sharp, sharp teeth. Wounds on his arms and hands were leaking dark strings of blood but he couldn't feel them just yet. He would have a dire need for a hospital visit in the next twenty-four hours but for now the adrenaline was too much. He couldn't even feel them. Later he would notice that he was missing a rather large chunk of skin from his collarbone. Mere inches away from a devastating blow to his throat.

The gun was to the back of the killer's head. Winston's heart couldn't possibly beat any faster than it was at this single moment in time. He took a few breaths to calm himself. His finger was on the trigger. Ren simply knelt there, silent and still. The ever-elusive Ren Rockey was a careful and dangerous predator. A man who could disappear from a locked room, Avery always said. Winston considered Ren to be a type of arch enemy. Perhaps it was because most of the time, when Winston found his man, he didn't lose him. Not like he lost Ren.

But now he was here, caught, and so real. Just a bloody-mouthed rottweiler with the muzzle of a nine millimeter to the back of his head. His hat had come off in the struggle and was laying just a few yards away, the hair that had been underneath out of control and spiked into absurdity. The tips were blood red.

"Put your hands up. Either side of you, open."

The killer did what Winston asked of him, slowly and methodically. His hands didn't tremble even the slightest bit. His knees must hurt. Winston shook his head. What the fuck did he care about Ren Rockey's knees?

"Alright, now you're going to get to your feet, you're going to keep your hands where I can see them at all times and you're going to stay with your back to me. Understand?"

"Yes." It was a clear word. Winston had expected something different but he couldn't exactly say what that was. Ren leaned his head back just so slightly, putting pressure on the tip of the nine millimeter, like he was begging Winston to just shoot him. Then he got up. The gun followed the back of his head carefully. Winston couldn't stop it from shaking at least a small bit.

With his other hand he managed to secure Ren, whose head was down, with his standard issue zip-ties. Big red circles were gathering on the grass under his face and the agent was somehow surprised to see Ren's nose was gushing blood down over his lips off his chin and soaking into the front of his shirt. With his hands behind his back he looked at least a small bit pathetic, refusing to make eye contact.

"Sit down, on the ground, right now." He was completely and utterly unsure of what he wanted to ask but if he did ask it, it had to be with conviction. When he side stepped so he was in front of the young murderer it was really to make eye contact but Ren wasn't biting. Goddamn, if only Avery were here. He'd know if the bastard was lying. He'd know. Finally he simply had to do it. "Where is she?"

Ren didn't make eye contact with him. He remained staring at the ground. But he laughed a small laugh and grinned, the blood coming out of his nose rushing down over his teeth, mixing Winston's blood with his own. "You're just a fuck-up, aren't you Winston?"

Winston could feel a little case of the shakes coming on from all the adrenaline that was rushing through his body. It coupled with the anger he felt at this one daring to accuse him of failure. So what if he wasn't as talented as Avery? "I still got you down on the ground, didn't I? Who fucked up this time?"

Ren shook his head and made eye contact. His grin was even more fearsome with red lines of blood lining each and every tooth while more spilled from his nose. "Should have called for back up, Clarice. Now you're gonna lose. You'll always lose against me."

Winston didn't have time to understand.

Tomi had him sitting with his back against a tree in a heavily wooded area. The bastards would need dogs to sniff them out. The detective had been alone. Her heart was beating so hard she could hear the blood rushing in her ears. Ren was licking his own blood off his lips. There was too much of it. It gushed from his nose like a firehose in a flow down his lips and chin. When he'd gone for a piss in the woods she hadn't thought anything of it. That was until she'd heard the scuffle. It had been easy to sneak behind the detective. He'd been so very focused.

"You think it's broken?" he asked her about his nose when she stared at it.

"Not sure. I'm not worried about it yet. What about the zip tie?"

He wiggled a little and tried to look over his shoulder, sending blood down his bicep. "It's tight. It hurts a bit."

She nodded. Her hands were shaking. She'd never hit anyone that hard before. Could he still be alive? "Ren?"

"Yeah babe?"

"Will he be okay?"

"He'll be fine." It was a calm statement. She could tell his mind was otherwise occupied. Would the agent really be fine? Could that possibly be? She'd hit him over the head *really* hard. "Sweetie, do you think it would be possible for you to find something that could either cut or saw through this tie?"

"I'm sure. Ren?"

He sounded a little exasperated, "Yes darlin'?"

"I hit him really hard."

"Not hard enough."

He would know wouldn't he? He was the killer. He had no reservations. If he'd been able Tomi had no doubt the agent would be a dead man by now. Very very dead. She'd practically saved his life by being there. And not having a pair of scissors in any case. She knelt in front of him and caught his eyes with hers while she gently put two fingers on his nose.

"Think it's broken? It feels broken." She could tell. There were tears in his eyes but he didn't sound choked up. It was just the pain and reaction from his nose getting a good beating she supposed.

"It's probably fine." Maybe. She wasn't sure. It was bleeding an awful lot. "What...what happened?" He'd gone off to pee. That's what he'd said. He'd gone off into the woods to take a piss and of course she'd come around just at the right time. Just when Ren was about to get taken away from her forever. It had been panic. Panic and fear had driven her to nearly kill a man. For what? To see her brother? She could feel the lump start in her throat and the tears well up in her eyes.

"Winston?"

A blurry too-bright image swam before his eyes. Avery was sitting next to him. He reached out and Avery took his hand. "Avery?"

"Yeah Trent."

"I'm in the hospital."

"Yeah you are."

"Who found me?"

"Officer Crawford."

Winston didn't try to nod. His head hurt. He swallowed and simply lay and breathed.

"You looked like you got in a fight with a dog."

"I did," Winston groaned. "A rottweiler."

Avery's whole body tensed and he leaned forward, his eyes wide, searching Winston's face. "You...no...just randomly out in the woods? Why? That's...that's insane. What did he say? What did *you* say? This whole time I was thinking you ran into poor Tomi and got yourself bushwhacked."

"Well I was bushwhacked all right, but I didn't run into Tomi." He looked around himself for the little remote that called the nurses, fully intent on getting more pain medication for his pounding headache. "I don't think he was expecting me. I think he was pleasantly surprised by me. But why he was in the woods at all is just baffling."

Avery tapped his lips. "Did you get a good look at what he was wearing?"

"No. Even if I had, all the details are fuzzy. Whatever or whoever knocked me over the head got me hard. Knocked some of my braincells right out my ear. I do remember something you'll find interesting though."

Avery's eyebrow lifted.

"Black and red. His hair."

"No shit?" Avery looked impressed. "That means we can place him in places where Tomi has been. But..." he frowned.

"I know what you're going to say. It makes sense and then it doesn't make sense."

Avery nodded. "There is something else, Trent."

"What's that?" He was distractedly pressing the button for the nurse, pressing it in with his thumb as hard as he could.

In a grave tone Avery mentioned, "We found another body."

"Son of a bitch," Winston ground out, pressing the remote so hard his thumb hurt. "What the fuck, goddamn cuntwagon son of a motherfucker..." A few more choice cuss words spilled from his lips in a seething rage. "Fucking *Ren*."

"But it doesn't make sense. Ren..." Avery put up his hands, palms up, obviously at a loss. "She was sixteen this time. Aubrey Lawn. Brown hair, brown eyes, adorable, same M. O. as the ones before.

Strangled to death."

Winston closed his eyes and accepted the fact that he would have to wait for maybe a long time before a nurse came. He looked at Avery, "I know how much it doesn't make sense. I know how weird it looks. But he was *there,* Avery. He was *there.* As far as we know, he's been there this whole time. There has to be some *connection.*"

A familiar voice floated in from the doorway, deep and smooth. "You shouldn't be working on your case right now anyway, you should be resting." Rayne Wilson's dimpled grin greeted him from the door. He leaned against the frame easily. "I came to wish you to get well soon but it looks like you're as riled up as you always are. Is your Dr. Lecter driving you to madness yet?" The suave profiler sauntered into the room as if he had always belonged there, sharing Avery's ability to appear as if he had not a care in the world.

Winston sighed, resigned to a fate of inconsistencies. "Rayne, we have this problem."

"What's that?" he smiled.

"You did the profiling for Ren Rockey, right?"

"Indeed I did, and I have yet to be proven wrong." He was still grinning.

"He's a lone wolf, would you say?" Winston reluctantly sat the nurse-calling remote on the bedside table.

"Yes. I would be hard-pressed to find a situation in which Ren would take to a partner. He's a disorganized killer. He's rather on the intelligent side when it comes to disorganized killers but he's got all the traits of an excessively violent teeming-with-rage serial murderer." Rayne's brows furrowed just a little and his grin faded. "Why?"

"Well I had him on the ground," Winston recalled, "And I ended up hit over the head. Now...if it weren't a ghost who hit me over the head, Ren must have someone sympathetic to him who did it."

Rayne seemed to ponder this for a few minutes, the side of one finger to his upper lip. "When I came in here you two were talking about connections. This isn't what you meant."

"No," Avery murmured, "it wasn't. Someone's been killing teenaged girls. And Winston ran into our Rottweiler not a hundred yards

112

away from another body. I'm not sure if we can count that as a coincidence."

Rayne's eyes flitted between the two detectives and he was clearly thinking hard. "The M. O. is wrong."

"That's what's killing me," Winston groaned. "The M. O. is all wrong. It's nothing like him. It's nowhere close to his personality. Could he change? Could he be willing to have a...friend?"

"Change so drastically as to have a friend with a different M.O.?" Rayne shook his head, "Unlikely."

Winston nodded, "We're dealing with two. Two killers. Not one. Two *separate* killers."

Avery took Winston's hand and squeezed. "Forget about Ren for now. One thing at a time. We need to find Tomi, get the strangler, and then we can think about Ren again. You know he's probably just waiting for you to go after him again. Don't give him the satisfaction of that. Feign disinterest."

Rayne agreed. "Ren's a clever killer. He'll wait until you've got nothing better to do. He wants all of your attention or none of it."

Avery nodded. "The only killer we need to be concerned about right now is our strangler. He finds his victims, takes them somewhere, kills them, and dumps their bodies. He's organized, he's smart, he's controlling, and he's damn straight one crazy son of a bitch. Not to mention the task force for Ren's capture with the local jurisdictions has almost completely disbanded at this point since he's been dormant for long enough that the administration got distracted and the guy who hired us in the first place died of a heart attack last year. Let's get the guys together again around the table for this guy and figure this one out first. I know you want Ren. I know how bad you want him."

Could he? Could he ever really know how bad Winston wanted him? He focused on relaxing his jaw. Grinding his teeth would only make his headache worse. "Ren knows who she is. He knows where she is. Goddamn it. Ren's mine. He's mine, you understand?" He closed his eyes and balled his fists in his lap then gave Rayne and Avery a warning look. One hand was heavily bandaged. Ren had gotten the best of him. "He could find her. He could probably even find our killer if he was so inclined."

"In another life maybe he'll be an investigator." Avery was smiling as if he knew that in a past life he had been such a lost soul.

It was then that Patten decided to make his appearance, sauntering into the hospital room just as Rayne was leaving, giving him a curt professional nod before moving his attention to Winston and holding up a bag of chips. "I thought you might like a snack since these gorilla nurses don't seem to hold these in very high regard."

"Thoughtful," Winston grinned. He caught the bag when Patten tossed it and pulled it open with a little difficulty due to his injured hand. "Be sure to thank your lackey for finding me."

"No worries. Now let me in on this little thing that occurred. You know, since you haven't exactly been debriefed on the incident."

"Not gonna take out your little notebook and jot this down?" Winston chuckled.

Patten pulled out a tape recorder and set it on the little table that sat next to the bed. "I thought a recorder would be easier since this is going to be rather official when we get our guy."

Winston smiled a wicked smile and winked at Avery, sure that Patten had seen it. "I'm not sure you'll be getting this guy. We could race for him if you'd like."

Patten pressed "record" and mentioned the people in the room and the date and time and all the other formalities of tape recording a police interview before he started in on the questions. "In your own words, Mr. Winston, could you tell me what happened in the woods when you were looking for Miss Balekowski?"

Winston crunched his chips with his mouth open earning a narrow-eyed stare from the surly police detective. "Well..." he started easily, noting Avery's sad attempts at holding back a chuckle. "I was walking through the woods looking for Tomi when all of a sudden I look up and there right in front of me is Ren Rockey, serial killer extraordinaire. Probably heard of him once or twice considering he's the Roanoke Rottweiler and we've tumbled once before."

Patten swallowed, staring at Winston as if he wasn't sure if the other investigator was jerking his chain. "Are you...being serious?"

Winston was still grinning that sick grin. "Do these bite wounds lie to you, sir? There is a *reason* he is called the Rottweiler. And the sick fuck is definitely turned on by me or else he wouldn't have gone out of his way to see me. He's mine, Patten. Don't even think about this one. I'm going after him. You can have your serial killer. I want mine."

"I don't care about your history with this man, Winston," Patten glared, his voice filled with venom. "I need him out of my territory and behind bars. Now tell me what happened."

Winston leaned backward and settled into his pillows. He couldn't tell Patten what happened. Not exactly anyway. He would find Ren first. Before the no-good son of a bitch police detective even got close. "I attempted to get him to give himself up. He didn't like that idea much and attacked. As was the case last time we had our little tango, I didn't end up the winner. Gotta work out more I suppose."

Patten was grinding his teeth together. "Are you telling me the truth, Winston?"

"Of course," he was still smiling. He wanted the detective to know he was fucking with him. He wanted him to know that there was something he had control over. He wanted to win. Ren was going to be his prey from now until the bastard was dead at his feet. Patten be damned.

"You do know that if you're interfering with my investigation that you will be prosecuted at the fullest extent of the law. Correct?" Patten raised a brow.

"So prove I'm lying to you. Do you have a reason to think that I am? Would I?"

"I don't know what your motives are," Patten's voice lowered and he leaned forward, "But I'll find out. I'll find this killer of yours. I'll find this killer of mine, and I'll find this girl too."

With that the detective stood, grabbed his tape recorder, and left, stomping out of the room like a two year old who was just sent to his nap without a snack.

"Do you think," Avery mused, "That it was quite wise to anger him?"

"No," Winston sighed, picking up the nurse calling remote and pressing the button again. This time a woman walked in and asked him what was the matter and rolled her eyes when he requested more pain killers. When his attention was back on his partner he settled more comfortably into his pillows and wriggled his body deeper under the flimsy hospital blankets. "The man is a menace. He'll fuck everything up. If I challenge him man-to-man then he can't start using resources that I don't have. He'll want to win fair and square. Which means me or him. We've had this little thing going, Avery. We've had this nice small operation that didn't go into any huge kind of mass man hunt. That was what was necessary. *Is* necessary. Patten won't bring in any huge kind of hunting party if he thinks for one second that *I* would be able to do it alone."

"But you can't," Avery countered.

"I know that." A twinge of annoyance tugged at his gut. "But it's a matter of convincing *him*."

His partner put a hand to his mouth and sighed. "So what do we have?"

"Ren knows we're out here. He knows we're looking for Tomi. The other killer might know too. But if he does then he isn't letting on to that fact."

"You're saying that the killer is the size nine."

"The Nikes. Ren's the guy who walks on the balls of his feet with the worn treads. He's the guy with her. The two of them are being followed by our killer. Ironic that it might be that he's following another killer." He shrugged to himself and laughed at the sheer absurdity. "Now that Ren knows we're onto him and Tomi's trail he'll hide it. Patten would be lucky to get anything after this. Ren's a careful son of a bitch. He'll slip away like he's never been there at all. But I have a feeling I know exactly where he'll be."

Avery was silent, watching Winston with a contemplative gaze.

Winston nodded to himself. "Yeah. I know him too well. I know the way he thinks. As crazy as that sounds." He tapped his forehead with one finger. "The bastard knows me too though. It's a fair trade."

116

It was a chilly night. Ren's nose had finally stopped bleeding and was swelled around the bridge. They were huddled up to one another under a dirty rug Ren had pulled out from behind some trashcans. Tomi tried to ignore the smell that emanated from it but every so often she had to turn her nose into Ren's side to get nothing but the scent of him. His blood had gotten everywhere. It was all over his clothes. He would need new ones. When she looked down at herself she realized that she would as well. She was smeared with it.

At least it's his. She shook her head to rid herself of the thought. It wasn't any better. Wasn't this the man she was both in love with and afraid of? Was blood any better when it was his? Did it stain her any less? Did it make her any less impure? She snuggled him tighter and closed her eyes when his arm tightened around her small frame.

"Ren?" she asked in a soft voice.

"Yes?"

"Are you warmer now?"

The cold that had radiated out of him for the few hours after his encounter with the detective had subsided at least a small bit. He had held her hand again and kissed her sweetly. His voice was a little stuffy sounding because of his nose. "I hope so, sweets."

"When you were a kid, did you have any pets?"

The corners of his mouth tipped up a bit and a soft look came to his eyes. "I had a little sand crab I kept in a ten gallon tank. I fed him little pieces of fish and whatever else I happened to pick up on the beach. He was a snipper too." He shifted. "You?"

"No. I never had a pet. My father gave me a few hundred dollars for a puppy though."

"What'd you do with that?"

She bit her lip. Would he dare take it from her? He hadn't been interested in her bag thus far in their journey. He had barely looked at it. He probably thought that whatever was in there was useless to him. She glanced at it.

"You didn't buy a puppy. You bought a way out," he deduced. It had been so easy for him to see her small glance. "I'm impressed."

"I thought I might get us some clothes," she supplied. "Ours seem to be covered in your blood."

"Good thinking."

There was a pause before she asked, "Favorite food?"

"Steak."

"Blue?"

He laughed, "Actually I'm rather partial to Medium Rare."

She smiled at her small bit of foolishness. "I'm sorry. Tell me about your mother."

"My mother." The soft look in his eyes turned warm. "I like to think that I look more like her than my father but you can't ever escape your father. I have his eyes."

And his teeth?

"She liked to read and she was a wonderful cook. She loved daffodils and daisies. She kept pictures of me on the walls. When I was young. The times I was happy. Her little kid." His smile faded a little. "About the time I turned thirteen I really understood her. She was a little off. She murmured to herself a lot when I was a kid. But it got worse as she got older. It made my father angry. I think he was more angry with himself than anyone else. But what could he do?"

"Your mother..."

"Went insane." The word was stiff out of his mouth. "Sometimes she would brush her hair for hours at a time while just looking out toward the ocean. The only thing my father could do to make her happy was buy her more books. He didn't know what to do with her. Or me." Ren put his fingers up to his nose. "I was just a kid. How could I have known?"

"You couldn't have."

"She loved me so much more than he ever had. She doted on me. Even when I was sixteen she treated me like I was still just eight or nine. She would admonish my father if he punished me where she could see. He would just take me somewhere she couldn't."

"He beat you," Tomi recalled. "Just awful, Ren." She pushed her face into his chest.

"When I killed him she was there."

Tomi's ears pricked up but she tried not to move. This was the very

118

story she was most interested in.

"She told me to run. So here I am."

"You knew that investigator."

Ren sighed and closed his eyes.

"You did. You knew him. Or..." she frowned, "You know him. Since he's still alive. You know that detective. He's been following you. He's the one who's after you."

"He was hired to find me. He's a private investigator and his name's Trent Winston. He's a little over thirty, he smokes like a chimney, and he's got a serious boner for me. Did you manage to see those little silver hairs on his pretty head?" Ren's grin returned from Hell and spread his lips to reveal his teeth. "I gave him those."

"He almost caught you."

"He wasn't after me. Not this time. Their search party was for someone else. He told me that I was just a coincidence." Ren spat out the last word with distaste. "The fuck does he think he's doing, capturing me by just *coincidence*?" His voice dropped to a murmur and he tilted his head. "Fuck Winston. Fuck him. I'll fucking steal his stupid Marlboros. Then where the fuck would he be?"

"Who was he after?" she asked, wondering where exactly Ren might be if Winston stole his Camels.

"Who was he after?" Ren blinked and looked at her. "Well. He was after *you*."

CHAPTER 6

He was dreaming. He had to be. He looked around himself into the darkness. The deep pervading horrific darkness that surrounded his whole being. Body and soul. The sound of a growl made him blink and suddenly he was in the forest, surrounded by trees that were merely black and white, illuminated by the white light of a full moon. They whispered above him, knowing his secrets and telling all that could speak their language of leaves. He swallowed convulsively and his hand went to his chest. He was bleeding. The wound from Ren's vicious attack was open and seeping, his blood like chocolate syrup in an old Hitchcock film. Colorless and sticky. It smelled like pennies and rust.

The growl sounded again. Behind him. He turned and found nothing. His breaths came in quick pants and fear settled low in his belly. He was here. He was hunting. Winston was his prey.

He ran. Deeper into this black and white forest. Deeper into the darkness. The moonlight grew dimmer and dimmer as he ran, pushing limbs out of his way and sprinting through patches of dense fog that felt cool on his heated flesh.

He stopped when it loomed before him. A memory so vivid it almost stopped his breathing. A tall tower. A rustic red, the only thing that could possibly have color in this nightmare. It was taller than the trees and it was old and had patches of gray near the base. He cried out but there was nobody to hear him. Nobody but the tower and Ren somewhere behind him. Somewhere still in the woods waiting to capture him. Waiting for the ideal time to strike.

"No." He fell to his knees, his palm to his chest, panting hard from his sprint. He could feel the warmth of the blood through his shirt. "Please no." His tears were burning hot in his eyes and down his cheeks. "Don't. Don't do this to me."

The tower did not reply. Neither did the distant presence that he could feel in the forest behind him. Ren. The rottweiler. The devil with white teeth. The image of Ren's teeth lined with blood flashed in his memory and he cried out again, pressing harder on his wound that itched like mad. Suddenly around him were bodies. He recognized one as Collie Landall. She wasn't strangled anymore. Her throat had been ripped out. Torn to pieces. She was missing her left arm at the elbow, shredded. Her glazed eyes were staring up toward the light of the full moon, glassy and white. Another body he recognized but could not recall the name. He was around thirty years old and had been some type of drifter in the city. His death had been of natural causes. Here it was not. His intestines were draped over his face and piled around his body, his abdomen caved and open, gaping wide and dripping that chocolate syrup substance that resembled blood in so many ways. The smell of decomp was intense. The bodies doubled when he blinked. They were all torn. All shredded. All of them were Ren's doing.

"Ren," he cried toward the moon. "Don't," he sobbed. His tears blurred his vision of the tower. "Stop."

"Stop?"

The word was so sudden that Winston whirled around and crawled backward in a panic, finding himself pushed hard against the rusty side of the tower. Ren was standing among the bodies. He was wearing a black suit that resembled Winston's, perfectly fit with a white shirt underneath and a sleek black tie. His hair was an artificial white and his eyes a clear chilly dark blue. He had his hands tucked into the pockets of his black dress pants. He was giving the detective a curious expression with one dark brow cocked.

Winston stuttered, "St-stop. P-puh-please. Don't do this."

"Don't do what?" the killer asked, looking about himself at the

121

carnage and gore with indifference. When he met Winston's gaze again his eyes were black, his mouth curving upwards slowly and spreading across his face until the gape of his mouth had reached either ear and opened to reveal rows of sharp white teeth. The thing that had been Ren just a moment ago spoke in a voice that had not changed but still filled Winston's chest and bowels with pure dread. "You're the one who should stop, Winnie. Boo hoo, Winnie the Pooh." It smiled, the mouth dipping until Ren's face didn't appear very human at all and its voice heightened. It sounded like Grace. A sing song tone that utilized her soprano talent. "Winnie the Pooh," it taunted as he pushed back into the rust, "Stop Trent," Grace's voice said, "Stop, you're hurting me. Stop. Don't hurt me, Trent."

"No," he closed his eyes and turned his head away from the thing that teased him.

When he opened them again his heart was pounding hard in his chest and his body covered in a fine sheen of sweat. The blip of his heartrate monitor told him that it was fast. Too fast. He looked over at the screen. The number was in the triple digits. He breathed steady to calm it into the doubles and looked about the dark room. His roommate was still in his coma. The door was open and the light from the hall shined in as a comforting icon of sanity.

The memory of Grace's voice was still haunting him. Echoing in his mind. He thought he might throw up. He rubbed his eyes with the heels of his palms and stared at the light coming in from the doorway. He ached. His whole body, as if he had tensed every muscle while he slept. He looked down at himself. His chest. His collarbone hurt. The latest and greatest wound. But the shooting star-shaped scar on his chest was intact. There was no blood. Not even any chocolate syrup.

He sighed and tried to relax back into his pillows, shoving his head back until he could hear the woosh of air escape the spaces between the lumps of cotton. He needed a shower. He needed a cigarette. He needed a little something better to cure the pain. Mental pain. He grinned at himself then suddenly lost his humor.

That red tower haunted him. He frowned. He'd tried to forget the way his blood had looked at the base of that rusted pillar. Obviously his subconscious hadn't forgotten anything about the way he and Ren had fought like dogs, growling and screaming and gnashing teeth. The way the bodies had looked when he'd found them, torn apart in places, guts strewn over floors and ground. There had been three that had really stuck out in his mind, the rest fading together. The first had been a coincidence. He'd strolled past the police tape and had observed like a good little Detective. The second had been a discovery. A murder yet to be seen by anyone. First on the scene. Interrogated, interviewed, supported by Avery. All the while considering his target.

The third had been a taunt. Peyton Hoolahan, 44, death by disembowelment. Staged. Propped up against the white washed wall of an old warehouse where Winston had been sure that Ren was hiding out. Hoolahan had been a drifter, a bum without a single thing in the whole world save a daughter who was living halfway across the country raising two children alone on Food Stamps while she wasted her life on cocaine. His bowels were strung out around the room like a horrifying spider's web. His lower jaw had been removed. Never found. His top teeth white, hanging out of a mess of red stringy ripped flesh. Above his head was a message. Written like a child with fingerpaint.

"Before beginning a hunt, it is wise to ask someone what you are looking for before you begin looking for it."
Boo-hoo, Winnie the Pooh

He remembered the way his eyes followed the trails of blood and splatters. The way the voice on the other end of the phone sounded dull and fake. It had been a police detective named Maldeen. He'd been a helpful sort. Reminded him a little of Patten, but much too lenient on Winston and Avery. The team had jerked him around a few times on procedure. It didn't matter anymore. Maldeen was dead now.

The way the detective had asked him all the standard questions and had asked him to work with the police as best as he could floated by. There were no threats. No suspicious glances. Just trust. Pure trust. Dangerous trust.

He sighed and rubbed his forehead with the hand that wasn't

bandaged.

"*He's dangerous. You have to listen to me.*"

"*I am listening, Mr. Winston but you also have to listen to me. I appreciate your input on the matter but I assure you we have it handled.*"

Maldeen's soft green eyes didn't look tired or worn. It had been the first time he'd been assigned to a murder investigation. The fact that there was talk of putting together a team of investigators to track down Ren hadn't swayed him in the least from putting his all into trying to find him.

"*That message is for me.*"

"*We don't have any evidence of that.*"

"*Winnie the Pooh, come on, please just listen to me.*"

"*Mr. Winston the quote is from Winnie the Pooh. It's something that little yellow bear said.*"

He recalled the frustration that welled up in his throat. He'd been so angry he could have punched the young detective right in the kisser. Maldeen had known that Winston was chasing this killer up the coast. He'd known perfectly well the kind of relationship that Winston had with the case. But he'd blown him off. Like there was nothing strange about Ren suddenly quoting Winnie the Pooh. He balled his hand into a fist, pulling the hospital sheets into its grip.

The police detective had signed his own death warrant in that warehouse. Finally pushing Winston to the wayside and exerting his dominance. Ren figured that one out quick. He was a smart little pisser. He'd had fun with Winston, tugging him along on trails, dropping hints, leaving dead ends with just a little clue left behind. It was like a big game. Ren dropped little bits of cheese and of course the mice would move through the maze predictably. It had been fun for him. That was until Maldeen took the mouse out of the maze. Their interactions later on had been more of the same.

"*What aren't you telling me?*"

"*This is a police investigation, Mr. Winston. I cannot tell you anything that is considered to be classified information. I urge you to remove yourself from this. For your own safety.*"

"*I have a client you know.*"

"I will not cater to your whims anymore, your poking around has gone far enough. I let you get away with too much and it's cost us at least one man's life."

Winston had stormed from the office and through the bull pen, officers turning to stare at him until he'd slammed the door behind him and lit a cigarette before he was even out of the lobby. He'd brooded for the rest of the evening. Even Avery and a cup of hot English Breakfast couldn't break him out of his funk. All he could think about was the case. Ren, where he might have gone, what he might be doing, and what Maldeen was going to do about it. He obviously had a plan or he would have still allowed for Winston to play his little game. That was why he'd allowed it for so long. Because he didn't have a fucking clue.

He looked around to his left for the bag that Avery had left him. Digging through it he allowed himself a little smile when he found the nicotine gum. Popping a piece into his mouth, he sighed with relief. At least he could get a fix without any big problems. He was calmed by the sound of his roommate's monitor and the now-steady blip of his own. He smiled when they were almost in tandem with each other. Almost but not quite. His roommate was in a coma after all. His roommate also wasn't a P.I. with a knack for getting himself into bad situations with very bad people.

"Before beginning a hunt..." His mind whispered to him, the voice inside his head not quite his own. *"Before beginning a hunt..."*

"...it is wise to ask," he whispered to himself, closing his eyes. He wasn't sleepy. The clock on the wall read about four o'clock. "It is wise to ask someone what you are looking for before you begin looking for it." He breathed for a few moments and allowed his mind to go blank. "Before you begin a hunt, it is wise to ask someone what you are looking for before you begin looking for it." What was he looking for? "Ren" was not the correct answer. He knew that already.

The words he'd said were still ringing in her ears two days later. *He was after you.* She chewed her thumbnail. The new shoes she'd bought herself were snug on her feet. He'd advised her to get a dark color and she had. A dark brown. She had replaced the white laces with black ones and had jogged in place a little to make sure they didn't rub anywhere. She had also bought herself a new pair of jeans, shorts, and two new tank tops. Not to mention a brand new hooded sweatshirt— double layered with a faux fur-trimmed hood. After that she'd picked out a pair of cheap sunglasses from the dollar store and toyed around the with the idea of dying her hair. She nixed it when she saw him standing next to a rather expensive-looking Beamer as if he owned it.

He was still a little ratty despite having cut off the ends of his hair, the blood red now just a memory. His do-it-yourself cut job had left him looking a little more punk than she was used to but his new, tighter sweatshirt, T-shirt, and jeans made him appear nothing short of a rag-tag brand of handsome.

"You clean up well," she noted when she walked by him through the parking lot.

"I do what I can," he replied, a lit cigarette dangling from his lip. When he started walking next to her she realized that he'd gotten himself a new pair of *Toms* and grinned when she realized how perfect they were for him. The tight, form-fitting shoes would be perfect to slip around silently.

"How can you be so human?" she asked, grasping his hand and swinging it.

"What do you mean?" he chuckled.

"I don't know." She swung his hand with hers and decided not to pursue her question. He was human. And he was an animal. She just wasn't sure if she wanted to know the truth behind it. "You're cute."

He didn't reply. He just smoked as they walked together and squeezed her hand with affection.

On the street in this small town they didn't look in any way out of the ordinary. She smelled wood smoke and cedar and watched the old people shuffling in and out of shops. One day she would live in a town like this. In a small place with specialty shops with wide front windows and a lively Main Street. One day her life would be a little more normal. Her heart gave a little pang of grief and she once again squeezed Ren's hand, taking comfort in his answering one.

He could never be with her. They were on two separate playing fields. They just happened to meet somehow. Fate had thrown them onto the same bus. Her father would never forgive her if he knew. But he never had to. Because her and Ren were just some passing phase.

"Tomi?" His deep voice caught her attention. "Would you like something to eat?"

She nodded. "Yes. That would be nice."

"You were thinking."

"Oh you know, just girl things. Hearts and flowers."

He tried to smile but she could tell it pained him. The swelling around the bridge of his nose had yet to subside completely and she was sure it was broken. "I know better than that," he said. She wondered if it was Spring already. He didn't push the issue.

Winston was again grateful for his roommate's coma. The gentle blip of the heart-rate monitor relaxed him. The photos of the girls were laid out in their folders in front of him. The circumstances surrounding their discovery were written in the notes. He chewed his nicotine gum and pondered them but his mind was often distracted. His rash thought that Ren could have been killing all these girls was still floating at the back of his mind. His cheeks flushed when he thought about it. The frustration of looking him in the face kept burning in his chest. It would have been so much easier if there had just been one killer to deal with. Now he was trapped inside this horrid situation. It wasn't just Ren he had to be concerned about. It was Tomi. She was in the middle. A girl. Just sixteen.

The girls' dead eyes stared up at him. He put his palm to his forehead and whispered, "Where is he?" He wondered if they'd seen Ren. Their dark shining eyes flashing for a moment on a rugged young man. Appreciating him. Maybe not even giving him a second thought. "Who killed you?"

His mind couldn't help but recall how Ren had stared at him. Not as an enemy, not as an opponent. Ren's cold dark eyes had looked at him as prey. It was as though he had stared a cobra in the eyes, even been bitten, and survived. He shuddered despite himself. He had never been afraid of any killer before. He had dealt with a few. Most of them were one-timers. They had killed out of passion or for a singular motive. Ren killed with one motive: cold blind rage. He wondered about his other killer. The media had dubbed him the Mad Strangler. Their unoriginality never ceased to amaze him. At least Ren had managed to inspire from them a more original and fear-inducing name. The Roanoke Rottweiler. Of course he was, Winston thought, a rottweiler. Typical murder didn't spark the imagination quite like those in which a serial killer ripped apart his victims with nothing but his *teeth*. Winston was vaguely aware that his fingers had become cold.

A nice doggie. A good doggie. Surely a rakishly handsome young man like Ren could have found himself plenty of support along the way. A girl here and there to give him scraps. Or was he too cold for that? He wished that he had Ren's file here in the hospital but he would have to wait until his discharge. Ren's personality did not account for any company.

The girls continued to stare up at him and he felt defeated. He sighed and stared at the photos a little more. Their underwear was gone. He liked to keep something. He had a place to keep something. He was organized. Ligature marks on their wrists and ankles. Less sporting. He closed his eyes and felt suddenly foolish. Their bruising was on the left side of their throats. Classic *To Kill a Mockingbird* moment. Winston wished beyond anything he could just smoke a damn cigarette.

His other killer was out there. Ren was out there. And poor Tomi seemed to be stuck somewhere in the middle. Was she aware? Did she know she was in danger? Avery was doing everything he could to track her down while Winston was stuck in the hospital but no progress had been made. He was kept informed but they seemed to have lost her completely. No more tracks could be found. Nothing. Avery's constant downcast expression was disheartening.

He heard a soft knock at the door and looked up from his notes and photographs. Mr. Balekowski was standing in the doorway. He was clad in khakis and a dark green polo. He was trimmed and proper with his back straight. His shoes and belt matched in color and on his head was a dark gray golfing cap. His gold Rolex glinted in the sunlight that stretched across the room.

"Detective." He nodded his head. "I came to apologize."

Winston frowned and motioned to the chair beside the bed. The one Avery had spent so many hours in. The old man moved toward it but didn't sit down right away, his hands laced together in front of him.

"Searching for my daughter wasn't meant to be a dangerous job."

Winston closed the folder on his lap without looking down at it and gave Mr. Balekowski a blank stare. "It's my fault."

"Your fault?" The man looked confused.

"I have a history with a particular killer. He's the Hannibal to my Starling if you get my reference." He tapped the top of the file folder with one finger. "I lost him a while back and I'm supposing he lost me as well. But being back here at the old homestead kinda threw us back together and of course it all ended up predictably with him at large and me in the hospital. It's the way he prefers it." He allowed himself a grin to disconcert the irritating politician.

"Is...is that so?" The older man took off his golfing cap and sat down in the chair. "Does this other killer have any connection to your search for my daughter? You *were* searching for Tomi when you ran into him, right? That's what the police detective implied."

"And Patten would be correct. I'm surprised he ended up telling you that."

"He didn't exactly tell me. He was skirting the questions I was asking and it was enough for me to deduce."

Winston raised a brow. "Well, it looks like you have a little bit of an investigator in you, Mr. Balekowski."

He smiled a sheepish little smile. "I did my best." His gaze fell again into a tangle of worry. "But this has gotten me no closer to a resolution. My girl is out in the wilderness and there is a killer out there too."

"I hate to be the bearer of bad news, Mr. Balekowski, but considering you're my client I believe I have a right to tell you that I'm also working on another case down here. One I took before you proposed a payment to find your daughter." When the old man's attention was focused fully on him he said, "There are *two* killers in this territory. Not one. And the one who put me in here is the *least* of your worries."

"The least?"

"I have a history with a killer who only kills men aged thirty to sixty. That doesn't sound quite like your daughter. But there's another one out there. I don't mean to panic you, sir, but it's not looking very good."

It appeared as if Nathan Balekowski was getting more and more frayed the longer he sat in that seat. He rubbed at his forehead with his fingers and his teeth gritted. "I figured after they said that you were in the hospital...that something...that it was getting to be a little out of hand." He wilted in the chair, lost and hurt and alone. "I don't even care if she comes home."

Winston, alarmed, sat upright. "Sir?"

"What I mean is that I don't care if she doesn't want to come home. All I need is for her to be okay."

"This isn't about lowering your standards, sir." Winston put out his hand and touched the back of the politician's. "We won't give up on finding your daughter. It's just a matter of determination. And...and strategy."

"And what is your strategy, Detective?"

He looked down at the closed folder in his lap. "Right now?" He met the icy blue gaze beside him and his voice sounded like it came from someone else. "Pray."

He scratched at the wound on his collarbone tenderly after Mr. Balekowski had left, a little more hunched over. A little more hopeless. They itched in a fierce way and often he found himself touching his bandages. There were two possibilities in his mind. That Tomi had somehow slunk away with some kind of wilderness prowess, or she had been taken. She was truly missing now. Nadine had already expressed a kind of surrender about the whole ordeal. Admitting defeat was not one of her strongest points. It was something they had in common.

When Avery walked into the room he couldn't have had better timing. Winston was just finished with his god-awful hospital dinner and

130

was flipping through the channels on the TV hanging in the corner when the other man walked in. The sun was starting to set, casting a hazy yellow light into the hospital room.

"Hey tiger." Avery grinned. "Heard you had a visitor today? Hope that all went well?" His dark brow was lifted as he made himself at home, tossing his sweater over the back of the visiting chair and sitting down in it, his arms on the armrests and his legs spread comfortably.

"As well as it can go when you're essentially telling a man that his daughter is probably rotting in some ditch somewhere."

Avery frowned. "You didn't say that."

"No. But I didn't say it was going to end very well either. I'm trying to formulate a plan but unfortunately they're not letting me out of here until they've made sure of one thing or another. I am fully annoyed by this whole ordeal and I am also convinced that this is all Patten's doing."

Avery chuckled. "I wish I could say you're wrong but I'm pretty sure the guy had to get you out of his way some way or another. Got you on lock in this hospital by telling them that they need to test you for communicable diseases."

"Oh for the love of Christ."

"What did you expect after you annoyed the shit out of him like you did? He's out to find all of them. The main course and both the sides. Looking to take you right out of the game." There was a small pause in which Avery scratched the side of his jaw. "Of course one has to hope Ren doesn't actually have any plans for you. That wouldn't bode very well for the nice detective. Didn't for the last one anyway."

Winston's bowels squirmed. "If it's a game now, it's only just started."

"You would hope so anyway. Maybe Ren's just looking for a game to play. And I have to say, Winston, you seem to be his favorite partner."

His nose wrinkled. If it hadn't been for Ren, Winston would still be living a few miles from the coast in a cozy little cabin. He'd be eating eggs for breakfast every morning and making love to his woman every night. "Well if I don't have to be involved in any more of his games then count me out. I fold. I give. I don't wanna play." It had cost him everything. Everything except Avery. The two of them packed up and went North, getting taken in by a practice in D.C. that had use for a good tracker and didn't mind taking in the tracker's tag-along investigator while they were at it.

He'd thought that dealing with murder would have given him an edge in dealing with the killer. He'd been wrong. He'd thought that he could protect himself. He was wrong about that one too.

Avery's chin was scruffy and he rubbed it a little with his palm. "Rayne called. Said we got a few offers up in the district if things don't work out so well down here. He put the files on your desk for when we get back."

"Fine, but you know I'm not going back."

Avery leaned forward, his elbows on his knees. "You're not going back?"

"Not until this thing is resolved. My way or Patten's way. Don't care. I can't leave here until I'm satisfied."

"Well you'd better hope Patten is doing all he can. Because you're gonna be shit out of luck if he's sitting around with his thumb up his ass."

"There has to be something I can do," Winston groaned. "Something I can say, someone I can talk to. What do you know about the investigation? Did you find out anything?"

Avery shrugged one shoulder. "The nice detective is avoiding me. I tried to find out everything I could but the guy has about diddly on your guy and close to diddly on the other guy. So let's lay down what we know and mull it. We know that Ren and Tomi have been in contact. They might even be traveling together. In fact that is a distinct possibility. Ren's tracks are about size thirteen and he walks on his toes. Our killer has Nike's, size nine, he's possibly around five six or seven. He's most likely older than thirty but younger than fifty. He's right-handed and was possibly a Boy Scout. I'd be looking for an Eagle Scout considering how well he can move around a wooded area. He likes to keep a souvenir, underwear, and generally kills very soon after capture. He catches girls by hitting them over the head or choking them until they pass out. Then he takes them to a secondary location where he kills them by strangulation and takes his souvenir and then brings them to a third location where he dumps them."

Winston nodded when Avery was finished and looked over at the file folder on the bedside table. The photos of the girls flashed through his mind. So did Grace's voice. *"Please don't hurt me."* He took in a deep breath. "Ren's only killed one person so far. And someone who might have meant him harm at that. I'm actually impressed by how well he's done in keeping on the down-low."

"Don't start admiring him now." The side of Avery's mouth turned up. "All killer's have a motive for killing. Just because he hasn't had a need to kill and thus hasn't doesn't make him any less of a threat than our crazy-strangler-guy."

"But you guys are right when you say I shouldn't get twisted up over him."

"Thank you."

"I'm focusing on the wrong thing here. I'm focusing on him as a wild animal. He's not a wild animal when he has direction."

"Right."

"What if...I gave him a direction?"

Avery appeared as though he'd been spritzed in the face with cold water. "What?"

He wished Ren could have been on his side. He wished Ren could have been a real Hannibal Lecter. He wished the dog wasn't out to get him. Then, as Avery looked on, something happened in Trent Winston's little brain. Something clicked. Exploded more like. Somehow the proverbial light bulb flickered and stayed on. And then he wondered if Ren could end up on his side after all.

He was kissing her breasts. The heat of the evening was stifling and it seemed a bit too early for his Spring mood to have emerged. The sun was low in the sky and the world took on a hazy feel. She focused on his touch. Slow pressing of his lips against her soft flesh. She breathed deeply and held in her tiny mewls when he suckled her. How did it get to this? One moment he had been cold and distant, staring off into the fields of soy, and the next he had been nipping at her ear and whispering proclamations of her cuteness. She may have let him push up her shirt because she was curious as to what he would do—his delicate kisses on her sensitive belly had been giggle-worthy at least. But she had let him push down her bra for another reason.

She throbbed between her legs and shifted in a vain attempt to relieve the pressure. If anything she had made it worse by calling attention to it. His hand found her and rubbed the outside of her shorts. She groaned in protest and pushed her thighs together.

He lifted his head up, his shining saliva on her breasts cooling quickly and uncomfortably. The question in his eyes was sincere.

Tomi's face was red. She didn't know how to express what she felt. He had asked her if she was a whore. Could he have forgotten what he had said so soon? The intense look in his eyes was one clouded by lust. Men didn't understand themselves when they were consumed by their needs. Surely Ren's actions, put in the body of a female, would have been considered slutty. As a woman he would have been considered a temptress. A whore even. And what had she done? Merely told him that she wished to have sex with him.

"Tomi?" His voice was not impatient as she had expected. It was concerned. He truly was Spring.

"I'm sorry," she said, tears brewing. She cursed them silently.

"Are you afraid?"

"No." She rethought this. "Yes." Her tears slipped out and she sniffed, her breath coming in quick pants.

He moved to her side and pulled up her bra for her, easing her shirt down over it and pulling her to him. She turned into his shoulder and let him hold her.

She felt the need to clarify. "I'm just afraid of what you'll think of me." She felt stupid. He didn't reply so she continued, "I don't wanna be a whore."

He hugged her tighter. "I didn't mean that when I said it. I was angry. All men say stupid things they don't mean when they're angry." He put his hands on either side of her face and pulled her away to kiss her on her lips. "It was wrong of me to say anything remotely close to that. You're a lady, Tomi. About as close to a lady as I've ever met anyway."

"But...what if...you..."

"I don't think you're a whore, Little Miss. I never will."

The thought that he was simply saying such a thing to make her go further at the moment was foremost in her mind, but he didn't make any other movements of a sexual nature. In fact he merely held her for a little while before getting up with the small claim that he needed to pee. Her blush gave away that she knew what he was really going to be doing out of her sight. He pretended not to notice it.

When he came back he pulled out his decks of cards and laid them out on the grass between them, dealing out a game of canasta. In a casual tone he said, "They're taking great pains to find you."

"What?"

He glanced up at her before going back to the cards in his hand. "Winston and his partner are considered very good at what they do as detectives. They're good at finding. His partner is a seasoned tracker. They've been successfully following us for a while."

"But..."

"It's easy to follow you, sweets, you make it too easy."

A flash of shame squeezed her heart. "I don't mean to."

"Nobody means to. You can't help it. The real question is why they're tracking you. Why would they bring those two in to track *you*? Aren't you just some runaway? It happens all the time. It's really no big deal. Send out flyers, post them at truck stops, gas stations, give them to the local PD but to bring in the big guns so easily? Where does that fit in?" His lips pressed together and he stared at her. "I guess I never really asked you where you came from."

She shrank under his gaze but gathered herself and put down some cards. "My parents are kind of...high class."

"How so?"

She bit her lip and didn't look into his eyes. "My father is a politician."

Ren sighed. "Congressman or Senator?"

"How did you--?" She stopped when she saw his expression. Of course. Winston and his partner could only be involved in something so important. "Senator."

He nodded and put his eyes back to his cards, making a play easily. "He doesn't know you're with me. He was genuinely surprised to see me. Good news for us. Your father is a Senator. Very bad news for me if they find out that we're together. You'll never be seen as an accomplice. You'll be seen as a captive. Good news for you. Play that up if it happens."

While he spoke she was formulating her next move. His words scared her too much to truly focus on them alone.

"We took Winston out of the game for a little while. That's good. But he'll be back. He always comes back. I could probably kill him and he'd come back. Stubborn fuck." He put a few cards down and then scratched the back of his neck where he'd been bitten by a mosquito.

"He's like you, you know," Tomi managed a small smile.

"What's that?"

"The way you describe him. Stubborn. Relentless. Malicious. He's very much like you. I would expect that he's a little rash, clever, and maybe a pinch of a romantic too."

Ren frowned at her. "Don't go falling in love with him now, you hear?"

She giggled and held her cards to her chest. "Goodness gracious are we a little jealous?"

"More than a little," he grumbled in good humor. It was getting a little too dark to continue their game of cards so she put hers down and stared at him. He was trying not to look at her, pretending that grass was more interesting, picking at it with nimble fingers. He was more human than ever in the fading light of dusk. His muscles under soft skin did not ripple or move like a dog's like she had seen them before. He was calm and all tension was gone. It was a state he was rarely in. Her heart swelled in her chest and a dull pain was present in her throat. He was her true soulmate. A frosty violent rogue who seemed to have in his mouth a plethora of ripping teeth. She loved a killer. She continued to stare, the corners of her mouth being pulled down by circumstance. The tightness in her chest refused to let up. A desperation filled her stomach and suddenly she felt a wave of vulnerability.

She looked around them again. Through the darkened woods. She again felt as if she were being watched. When she looked back at Ren he was still staring at the ground but tension was back in his shoulders and his eyes were not looking at his fingers. She whispered, "We should go."

He looked up toward her and nodded his agreement.

CHAPTER 7

It had been pure foolishness. The whole idea had been pure foolishness. They wouldn't notice that he was missing for a good few hours. He could be dead by then. He pulled in a long drag from his Marlboro and relished the feeling of the smoke in his lungs. He looked at it between his fingers as he blew out. "Gonna die anyway, right?" he whispered. The forest was still, the only sound the whispering of the leaves above him. He knew he was in the right place. Somehow he knew. All he had to do was make himself obvious.

It had taken him hours. Almost a whole day. He consulted maps and memory, thinking about where he himself would have gone had he been a rakish young man on the run. It was stupid. He probably wasn't even here. If he was...well that was another thing burning in his mind. If he was here there was most definitely a large possibility that these could be the last moments Winston would ever have on God's green Earth. Sounds seemed amplified. He tried to put his fear behind him but when dealing with a man whose teeth had sunk into his flesh, Winston wasn't exactly the bravest soul. He licked his lips and shuffled about the forest with his hand on the butt of his pistol. He was banking on his predator being able to smell the cigarette or see the orange prick of light from the tip. Holding it between his fingers he made a soft whistle and two little 'tsk' sounds before giving a soft call: "Here pooch. Coooome on doggie. Come'ere."

The forest answered him with silence.

"Come here doggie. I got a little treat for ya. Nice tasty little treat for you." He took off his backpack and pulled the carton of Camel Blues out before swinging it back on and raising the package above his head. "Come here pooch. Not gonna hurt you. I got a proposition for you."

He stood there in the hot early August dark for what seemed like forever. His cigarette was down to just the filter before there was a rustle somewhere to his left. "Ren?" he asked. He was met with silence. "I need to talk to you." The wound on his collarbone itched incessantly under the heavy Kevlar vest. But what if he wasn't talking to Ren? What if he was talking to his other killer? The thought made a slice of panic run through his heart and tighten his chest. His breathing was a little more harsh. "Ren, please," he murmured. "This is a matter of life and death. I know you're very acquainted with the latter." He waited a little more before he dropped the butt of his cigarette to the ground and put his arm down, the carton bumping his thigh. He stepped on the smoldering butt and ground it down, taking a long sweeping look into the dark before he took a step to go.

"Wait."

He paused. Had he truly heard it? He turned around but still could not see anyone. "Ren?"

"What are you doing here, Winston?" The sound of his voice was up higher than Winston had thought and as he raised his eyes upward, Ren dropped down, landing easily on his feet. He had been in the trees all the while. "How did you know where to find me?" The unease in the killer's voice gave Winston a smug little feeling in his stomach. He fought back a triumphant smirk.

"I brought these for you."

"*What are you doing here?*" There was a threat in his tone.

"Calm down. I'm alone."

"I know."

Winston smiled. "You shouldn't have let me sit idle in a hospital bed, pooch."

"I shouldn't have let you go to the hospital at all."

"Well this is what you get."

"A reward?"

"A bribe."

Through the darkness he saw Ren's head tilt in question and his dark eyebrow arch. He had successfully interested the young killer. Now he just had to get out of this alive. Ren wouldn't kill him until he'd made his business known. And only if he chose to reject it.

"I'd like your help with something. I think you'll find it a little sporting." Winston took the time to light another cigarette and take a drag. "You fancy yourself outdoorsy, right?"

One side of Ren's mouth lifted in a grin.

"There have been murders happening around here. Young girls. Fourteen to eighteen."

Ren put up his hands and his grin disappeared.

"Don't worry," Winston laughed, "We know it's not you. But you admitted yourself that you've been in contact with a little blonde teenager. Were you lying to me?"

"Tomi?" Ren teased with a full-blown smile.

Winston's heart started to race in his chest. He knew her name. He swallowed but tried to act nonchalant. It would do him no good to have Ren know his weaknesses. Not that he didn't already. He took another drag of his cig. "Yes. Tomi. I trust you've seen her recently?"

He shrugged one shoulder. "Maybe. Concerned about her, are you, Winston?"

The detective took in a calming breath. "Our killer has a tendency to adore teenaged girls. She's a prime target out here. I'd be stupid if I wasn't worried for her safety. Aren't you worried for her safety, Ren?"

"I'm not as invested in her as you are."

"Aren't you?" It was a game they'd played before. Trying to guess each others' intentions and feelings. Winston was sure he wasn't misjudging. Ren knew her name. He'd had contact with her. There was more to this story.

"Should I be? She doesn't cry diamonds from what I've seen."

Winston narrowed his eyes. "So she's safe then. Help me find this other killer."

"For a carton of cigarettes?" Ren scoffed.

"For a ten day head start."

Ren blinked. It meant that he could go anywhere. It meant that he could do anything. It meant almost complete and utter freedom. That was until he started killing again. Then there was nothing Winston could promise him. It would be up to him to stop this madness. It would be up to him how long he could stay free.

"Does that sound fair?"

Ren murmured, "How do I know you're not lying to me? How do you I know you're not going to welch on this deal?"

"Would you?"

"Maybe."

"I know you, Ren. You wouldn't. Don't do this to me. Help me find him. Help me solve this case. Help me save some lives. Wouldn't that be a little bit of a fun game for you?"

Ren's nose wrinkled a little on one side. "What happens when I find him?"

"Whatever you want to happen. You can tell me where he is. Who he is or..." Winston left the sentence open ended to imply what would inevitably happen in any case. He didn't want to give him expressed permission. It was almost like murder in itself. He watched Ren think and said softly, "You already have a plan." Ren's eyes met his and suddenly Winston knew exactly what he had in mind. Those cold ocean depths spoke to him as clear as a warm sunny day. Horror clenched his chest. "Don't do that."

Ren's tiny kitten smile feigned innocence. "I don't know what you're talking about."

"Don't do it," Winston warned again.

"You never specified how I was to find him," Ren growled, obviously irritated. "I can find your stupid killer. I can get him. And I know exactly how I'm going to do it." Ren advanced on him with liquid movements. He brushed Winston's side while he ripped the carton of Camels from his hand and made a soft animal sound in his ear. Still so close Winston could smell tobacco from his hair, Ren stated, "You're a lucky fuck, Winston."

"I know."

In an instant he was gone. If not for a missing carton of cigarettes and the fading warmth from his brush against the detective's side, he might never have been there at all. Winston finished his cigarette and stamped it down into the ground, reaching in his pocket for another. His fingers found nothing.

"Son of a fucking bitch." He glared into the darkness with cold fury.

He was smoking when she woke up. The dangerous scent of it wafted to her and when she sat up, he stared at her interestedly as if he meant to say something. His fingers were on the grass, curled around a red and white packet of cigarettes. A kind she'd never seen before.

"Where'd you get those?" she asked, rubbing her crusted eyes.

"Around." He put them back in his pocket before she could read the name of them but she didn't miss the tiny smile that curled his lips when he hid them. He looked at her with a soft kind of expression. Not amused or contented, but perhaps a little worry etched in his forehead. He gave a short little sigh, she wasn't sure why, and moved toward her, his cigarette in his mouth. He lay down next to her and extinguished it in the dewy grass.

"Ren." It was a statement. She felt the warmth of his body as he lay inches from her.

"Tomi," he responded.

"I think..." she started and then paused for a few moments.

He reacted quickly, before she could finished her sentence, pushing his finger against her lips and smiling a small smile. "You shouldn't say things with 'I think' in front of them when in reality you haven't thought at all."

She stared at him, her bright blue eyes wide and clear in the morning light. His smile was condescending at best and she knew that he was perfectly aware of what she was going to say to him. He knew where her heart was. He couldn't bear to hear it. Did that mean that he loved her too? Or that he didn't? Her brows began to come together with the thought and her hands found his, his finger still on her lips. She kept his hand there and lowered her eyes to his throat where his pulse beat.

"Did you dream?" he asked, pulling his finger back into his fist which she continued to hold.

"Yes."

"Of?"

"My father."

Ren released his fist and held her hand. She felt stupid. Ren's dreams of his own father were probably a hundred times worse that the dreams she had experienced with hers. His icy blue eyes tinged with a slight form of madness when he'd told her that she didn't even have a brother. He'd been so calm. But there was a fire in him. She *did* have a brother. His name was Bo Balekowski and he was *her* brother. He had been the most important man in her life. But as she felt Ren's hand squeeze around hers she had to think twice.

She loved him. And not just that but she was *in love* with him. It was that stupid crazy thing that high school girls were so concerned about. Loving and being *in love*. When she had to go back to school they would ask her. How it felt. How she did it. How was her *summer fling*? What would she tell them? That she could never love this fiercely again? That the emotions of being caught like a mouse in a cat's paw were both terrifying and exhilarating at the same time? It was love and it was fear and it was joy and it was horror. A gathering of all of Tomi's most complex emotions rolled up into one little sushi roll she had to try to chew all in the same summer. Almost in every single moment she had with him.

He exhausted her. Every fiber of his being thrummed with an untapped energy and potential for rage and violence. Every word he spoke could have been replaced with a moan of frustration, pain, or pure agony. His eyes held nothing. As if he were soulless. Empty. A shell on the beach. Every beat of his heart pumped blood and energy through a body that had but one function: to convey anger. Rage. Lust. Frustration.

He could not love. It was not a new realization to her mind but it was in this moment that she had to face it. She must accept it. Ren could not love her. Not as he was. Perhaps there had been a time when he

could have loved her. He could have been what she needed. A time
before he had become nothing but a dog. A feral dog. He acted human.
But he wasn't. He acted civil. But he wasn't. He was in a play. *All of
life's a stage.* She put the back of his hand to her lips and stared at the
place where his pulse beat in his throat.

Wild thoughts began to run through her mind. Wild, brutal, and oh
so very fucking clear. Her mouth on his throat. Her teeth scraping his
flesh. The coppery overwhelming taste of his blood filling her mouth.
The inevitable push that would rip her from him. That would force her to
either let go or clamp down. Which would she do? Which did she have
the stomach for? She could kill him. She could end him. She could own
him forever. A part of him. He didn't have to love her. He merely had
to be hers.

She closed her eyes, blocking out the image of his pulse. She was
too weak. She was too human. She couldn't own him. It was the same
to her as shooting a dog just because his temperament made him unfit for
the leash. *Let him go.* She closed her eyes even harder until her nose
wrinkled with the effort. Go away, thought. Go away. But it was there.
It would stay.

"Tomi?" he asked with humor.

When she opened her eyes again and took his hand away from her
lips, she found him staring at her with laughter in his expression.

"You're a little clown," he mused before pulling her closer to him
and kissing her. He tasted like cigarettes and she wrinkled her nose for
that reason instead. He chuckled at her. "Sorry." His sheepish smile
was enough to make her nuzzle into his chest and push her body against
his warm one. "Tomi?"

"Mmmhmm?" she murmured, muffled by his clothes.

"What will you do after you've seen your brother?"

She shrugged. "I dunno. I'll probably just go back home. I'm sure
my parents are worried."

"What about your friends?"

"Didn't I tell you that I don't have many friends?"

His body shook with silent laughter. "Oh yes. You did. Because
you're such a sour princess you have no friends."

"If I'm so sour, why do you always call me 'sweets'?" She frowned and pinched his side so he would laugh more. She liked it when he laughed. It made her think that there might be something honest about him. Something she could trust. She curled into his body with tension in her stomach. *Trust* was the wrong word.

But then again, it would have to do. Because he was all she had in the world.

"Where have you been, tiger?" Avery's smooth voice came casually from the visitor's chair as he wandered back into the hospital.

He gave his partner a tiny little grin and threw him a wrapped taco from the Taco Bell paper bag he carried in. "Couldn't handle this fucking food anymore," he explained. He had changed his clothes with an extra set he always kept in the car so he wouldn't smell like the forest. His shoes he had wiped hard on the little carpet at Taco Bell. To the point where he thought the cashier might have assumed he had OCD. Locard's exchange was a silly thing he knew so he went over his body with a lint roller. Just in case one of Ren's black hairs had ended up attaching itself to his skin or hair. Avery had hawk eyes. But Winston had wonderful lies.

"Brilliant." Avery grinned while opening up the taco and taking a bite. "You're a sly dog. I knew you'd come back. Clever putting your SAT monitor on your comatose roommate's other finger. Of course I'm pretty sure your heartbeat is a little more intense than his considering you've been running."

"Well I had to get back here before someone raised some kind of alarm. I don't want to cause a ruckus just for a Jonesin' for Taco Bell." He rolled his eyes, the lie slipping easily out of him.

"Well hurry up and get back in bed. I don't want Patten on our case. Besides, I think we should talk about this."

"About what?" he asked, shoving a taco into his mouth while simultaneously easing out of his shoes and into the bed.

"About Tomi. And about the Strangler." Avery was looking oddly morose, as if he had just heard bad news. Winston's throat started to constrict. Had he been wrong about Ren? Had Ren only seen the girl beforehand and had lost her? Avery continued, "I think we're going to

145

have to come to grips with her as a *past-tense*." He took a breath in and let it out through his nose in a sigh.

"Why?"

"Winston." Avery gritted his teeth. "I think she's gone. I know you think Ren and her were together but we've lost them both. Whether or not she's dead, I don't know if we're going to find her."

He put his hand out and Avery took it. "He's gonna get his," Winston told him with hard eyes. "We'll make sure of that, Avery. This one isn't going to get away."

Avery let one side of his mouth raise. "You're a one nemesis kind of guy, huh Winston? If you love him so much, why don't you marry him?"

Winston chuckled but moved his eyes away from his partner and best friend. He stared at the lumps that were his feet under the hospital blanket. He *had* married him. He'd made an oath. An oath that would be sealed with Tomi's blood if Ren truly went through with his plan. He bit his upper lip. Now the question was: How in the hell he was going to come to terms with that? Avery had already counted her as lost. Nobody would think anything of it. Except him. He knew in his heart that she was still alive. That soon, if Ren had his way, she wouldn't be.

How do I know you're not lying to me? How do you I know you're not going to welch on this deal? Winston shook his head and closed his eyes. Avery was fully absorbed in eating the rest of his taco, oblivious to Winston's inner thoughts. His deal with the devil. Could he let it happen? Could he allow one girl's death to get this killer? Was neutralizing a killer with little to no effort on his part the most appealing factor? Or was it all the lives he would save? And yet how many more had he condemned by allowing Ren to leave? He could feel tears gathering, stinging the backs of his eyes.

Why had he even gone out there? Questions flooded his mind so he laid back down on his lumpy hospital pillow and stared at the ceiling. "I'm tired," he said to the room.

"I'll go," Avery got up, balling the little wax paper wrapper and tossing it into the tiny waste bin. "But Winston," he continued without looking at him. "Don't think you'll catch him yourself."

"What?" Winston breathed, his eyes wide at the ceiling and his heart thumping in his chest.

"Ren," he elaborated. "You might know where to find him because you and he are very similar creatures." He wiped his bottom lip with his thumb, it was a trait he'd had forever. Probably a mannerism from his parents. "You two might even have the ability to come to an understanding. But you will never *ever* catch him alone."

Winston was staring at him now. At the back of his head. He couldn't form words.

Avery's voice lowered, so that Winston had to strain to hear him. "I won't pretend to understand the two of you. I'll let you have your secrets." He left. A cloud moved over the early-morning sun and darkened the room considerably through the white venetian blinds. He could hear the wind start to blow through the tiny decorative trees that lined the outside of the hospital and he knew that a storm was coming.

They were sitting together side by side, their shoulders touching. She was warm and the bugs were leaving her alone. The sky was a curious yellow color, almost green. A storm was brewing. They had no shelter but for the forest. Tomi listened to the wind rustling the leaves in an ominous manner. What would they do? There had been plenty of gentle rains they'd weathered under the thick canopy of leaves above but a storm? Wind, rain, hail maybe? Lightning? She shivered when a cold gust whipped her hair around her head and into her face. She leaned against him. His shoulder was hot.

When she looked over at his face she was surprised there wasn't a cigarette in his mouth. He looked pensive. Almost lost in thought. His ebony brows were knitted and he was staring off at the horizon. Perhaps they shouldn't have been sitting at the end of the woods. The storm was coming from behind them, the sun already lost in it.

"What are you thinking?" she asked.

For a little bit he didn't move his head. There was only a flicker of something in his eyes that told her he'd heard her. The wind picked up again and rustled his hair and he turned his head to look at her, the same look still marring his handsome face. She wished to sooth him from

147

whatever unseen demons haunted him but she feared they were much too much for her to handle. So she kissed him. It was quick, a silly little peck on the mouth that was meant to surprise him. Somehow she had expected him to have his eyebrows up but they remained cemented in worry. She scowled at him. It was a silly scowl. He didn't react.

Finally Tomi let her face take her true feeling. Desperate. Ren wasn't himself. "Ren," she whined. "Don't be weird."

Finally his mouth twitched at the side. At the same time a bolt of pure white light flashed and left spots in the blonde's vision. A clap of booming thunder shook her but she smiled at him and laughed a little. Laughed a little and then quite a bit. Her heart flurried. He found his smile. It crinkled under his eyes and warmed their ocean cold depths. His deep voice answered her and she was a little shocked when she heard it. "I'm not weird."

She didn't quite know how to explain to him what it was that was making him weird.

He was smiling at her though, which was almost always good. He didn't look right without a cig on his lip. She kissed him again. This time it wasn't silly. She could feel his arms wrapping around her, sliding warmth against warmth to cuddle her into his larger body.

When they quit kissing, he was holding her tight against him and her face was so close to his that her lips touched his as she spoke, "I didn't know you could be worried. I learn something new everyday."

"If you knew what I was thinking, why did you ask?" There was a chuckle hidden in his voice.

"I wanted to know if you were worried about me."

"What if I said that was true?"

"Then you need to listen to me right now, Mr. Ren." She backed away as his arms loosened to allow it. She put her palms on either side of his face and then pushed to pucker his lips like a fish. "We could die tomorrow and the world could move on without us."

He laughed, "If you died tomorrow I..." His voice cut off and he looked forward, his teeth gritted together in a terrifying grimace. "I wouldn't know what to do with myself."

It was those words that most frightened her and her heart pounded in her chest. It was probably true. He had spent nearly a month doing nothing but assisting her in her whirlwind journey that felt more like an ill-prepared camping trip at this point. Did he even *have* a life to go back to? Lightning flashed around them and the wind whipped her hair around her face. His expression was hard and he was deep in his thoughts. The odd mood that surrounded him was putting her on edge so she decided to change the subject. "Ren, sweetheart, maybe we should find some shelter."

His eyes flitted toward the sky under his furrowed brows. "Yes. You're right. Come on."

They were sitting under the canopy of a gas station when the rain started. It was hard enough to spray them with mist as it hit the parking lot. They huddled together with their hoods up and their hands clasped tight together. Ice cream sandwiches had been two for a dollar and her cheeks still felt sticky despite much desperate licking.

The sky was almost black. It was only one in the afternoon but the darkness that surrounded the world made it look like it was eight or nine at night. The rain was so heavy that where it fell from the sides of the canopy looked as if they were walls of water or curtains that could be drawn. He sat next to her silent and brooding.

"Why do you think about him so much?" She asked him, her lips close to his ear.

"Think about who?"

"That detective. The one who got you. I saved you. You don't have to worry about him. You're not weak."

"It's not that."

She pouted. "What is it then? Why does he steal your mind?" She pushed her face into his neck and closed her eyes. He was warm. She whispered, "Come back to me."

He was pressing the button too hard. The crappy plastic might have broken if he hadn't realized it before that became a possibility. All he wanted was a root beer. He'd found the vending machine tucked down a dead-end hallway with a few vinyl couches with no backs and a sad looking potted plant in the corner. It only had *Pepsi* products which might have been a mighty bummer save the root beer tab on the bottom. He'd pushed it in. But he couldn't seem to let it go.

He couldn't help but wonder what it was he was looking for. *"...it is wise to ask someone..."* The root beer was sitting down at the bottom of the vending machine waiting for him to put his hand through to pick it out. If only it were that simple. To reach down and pluck what he wanted through a vending machine. To pick up the pooch by the scruff of his neck and put him right in his cage where he belonged. But no.

That wasn't right at all.

Because he wasn't looking for the pooch anymore. He was looking for the other killer. Tomi's predator. "What am I looking for?" He covered his eyes with his hand and leaned forward, his forehead touching the cool plastic of the humming machine in front of him. "I'm not even looking for a strangler." He could feel tears welling under his eyelids and he let them come and seep from under his hand to course down over his cheeks. He wouldn't respond if someone came along. Nobody would. "What am I looking for?"

Blonde. Blue eyes. Young with a smattering of freckles over the bridge of her nose. Probably sun-kissed by now. Instead of Tomi's school picture, Winston was thinking about another blonde. One from his own past. One who had seen the very worst of Winston and Winston's profession.

He wished that he could say that she had stayed. That she had persevered through the thick and the thin. But they hadn't been married. There was no bond that was meant to weather the for-better or the for-worse. She had gone because she was frightened. He didn't blame her. He could still hear her screaming sometimes. In the middle of the night. The way she had clung to him. His blood smeared across her arms and smudged into her shirt.

"Trent, please. Don't. They're coming. Don't close your eyes."
"I'm not going to die, Grace. It just hurts."

The rust had scraped against the back of his head and his neck while he sat propped against it. The front of his shirt was torn open and soaked in blood. It must have looked as if he'd been shot in the heart. He

couldn't fault her panic. He couldn't fault the way she'd looked at him
from the side of his hospital bed.

*"I can't just let him go. I have to capture him. Whatever I do. You
understand that, right Grace?"*

"Trent, you have to stop this." Her eyes had filled with unshed tears.
"Trent, don't hurt me. Please stop this. Stop."

"You know I can't do that, Grace."

The sting of her glare had pierced his heart. He never saw her again
after she left the hospital that day. Her friends had come to pick up her
things one by one. They'd given him odd looks. As if he had done
something wrong. He'd ignored them. He had returned the black velvet
box and ring to the jeweler's. It had been a stupid place to think of
proposing. It was just a stupid red tower in the middle of the woods.
They'd played there as kids. Nothing bad had ever happened there
before. Nothing could. Their childhood memories were too solid, too
strong, too positive.

What a stupid day to think of proposing.

What a stupid life he was living.

What a crazy stupid terrifying life.

"Why didn't you just kill me?" he whispered. "String me up by my
own fucking entrails like you did to Maldeen?" His forehead slid down
the plastic surface as he slowly crouched down into a fetal position, his
hand still over his eyes. He could reach forward and just get what he'd
wanted. Just push through the barrier and grab it. It would be so easy. It
would have been easy to kill him too. He'd fought hard but so had
Maldeen. So had the others. They'd fought him tooth and nail.

It must have been around midnight, she thought, her eyes focusing
on the graffiti on the opposite wall of the highway overpass. The word
"Swanks" didn't really mean much to her but she admired the way it was
written with deep curves, sharp corners, and lined with carefully defined
borders of red, purple, and an intense shade of pink. The inner color was
yellow and she wondered if a girl might have been responsible for the art.
Swanks seemed like a pretty decent name for a girl gangster. Or

whatever.

She was curled next to him and she put her hand under his sweatshirt that was unzipped because of the warmth of the night. His chest was hot and she could feel his heart beating under her palm. She wondered if he felt things there like other people did. Or in his stomach like other people did. She tried to imagine being devoid of all feeling, of all emotion. Not that Ren was, of course, as she had *seen* emotion from him. But she wasn't sure where he felt it. Or if he *felt* it at all. Perhaps he simply *thought* his emotion. She tried to put her thoughts in order but they were much too abstract for her to fully grasp despite them being hers in origin.

She tried to think about home. Or what had been home. She put her leg over his and put her thigh over his crotch, pushing a little on him until he shifted in his sleep, moving closer to her. The girls she sat at the lunch table with probably thought she was an idiot. Or they probably sat around in their little circle on Courtney's bed and chittered away about how she was most likely chopped up into little tiny bits of Tomi-meat and stashed somewhere in her father's study. His safe maybe. Maybe they thought he hated her.

None of them were dangerous. Or brave. Or even slightly daring. None of them could fathom having a brother like hers either. She tried to think about the breeze that came off the ocean. They were so far away from it now that she could no longer feel its carefree fingers sifting through her hair. The breeze that came now was different. From another direction. Source-less and contained. As if the ocean breezes were untamed and wild and these were somehow fenced in.

What he dreamed of intrigued her. She had never asked him. She wondered if his dreams were somehow like a replay of his life thus far. The people he'd murdered, the girls he'd fucked, the places he'd slept. One month of Ren's life was probably filled with more excitement than her entire life could ever produce. She had the reckless thought that it would probably take forever for him to die since there would be so much to flash over. She wondered if he dreamed of killing. If the small twitch of his upper lip every so often was a symptom of a dream of him sinking his teeth into some unsuspecting victim. Their warm blood on his

152

tongue. Streaking his chin and flowering in soft-edged circles on the front of his T-shirt. A rage that had broken loose and taken another and ripped him apart.

Ripped. The word floated through the darkness and goosebumps rose on her flesh. She could hear the long grasses around them shuffling in a dance, the wind an invisible participant in this tango. Other killers cut. Hit. Sliced. Choked. Deceptively clean-sounding words that implied efficiency and a clear mind. Ren *ripped. Tore. Shredded.* She swallowed convulsively when she thought about what they must look like. After he's done. Missing pieces. Blood seeping from gaping oval-shaped wounds. Did he...*swallow it?* She gagged a little, the sound causing him to stir beside her.

"-Omi?" he murmured, turning his body toward her. His mind was clouded by sleep. He wouldn't stay awake long. When she didn't say anything but cuddled closer, he once again fell into a pattern of even breaths and she knew he was asleep. Her lips were tight together and she watched his face while he slept, lit just slightly by the distant light of a lonely lamp that hung over some overgrown train tracks that passed a few yards from them. He didn't look capable of murder. In fact he didn't look like he could even bring himself to wap a puppy over the snout with a newspaper.

You're in a game. That little voice in her head wouldn't shut up. It wasn't a voice. It was her own brain trying to knock some sense into her. Nothing made sense. Nothing *had* to make sense. If he could be psychopathic then why couldn't her life be a little *psychotic*? Why did everything have to make sense all of a sudden? She rested her hand on his side under his hoodie and stared at the way his eyelashes rested against his freckled cheeks. He was playing a game. But what kind of game?

A game of strategy of course, she thought wryly. And he wasn't playing it with *her*. It was Winston. That damnable detective. It all came down to what kinds of cards they were holding. Of course, she silently giggled, cards. *Canasta.* She wondered where she lay in this. Whether or not she could freeze the deck or add extra points in the end for she was most certainly a three. No more. The difference was in her

153

color alone. Black and she could freeze the deck if only for a play and red--well red could go either way. Up or down. Who would catch her? And would having her hurt or help in the end game?

Who'll hold you in the end? She took a huge gulp of air. That's what she was. A strategy piece. A carefully held item of value that could turn the tides, however slightly, into favor of one player or the other.

She closed her eyes but doubted that she would sleep. His even breathing beside her was calming though and she eventually drifted into a light slumber which was broken somewhere in the morning hours after they had hit dew point and everything around them was covered in shimmers of moisture. There had been a snap. As if an animal had broken a twig somewhere in the brush. She would have attributed it to Ren taking a piss if he wasn't still beside her. His eyes were closed but she could feel a potential energy under her palm on his side. He was awake. His breathing was controlled. He was breathing through his nose very quietly, listening. She tried to listen with him, her heartbeat starting to pick up with a constant fast thump in her chest. It was so loud to her own ears that she was sure he could hear it. Could perhaps feel it through her palm.

There was a soft shuffling sound from somewhere behind her and she closed her eyes. Maybe if she willed whatever it was to go away hard enough, it would. Maybe it would feel unwelcome and slink away back into whatever dark hole it had crawled from. Ren's muscles tensed under her hand when he opened his eyes and focused intensely into the brush that was behind her. She didn't dare look into his gaze. He wasn't Autumn. He had gone immediately into predator-mode, his lips drawing back over his teeth. Without movement he searched the brush behind her with his stare and for a while she could feel an electricity in the air. As if Ren's challenge had been answered in some way. Soon it was gone and Ren had calmed, allowing the tension to fall out of his body in segments and he melted into an embrace with her.

"Is there..." she whispered but she stopped in the middle. She didn't want to ask the question. She didn't want to know the answer. *Is there someone there?* Stop it. Go away.

"Shh," he shushed her soothingly and petted her hair. She realized that she was trembling and she willed herself to stop but it didn't work. He continued to pet her hair for a long time and she held him close. When he stopped she dared to look upward and found warm blue looking back down at her. He smiled a closed-mouth smile and brushed a thumb against her cheek. She didn't know what to say so she just didn't say anything.

He didn't move until her stomach growled. It was then that he sat up with her and rubbed her belly with a small bit of humor. His voice gravelly. "I'll get us some food. You should wait here."

"Wait?" she squeaked, looking off into the brush around them with a nameless dread spreading in her chest. "But Ren..."

"Hey," he tried to soothe her. "Calm down silly, there's nothing there. It was just a dog. Some mutt that was rooting through the foliage. He looked a little shady but he's gone now." He pet her hair again once or twice. "Just be the boss if he comes back."

"The boss," she parroted, not sure if she was reassured or not. But she was hungry and if she wanted food, she had to let him go. She knew where he was going to go. That gas station that was just a mile or two away. He would be back in an hour or so he said. His smile calmed her heart a little and she huddled beside the concrete wall of the overpass and watched his figure as he wandered down the train tracks toward the town they had left the day earlier. She watched him until he was out of sight around a bend. Then she turned her attention around her. She looked carefully into the trees. She tried to think of ice cream sandwiches.

Two for a dollar.

It hadn't taken a lot to get into the map room. It was Patten's little hole where he kept the map for his work. But Patten had gone home for the night, cuddled warm in his bed trying to ignore the niggling sensation that he was probably supposed to be doing something. Winston and Avery had checked in with the night officers and had asked quite politely if they could take one more look at the map. They had been quite helpful, assisting the pair easily once they'd pulled out their D.C.

155

investigator licenses and explained that they had been working closely with Patten on his case. Avery had cocked a brow when nobody bothered to ask them if they'd be deputized but simply led them to the room. Perhaps Patten had left their names and descriptions with the staff.

The atmosphere between he and Avery was filled with a silent unbroken tension. It had been that way for a while. He'd been discharged just hours earlier and he was back to the map, the table underneath lighting it and red dots littering its surface. All those bodies. All those girls. Lost. Finished. Tomi was probably going to be joining them. He thought about what might await her. A club of murder victims? *The Lovely Bones* in "real" death? He was sucking on the end of a pen and staring at one particular red dot. According to its label it was the dump site for Collie Landall. That one had been found curled up as if she were sleeping as opposed to spread willie-nillie like the rest. Almost like he had posed her. Perhaps she had meant more.

Would Tomi mean anything to him? He wondered about what Ren had said. That he wasn't as "invested in her." Winston suddenly doubted it. But couldn't erase the idea that Ren was going to kill her. Indirectly allow her to die.

Avery wandered into the room and stared at the map as well, sitting in one of the chairs and eating a delicious-looking BLT he ordered from the specialty Deli down the street. They didn't say anything to each other. Winston knew he would have to break it. Apologize. Make amends. But there was too much that had been done. He couldn't admit to Avery that he had found out that Tomi was alive and well and that he'd sacrificed her to the devil in order to capture his newest obsession.

Avery munched and his eyes flitted from dot to dot.

"Look," Winston broke the tension like a pebble in a puddle. The air suddenly seemed too heavy around him when Avery looked up at him. "I wish I could catch him. I do. In fact I probably could. Just...strategically. He knows that. I know that. But he also knows that although he might be my pet project, he's not the center of the universe. There are other things out there."

"Why did you go try to find him?"

"How long did you follow me?"

Avery pursed his lips before answering reluctantly, "I didn't follow you into the woods. I figured you were trying to get yourself together. You've been bitter for quite a while about him."

"I'm over it."

"Are you?"

No. But he's going to help me. He closed his eyes and breathed. "Mostly."

"You saw him again."

Winston chuckled, "I feel like I'm trying to explain away some affair to my poor sobbing wife. So I saw him again, so what?" A bubble of fear and anger rose in his chest. "Do you want to know how it went? Is that it? You want to know exactly what he said to me? What I said to him? Is this an interrogation, Avery?" The fear grew exponentially. He recognized the tactics that Avery was using. The calm demeanor, the quiet stare, his ability to coax anything out of anyone. He swallowed. He was good at lying. It was just the matter of not saying too much. "Avery," he assured, "He'd said before that he'd seen her. That he'd had contact with her. I had to know."

"And?"

"I'm not sure. He knows her name. He spoke of her in the present tense."

Avery's eyes narrowed. "Knows her *name*?"

"He said it. Without a prompt. I was careful, very careful. He knew her name, Avery, he *knows* her. Present tense."

"Is that all you went out there, for? To see if Tomi was still alive or not?" His skeptical gaze threatened to break through Winston's tough outer shell of "genuine" truth.

"What can I say, I'm an obsessive bastard."

"You're also obsessed with Ren."

Winston shrugged. "He's a means to an end at this point."

"Why didn't you try to catch him?"

He was irritated and he was afraid his knitted brows would show it clearly. "And end up dead instead of just in the hospital?"

"How did you get away?" His voice was calm and monotone. It was another one of his tactics.

"Bribe. Carton of Camels."

"Blues?"

"Of course."

Avery nodded his head, seemingly impressed by Winston's ingenuity. Of course it was a total lie that such things would have been his ticket *out*. Avery didn't know Ren like he did. Ren had to be *enticed* before he could be *bought*. If he admitted what he had truly given Ren it was like signing his own pink slip.

Tomi wasn't even his case to begin with. He could still opt out of that deal. Mr. Balekowski had given him an out. That it was too dangerous. She would no longer be his responsibility. Nadine was still futilely trying to find her. She was sending out memos to departments all across the state and even in states neighboring North Carolina. She must be flooding email inboxes, causing headaches, eye-rolling, and soft chuckles from those who found her attempts to capture the rogue daughter of a politician ineffectual and tiresome.

But that would end. They would find Tomi. They would definitely find her. She would have had a small bit of a make-over of course. *Blue was such a good color on lips, wasn't it?* Paler, stone-like, a marble copy of her. Her hair not shiny but lackluster. Almost like a poorly made representation of her. A clone with no animation. A Tomi that had been left too long in a window, a document whose vitality was sapped by the sun. An over-exposed photo.

He bit his bottom lip. "Avery. Do you remember Peyton?"

"The bum?"

"Do you remember what the note was?"

"It was that line from Winnie the Pooh. The one about a hunt."

"What am I looking for?"

Avery blinked a few times. "You're asking me?" He frowned. "You're looking for a sixteen year old girl who has run away from home searching for her brother. She's young, scared, and being manipulated by a guy who would disembowel you as soon as look at you."

"It's not her fault."

"Maybe, maybe not. I'm sure if she didn't want to be with him, she wouldn't be. One way or another. You're looking for a kid."

"I'm looking for a body."

Avery pushed his lips together and his face darkened. "Could be, partner. But I think if you're right about Ren speaking of her in present tense, you might find that the next body you find could just be someone else's."

He closed his eyes and tilted his head upward toward the ceiling. "I'm looking for an explanation. For the reasons he does what he does. And the reasons I react the way that I do. I'm looking for the why. Not the who or the what. Not even the where. Just the why. Why am I even looking?"

"Because that's the right thing to do."

He pushed his forehead into his palms and put his elbows to his thighs, curling over. "My God, why can't I just *find* her?" He wasn't speaking to Avery. He wasn't even lying. Why *couldn't* he just find her? Why should he bother keeping a promise to a killer? There was no reasoning for it. There was making a promise to a mother, a brother, a friend, even a stranger, and then there was the promise made to the devil. He couldn't sell his soul like this. He would have to find her. He would have to find her before someone else did. "It's the right thing to do. I have to find her because it's the right thing to do." He caught Avery's eyes and said. "Because I'm the hero."

And that meant that if someone else already had, he had to find them too. And he had to kill them. Man or beast, he would destroy any who sought to harm her. A surge of ownership came over him and his shoulders tensed. She was *his* ward. *His*. Not Nadine's. Not Avery's. Not Patten's. His. He stood up. "Get up, Avery. Fuck this place, fuck this goddamned place. We're finding her and we're finding her *tonight*." With that he turned stiffly and walked out of the room. It was time to go to the motel to change into more comfortable clothes. He would follow his instincts. Maybe it didn't make sense to Avery or to anyone else for that matter, but his heart knew he could read Ren for what he was. He would find Ren at least. And then he would find Tomi.

And then this nightmare could finally be over.

She'd been dozing in the shade. She didn't know what time it was when she woke up. It couldn't have been too long. He was still gone. There were shadows spreading across the landscape around her. How long had he been gone? Could it only have been an hour? Crickets were chirping somewhere in the brush and she tried to calm her breathing. She curled her legs and stretched her arms outward, trying to crack her back.

The sound of the crickets pleased her and she reveled in them. The whirr of cicadas came to her ears as music and she wished that the tracks were utilized so she could watch the trains go by. She shifted to become more comfortable.

"Mmmmmmmmm," she hummed in a monotone to mimic the cicadas. It was a forced silliness so she quit.

She drew pictures in the dirt. She examined leaves and tried to figure out what species they were. She picked grass and arranged it into a flimsy log cabin. The crickets kept chirping. She hugged her knees to her chest and watched the shadows spread long across the dirt and gravel of the rails. He wasn't back. She should have seen him wandering up the railroad tracks, his gait and shape familiar to her. Possibilities floated through her mind. He'd been caught. By Winston. At the gas station. They had been waiting for him. Then they would come for her. He would tell them where she was. They would torture him in the back of a van and he would tell them where she was. Dread filled her. Her teeth gritted together painfully. Or maybe it wasn't Winston at all. Maybe he had been on his way back. Maybe that dog—whatever it was—had gotten him. Two ice cream sandwiches. Two for a dollar. Lying on the tracks melting pathetically in a patch of weeds. She started to cry as dusk approached.

The stars were just starting to peek out when the crickets abruptly stopped chirping. She raised her head, crusty tear tracks staining her cheeks and the well-rubbed skin under her eyes. Her first thought was that Ren had come back. That he had stunned the crickets from their duties. But she didn't see him. He wouldn't sneak up on her. He would know that it would upset her. She blinked a few times into the gathering dark. A soft rustling sound came to her and she sat fully straight up, her whole body tensing toward the sound. *Please let this be Ren.*

But it wasn't. That she knew. She got up, undecided on what she should do. She put her bag over her shoulder and gripped the strap tight in one hand. The concrete wall was to her back, the rustling from the west-facing opening of the overpass. She fled to the east. She followed the railroad tracks, her feet slapping madly on each rotting tie and then every other as she leaped in her strides. She ran hard and fast and her bag bumped her thigh. She continued to sprint, as hard as she could until she could no longer breathe. Until her chest burned with exertion and she could taste blood in the back of her mouth. She didn't stop moving. She couldn't. The panic was intense. It occurred to her that this was the opposite direction that Ren had gone. She shook her head as she walked briskly and swallowed in an attempt to remove the metallic taste of blood. If he still wanted her, he would find her.

It was dark now. The tracks stretched impossibly long in front of her and were eventually lost in the dark. Her heart beat had slowed down but she was still walking. Slower this time. She wished she had a flashlight. What would she do without Ren? She knew that tears would come but at this moment they didn't. She would have to find civilization. She would have to find a map. She would probably be caught in three days by some run-of-the-mill podunk town police officer who'd gotten her picture via some fax machine in his dinky little department office. She started to breathe deeply through her mouth.

There was no sound when it happened. It was so fast her memory only recorded it as a blur of motion and panic. Spots in the corners of her vision as her throat was constricted by an arm from behind. Colors flashing over the darkness of the world. Lovely pinks. Yellows. Purple. *Swanks*. It had been quick. Easy. Brilliant.

CHAPTER 8

Her toes weren't touching the floor. Her legs from the knees down were dangling. Her head hurt. With eyes not fully open she tried to see without turning her head. Her bag was in the corner. She was sitting on a high barstool with a stumpy little chair back, slumped forward with her hands tied behind her and to the chair. Her head throbbed. She'd had strange visions in her dreams. Whole segments of imaginary cooking in which she had to try to utilize her great aunt's obnoxious little microwave with the bum controls that burned popcorn and left Hot Pockets still frozen in the middle. All attempts to use the thing were futile.

She jumped a little when he came into her field of vision.

"Oh? Awake? Good."

She lifted her head. There was no use pretending to be in some coma. She looked around herself. She was in a small kind of earthen room with a concrete floor. Perhaps a basement. Her newest bestest friend was around five-six and perhaps in his late thirties, maybe older. His hair had a small streak of gray in the front that she thought could have been a genetic form of pigment loss. She would be willing to bet that if he tanned there were other spots of skin that had lost pigment as well. He was sipping from an opaque plastic Tupperware cup and his expression was nothing short of delightful.

"Would you like something to drink, sweetheart?" He smiled. It wasn't creepy. It was charming and inviting and simply normal. As if he were having tea in his backyard and it looked as though she might like some.

"Tea?" she asked with a small bit of sick humor she might have picked up from Ren.

He chuckled. "I was thinking water but if you're going to be so high maintenance maybe I should be making some tea. Hot tea?"

She ran with it. Ren would have been proud. "Yes please."

"Now don't run away while I'm making it," he laughed to himself. There was a stove in the basement. He was going to make the tea right in her line of vision. She tried to make herself laugh at his little joke but couldn't. Her head hurt too much. "You're an interesting girl, Tomi," he was still smiling. "You just seem to have a lot of luck on your side. I hadn't made up my mind about you. Sometimes I see a girl and I just have to have her. Do you know what I'm saying?"

Tomi blinked a few times before she said clearly, "I think so."

He flashed her an appreciative glance before going back to trying to find some tea in the cupboards. "Well I saw you. You were very pretty and I must say it, you were bathing. And I just watched you. Nothing perverse, just watching."

She nodded a little even though he couldn't see her.

"And then I just started seeing you all over the place. I can't say I wasn't following you. I did follow you sometimes. You just spoke to me. Everything about you, the way you move, the way you speak. Oh, just delightful." He clapped his hands together. "And I'd just like to make you happy of course, you're just such a young little thing. Just so cute and lovely. All blonde and pink. I've never...well..." He turned around and there was color in his cheeks. He was embarrassed. "I've never had a *blonde* before."

"You're charming," she interrupted. "You're very genuine. It works well for you." She found herself smiling at him and wishing he would just find the tea already. Her throat was parched.

"That's nice of you to say," He stood up straight with a small bag of tea in one hand. He was looking at her as if she was just terribly interesting. "In any case," he continued, turning around and starting to boil the water in a pot, "luck must have turned in my favor. You were

163

traveling with that awful... *creature*." He visibly shuddered. "There are evil people out in this world and any one of them could have just snatched you up."

"I would say I was snatched up fairly easily," Tomi sighed.

He stared at her and tapped the tips of his fingers together. "Yes. Fairly easily I suppose."

"And you're going to murder me," Tomi sighed again.

"My name's Larkin," he bubbled, ignoring her completely. "And you're Tomi. Cute, blonde, pink, adorable Tomi." He hummed a little and turned around, watching the water. "Oh this is all very nice. Maybe we could have some wine. Maybe...we could...oh...I don't know."

"Take a walk?" she joked.

He rounded on her, frowning lightly. "You don't seem all that upset about this turn of events. You should probably be crying and begging me to let you go."

"You said I was interesting," Tomi chided.

"Well..." Larkin tapped the toe of his shoe behind him and checked on the tea.

"You're most definitely interesting too."

He turned around again and tilted his head to the side. "How is this?"

Tomi shrugged. "You kill people, don't you? That is one of the most interesting things a person can do. Look at all the television shows just based solely around murder or murder mysteries. Why do you think people watch those shows?"

"For the puzzle?"

"No," Tomi smiled, "Because killers are fascinating. Normal people don't understand the type of mentality it takes to kill someone. Therefore they are left with this unsolveable riddle. Why did so-and-so murder so-and-so? Sometimes there is no reason. Sometimes there's nothing to blame it on. Like..." she looked around as she tried to think. "Look at Ted Bundy. Nobody really knows why he killed however many women he did. But they all kinda, sorta, looked like his ex-girlfriend. Coincidence? Maybe. Maybe it was just something that they made up to try to explain away the unexplainable."

"You think...I'm interesting then?"

Tomi snorted, "Of *course* I think you're interesting. I'd watch the Mystery Channel special about you if you were ever on it."

He tapped the tips of his fingers together again. "Really?"

"Yeah."

He looked down at the toes of his shoes and then back up again. "You wanna see something?"

"Sure."

He ran upstairs. She could hear him walking around on the wooden floor and traced his path on the ceiling with her eyes. When he came back down he was carrying a Reebok shoebox. He opened it before her as if he were performing some magic trick. "I keep their underwear."

"As a souvenir?"

He nodded. "Yes. It reminds me of them. You know, they're all special. They're all important to me." He paused and looked into her eyes. "You're important to me too, Tomi."

She swallowed but her eyes flitted back to the boiling water and he suddenly remembered it. With careful hands he poured it into a clean mug and let the tea steep while the water cooled a little. Tomi wiggled in the chair to get more comfortable. If this was the last tea she was ever drinking it had better be enjoyed to the fullest.

He held it to her lips while she sipped it. *Constant Comment* wasn't exactly her favorite but it was still tea. She had to savor the taste and the smell of it. When it was gone her heart started to race. It probably should have been beating harder the whole time but he hadn't had that semi-blank look in his eyes that made her stomach flip when he looked at her.

She bit her bottom lip. "So how do you do it?"

Larkin cracked his knuckles with his thumb on each hand. "I uh...I um...strangle. It uh..." He visibly lost his train of thought.

"Larkin?" she tried to say his name as sweetly as she could. "Does it arouse you?"

He swallowed a few times while looking at her. "Uh...yeah."

"Well I have a little bit of bad news for you, sweetheart." She tried to give him a sympathetic smile.

"What?" he asked, taking a step toward her.

"I'm not wearing any underwear."

He seemed to freeze in time, his mouth a little slack but still semi-smiling. It wasn't charming anymore. He'd crossed over some invisible line into slightly creepy. But considering the circumstances it still seemed a little uncharacteristic. He made a little high pitching whining noise before he turned around away from her with jerky movements. "That..." he started, "shouldn't matter. I...I could just..." He turned toward her again and this time she could see a shine of sweat on his forehead. "I could just...um...use...I...could..." He put his palm against his forehead and his expression turned to one of pain. "I don't...why?"

"Well the last serial killer who had sex with me took them." When she said it she wasn't sure why but she felt a little embarrassed and a little sympathetic. He had waited so long. *There were so many pairs of panties in that box.* For a blonde. Now she would deprive him of his souvenir. She felt *bad* about it. As if she somehow wanted to go back in time and force Ren to give her back her panties that said emphatically on the butt, "Cherry." He'd said that she wasn't a cherry anymore and that she'd graduated to "Peach."

"The last...?" His wide eyes turned toward her. "There was another? I'm not...?" His movements became fast and he very quickly duct taped her bare ankles to the legs of the chair. His eyes filled with recognition and he spat, "That *thing* you were with. I should have...I..." His face was even redder. She didn't know if it was because of his blushing or his anger. "It...it held you. It *had* you." She wondered if he referred to all men as "it." Or if it was just Ren. "It wuh-wouldn't have been j-j-gentle. I've seen what it can do. You're better off here. I cuh-care about you, Tomi."

Tomi stiffened when he poised himself between her knees. He wasn't going to rape her, she realized only a little too late. She didn't have that luxury of time. She pulled in a deep breath to scream as loud and as long as she could but his hands closed around her throat too quickly and choked it off. The pressure on her throat was painful and panic filled her mind. She thrashed, the insides of her knees gripping him hard as she struggled for breath. Spots started to form in her vision and she was aware of a burning in her lungs. It was slower than last time and it was tinged with finality.

And suddenly she was jerked forward as Larkin's hands were forced from her throat. The spots in her vision cleared with her first full breath of air. A whoosh of oxygen that seemed to suddenly make the world turn again.

A soft gurgling sound reached her ears and at first her eyes found her knees, still gripping Larkin's hips, small droplets of red dripping onto her white flesh. Her head tilted back and she let loose her trapped scream. It was flat and dull in the terrible acoustics of the basement, the sound absorbed completely in the earthen walls.

Larkin's mouth was open and his hands were around his own throat, blood flowing from between his fingers. The gurgling sound was from him. He was trying to breathe. He staggered backwards, his wild eyes searching around him but the dark of the basement hid his assailant. He stumbled backwards more and his back hit the wall. He slid down it, hitting his bottom on the concrete floor still gasping like a fish out of water, trying to breathe through his own blood. The front of his shirt was slowly looking like a painted red waterfall.

Tomi's scream was still echoing in her ears while she watched him struggle for breath. "Larkin," she cried out but a warm familiar scent came to her nose and his hand came over her mouth.

His cold deep voice grated into her ear and his warm breath made her shiver, "Don't say his name."

Larkin's wide eyes flitted between the two of them as he struggled, his legs wriggling as if they could help him breathe. He would drown in blood.

Winter didn't untie her hands. Instead he kept one hand on her mouth and cupped her breast with the other, pushing his nose to her neck and taking one long inhale of her scent. He turned her head and took his hand from her mouth in order to kiss her. It was gentle and warm but Tomi resisted.

His cold gaze found her eyes with question in them.

Tomi turned her head away and closed her eyes with a whisper. "You taste like blood."

"I came to rescue you."

She turned back to glare at him. "Don't act like a hero. Don't pretend you're some prince charming. Don't pretend like you're going to ride off into the sunset and live happily ever after." Tears escaped her and blurred her vision. She let them when she turned her gaze toward the still struggling Larkin.

If Ren's Winter could get any colder, it did. With nimble fingers he ripped the duct tape off her ankles, paying no mind to how much it hurt her. With that task finished she thought he was going to untie her hands but he didn't. He came between her knees and his hands found her hips. He gripped them hard and pulled her a little forward, grinding her against him. She could feel his hardness through her shorts and his jeans. He leaned forward and kissed where her shoulder met her neck then the soft sensitive spot under her ear, his hands still guiding her hips. She turned her head away from him again.

She could hear him let go a long sigh from his nose. A sign that he was frustrated. His gritty voice cut through the darkness with thinly veiled anger. "What the *fuck* is the difference between then and now?"

She let out a harsh little sob. "Will you please just kill him already?"

Ren looked over his shoulder at Larkin who was starting to settle down, blood trickling out of his lips with every wet cough he mustered. Her frosty killer left her and rooted around through Larkin's things before he came back with a small knife. He kicked Larkin onto his back and stepped hard on his chest, blood bubbling out of his mouth with the pressure. "Move your hands, fuckhead," Ren told the once-charming lady killer.

Larkin's brows pulled together and he looked like he was going to cry but he moved his hands away from his throat and gave a small cough. Ren leaned over him and with a quick movement and small mouse's squeak from the dying Larkin stood up again and met her eyes. "He'll bleed out."

The pool of blood around him grew exponentially and Larkin appeared as if he were falling asleep. Soon the slight gurgling sounds faded away and he was still.

Tomi started to cry. She lowered her head so he couldn't see her but it was obvious by her shaking shoulders.

"He was going to kill you," Ren stated simply as he moved around her to untie her hands. He picked her up out of the chair and carried her up the stairs. "Do you understand that?"

She nodded but couldn't stop her crying.

"Swanks" didn't quite mean anything to Winston but Avery spent a little while looking at it, his dark eyes studying in the contours of the letters. He then came over to Winston who was studying the area in which there were impressions in the grass. Someone had slept here. Two people even. Ren and Tomi? Together? Had he forced her? Had she been compliant? It was difficult to tell. There were deep slashing lines in the dirt from a panicked movement, when the sides of one's sneakers dig into the dirt in their haste to get up. Streaky footprints that indicated running.

"Hurry, Avery," he whispered, his eyes scanning the ground.

"They went in opposite directions. She went this way," he pointed off down the tracks to the east. "She was afraid of something."

"Then let's go."

"What about..."

"Forget him," he said. Ren had left her here. As bait. He'd known that the other killer was coming. He'd known very well that if he left her here she would be easy prey. How did he get her to stay? Promises? Drugs?

There was a rustle in the forest and Winston whirled about. A soft voice announced, "Out in the middle of the night, boys? Very dedicated to your work. I was called when you checked in with the receptionist." Patten's brow was lifted and a smug little smirk was firmly placed on his lips. "You know you two don't exactly make yourselves hard to find."

Winston snarled, "What are you even doing here? Don't you have somebody to interrogate?"

Patten chuckled, "I could only get them to stall your release from the hospital for so long. I knew you'd be itching to get back to this case.

You're probably my best lead at this point. Find anything useful?"

"None of your business," he mumbled, turning away again and staring up at the colorful grafitti on the wall.

"Well then you have the right to remain silent."

Without looking up he pointed down the tracks. "Ren went that way."

There was a pause in which he knew Patten was looking to Avery for confirmation. When Avery gave it with a silent nod, Patten snorted. "Smart move, bucko."

"Can you not have cops tramping all over the place around here, Patten?" Winston could feel the burning rage in his chest. If Patten ruined this. God. He would never live with it. "We were kind of trying to be sly. If you know what that even means."

"I don't have any back-up in the woods. Relax. I've only got two other cops on the night shift and they're still in the car on the road waiting for my orders. You coming with me or are you not finished analyzing the artwork?" He turned away in the direction that Winston had pointed and began to walk, his shoes crunching noisily on the rocks of the tracks.

"We're splitting up," Winston told him and Patten paused, looking over his shoulder.

"Now if this doesn't seem suspicious..."

Avery was the one who responded, "We're not pursuing Ren at the moment, sir. We're pursuing Tomi. And Tomi did *not* go that way. They split up here."

Patten gave the two of them a long hard stare. It was obvious that he thought he was being misled. But Winston needed Avery and him to be together. One of them had to be the broom and the other the dustpan. So to speak. Their strategies for capture never utilized just one person.

Winston took a step toward his adversary. "Oliver, listen to me."

Patten turned to face the two private investigators and he crossed his arms, his back straight.

"You think I'm lying to you. And if we are wouldn't you say that's a pretty damn bad one? Wouldn't you say that the truth sounds a little bit more awkward than a lie? Wouldn't you say to yourself that Avery and I could probably come up with a real doozy?"

Patten blinked.

"If you go off by yourself in those woods looking for that murderer, you're gonna end up like Maldeen. And don't even pretend you don't know who he was. I know you. You've read the file front, back, and upside-down. If you trampse off into those woods you won't come back alive. That's not a threat. Consider it your mental caution tape. Pride kills, Patten."

His brows tightened together. "And what would you suggest I do, Winston?"

"Bank on Tomi. You need an army to catch that killer. That or a whole bunch of dumb luck." There was silence in which Winston was hoping Patten was considering the options. Considering wandering his way with the P.I.s rather than risking his life in the dark woods alone with nothing but a heavy standard-issue flashlight and a nine millimeter he'd never use for company. He was also hoping that Patten was actually thinking. That maybe if he went and found Tomi there would be information that led to Ren. There would be knowledge that she might have that he could get at. It was a common thing for cops to think about. The interview. The girlfriend. The last true connection. It was his in.

Patten clicked his teeth and then spat in the dirt, uncrossing his arms and putting up his palms in a gesture of surrender. "Alright. I'm with you. But when we get her, I'm the first who talks to her." He jerked a thumb at his chest to emphasize his point.

He bit his fingernail while the three of them walked down the eastbound rails, the light of his flashlight and that of Patten's bobbing through the dark. It was down quite a long way before Avery gave a small shout and Winston turned to find his partner off the tracks and examining a gap in the brush.

"This path isn't natural, Winston. I think we've found our ticket in." His grim expression made Winston's guts shrivel. Patten looked at stoic as ever, peering into the brush like a wary dog.

"Let's go, buddy."

"It could have been you on that floor down there." His voice was so chilly she shivered. He set her down in Larkin's living room on a large deer pelt sitting in front of the brick fireplace that was soft and warm. He walked out to find some firewood and when he came back he began to build one. He seemed so calm. Collected. He almost seemed too normal.

"Ren," she said before gulping back. The memory of Larkin's blood bubbling up from his mouth when he'd stepped on his chest came back to her and she couldn't seem to open her mouth anymore.

He turned toward her and looked down at where she sat. His dark blue eyes were cold but he knelt down in front of her anyway and put his warm hands on either side of her jaw, cupping her face and bringing her a little forward so he could press his lips to her cheek and then her ear and then her forehead. He held her there, with his lips to her hairline for at least a whole minute, the two of them simply breathing together. Her hands came out to grasp either side of his tank.

His voice was dark. "I wish I could make you forget." Spring had finally come. She wondered what time it was.

She leaned forward and kissed his throat.

"You have to understand something before you decide to stay or go."

"I won't leave you," she whispered. Her heartbeat grew a little faster and a flash of panic went in and then out of her chest.

"Don't say that until you understand me completely." He sounded so serious she could hardly handle it. He pulled away from her and stared into her eyes. There was nothing inside him. "I'm not sorry for what I did. I'm not sorry for what I felt. I'm not sorry to know I'll do it again."

Tomi felt a few hot tears rush down her cheeks and meet his hands. His thumbs wiped them away.

"I am only sorry for what I've done to you. What I've made you see. The position I've put you in."

Tomi gripped the sides of his tank top harder and sniffled.

Ren paused. He blinked once, looked down at the floor, then back up at her. He wasn't cold anymore. His forehead touched hers as he leaned forward and he closed his eyes before whispering, "I'm sorry you love me."

She was suddenly kissing him. Hard deep kisses that made her whole body shake and heat to seep into her soul. His response was immediate. He wrapped his arms around her and pulled her against him. He felt like living fire—too hot. She gave a small mewl when she felt his teeth on her lip. He gripped her hips and pushed her away from him.

"Tomi."

She looked up. He was staring at her. "Whuh—what?"

He reached into their bag and pulled out a rather sizable bottle that thunked heavily on the wooden floor as he set it down. The flickering warm light of the fire allowed her to read it clearly. He had a strange expression that lingered on his face, halfway between laughter and sincerity.

"Jack Daniels?" she asked, puzzled.

The woods were anything but quiet. The rustling of the trees was so loud to Winston's ears that it almost could have been considered deafening. Through the woods he could see a faint flicker of light. He knew that Avery had also seen it. His heart began to pound in his chest. Thumping against his breastplate with impatience and anxiety. He was a racehorse at the starting line. He was the bullet in the gun.

Patten's whisper eased him. "What's the plan, big guy?"

"You're trusting me?" He raised a brow at his police companion.

"There are two of you and one of me."

Winston nodded. "You two go to the front door. Introduce yourselves as the police. I want Avery to do it just in case Ren's somehow in there so he doesn't think he can get the jump on you Patten. He knows Avery's voice."

"Somewhat logical," he sighed. "But mark my words, Winston, we need to be careful. We can't rush this. We don't know who's in there. We don't know if it's just Tomi, just Ren, the killer, or some kind of weird combination. We need to be careful."

The two P.I.s nodded their agreement. It was time to be sneaky. It was time to be wise about it. It was time to take their time and not get stupid.

"Hold your breath."
She was. She was holding it hard.
"Now swallow."
She swallowed air. It may have been difficult and she wasn't sure she'd done it right until she burped. The orange flicker from the fire illuminated his handsome face before her and for a second she was frightened. "Will you be drunk too?"
"Maybe."
Relief washed her mind clean. "Okay." She pulled in a deep breath and held it while he put the edge of the tiny shot glass to her lips. When she swallowed it the air whooshed out of her lungs and she took in another huge breath in an attempt to kill the burn in her throat and chest.
"Loosen up," Ren told her while he poured another shot. He held this one up too and she took another deep breath. "Loosen up, loosen up," he repeated.
The second shot put tears in her eyes and she shook her head to indicate she wanted no more than these two. Her throat felt as though she'd had a voice-stealing cold, raw and burning. She didn't cough. It was suddenly too hot in the cabin. The fire he'd made for them both was flickering off the glass of the whiskey bottle and making her feel as though she were burning up. With some urgency she pulled off her blood-splattered tank top and threw it to the floor.
With nothing but her bra and shorts on, she sat with her back against the wall, waiting for the alcohol to hit her. Ren was smoking a few feet away, watching her, the bloody streaks on his shirt from his hands a vague dark color in the poor light. The tip of his cigarette burned bright every time he took a drag and the smoke seemed a little surreal after he'd held it in a while, letting it coil out of his mouth like some ethereal dragon. The bottle clinked and she was vaguely aware that he was drinking from it.

It was getting to her. She didn't feel sillier but everything that nearly came out of her mouth would have sounded stupid. Finally there were no inhibitions. Finally she could say what she felt. Tomi was now a different person. "Ren."

"Yes?"

"Why did you do that?"

He was quiet for a little until he told her in a soft tone, "He was hurting you."

Tomi frowned and put her feet out in front of her. Any jerk of her head one way or another would make the image in her eyes blur and follow too slowly so she just continued to look at him. "Are you going to kill everyone who hurts me?"

"Yes I am."

She felt both flattered and repulsed. She wrinkled her nose so hard her eyes closed. "I love you, Ren."

"I know, sweetheart."

"Make me laugh like you do." She gave him a little grin and he returned it. She was more than a little frightened of him. His face looked a little bit meaner, a little bit more wild, a little bit more like a killer. She shook her head and laughed at herself. It was absurd, wasn't it? He'd always looked like that. She couldn't help but stay laughing. At least if she was laughing she wouldn't have the time to cry.

She felt him sidle up closer to her and watched him take another swig from the bottle. How many had he had? She shut her eyes and continued to giggle. He put a soft warm hand around her back and pulled her until she straddled him while he sat against the wall. His lips found her collarbone and he kissed her gently there.

"Ren," she whispered into his hair.

"Yes?" He was kissing her chest and the tops of her small breasts. His hands cupped her bottom and pushed her against him.

She put her face in his and kissed him very lightly before she breathed her next words close to his lips. "Please don't leave me again."

He didn't answer her. Instead he brought one hand to the front of her shorts and undid them, slipping his palm over her belly before reaching downward to claim his prize. She held her breath when he touched her, her body hitching up in response to the deliciously sweet feelings that shocked her senses. She clung to him closer and put her forehead to his neck while her hips started a slow rocking motion, begging him to delve deeper into her core.

When his fingers slid into her she gave a tiny squeak and gripped his hips between her knees.

"Did I hurt you?" she heard him ask.

"No," she sighed. "I really like it." As if to punctuate that sentence she tried to relax her body again, pushing against his hand with a sort of hesitant urgency.

He continued what he was doing, playing with her hair with his other hand. When she was trembling against him he kissed her ear and whispered sweet things. He'd never done anything like that before. He whispered about how he loved her hair and her eyes and the soft smell of her skin. When he kissed the flesh of her throat she shivered despite the heat of his body against hers.

He whispered easily, "Do you want me?"

She knew what he was really asking and she wondered why he even needed the inquiry. Wasn't it obvious from how wet she had become? "Of course I do," she breathed.

It wasn't long before he had her on her back on the rug in front of the fireplace. He was slow and methodical. He whispered sweet nothings to her and paid every attention to the details of her body, kissing every piece of her, sweetly lapping at her with a well-trained tongue in her most delicate of places. She was writhing on the floor in her want of him before he loomed over her, his strong, tan, animal-like body forming easily over her small pale one. She gave sighs and moans when he took her and he linked his fingers with hers when he kissed her. Every part of her seemed to need to burst with something. A giddiness that was tamed and yet enhanced by every one of his thrusts. Her peak was marked by a breathy little moan and a tightening of all her body's muscles. Spasms jerking her hips and stomach. It was something she'd never quite felt before.

When he came he growled hard and panted, his lips curling back for just a moment and his eyes tightly closed. He pushed his body to hers and rolled them both sideways, gathering her up into his arms and pulling her thigh over his hip. He kissed her voraciously and when he was finished he had to calm his breathing, his chest and belly working against hers to steady himself.

"Tomi," he rasped.

"Yes?" Her voice was meek and she expected the worst. That he would be leaving her.

"You're...you're the most beautiful thing I've ever had in my life."

She watched his closed eyes as he thought hard about what he was trying to say. She attributed his lack of eloquence to the mind-numbing sex they had just had and also to the fact that he was a *man* and men in general weren't exactly the best at forming eloquent sentences. He was a serial killer, not Lord Byron.

"I wish I was more. I wish I was what you deserve. I can't change who I am. What I am. I'm despicable. I've done awful things. In my past. In the past...twenty-four hours. I'm not what you need nor what you deserve."

"Don't make me cry," she warned.

He pressed his lips to her hair. "You've done too much crying, sweets. But I can't make you happy. I only ever make you sad."

"Not true."

He tightened his hold on her. "You have people who love you out there, Little Miss."

She wanted to say that she had one particular person right here who loved her. But she knew that would be a lie. She wondered about his reaction if she had said it. Would he deny it? Would he say that he loved her to placate her? She wasn't the type to make social experiments so she stayed silent.

"What I'm trying to say is..." he frowned and his head perked up. "Is...." Again his head twitched and she could tell he was listening intently to something that was a mystery to her. "Get up," he whispered, pulling her up. "Get your clothes on."

She did as he asked her quickly, stringing her bag over her shoulder as he pulled on his hoodie. He took her arm and very gently pulled her to his chest, away from the dark window. "Whatever happens, Tomi," he whispered, "don't panic."

"Why should I be panicking?" she whispered back, her heart rate already increasing.

"I smell a bear."

"A *bear*?" Her eyes were wide.

He chuckled a little. "A *cop* sweets."

"Winston?"

At the sound of Winston's name from her lips, Ren's expression grew darker, sinister. He was angered by this thought, more than if it were just any detective it seemed.

All her thoughts were erased when there was a bang on the front door. "Open up, police," was the standard cry.

Ren took her hand and ran with her into the only other room in the cabin. It had but one window. "Shit, shit, shit, shit," he breathed. He pulled her toward the basement stairs and although she resisted, he won, pulling her down the stone steps into the cold dark basement air that was now stifling with the smell of fresh blood. There was more banging on the front door and Ren looked around at the windows at the top of the basement. There were two on each side. The question would be which to use. He flew back to the top of the stairs and locked the door with the thick brass sliding bolt.

She tried to not look at the corpse on the floor but it was difficult. She found herself glancing at Larkin's cold body, what she could see of him through the dark anyway.

Ren guided her to one of the basement windows. One of the ones on the side of the building. He must have figured that there would be another cop at the back.

"Wouldn't we be surrounded?" she asked in a low murmur.

"That's Avery's voice," Ren calmly explained. "That means we have a fifty-fifty of whether or not he's with Winston or he's with the SWAT team. One or the other, we're probably going to get shot at."

She gasped.

"*I'm* going to get shot at. You're just going to have to avoid the crossfire."

"I don't want you to get hurt," she choked.

"Don't cry, for God's sake don't cry, I need your wits about you, Tomi." He turned to her and brushed her hair back from her face and kissed her lips. "You need to get away. If I don't...then I don't."

"Don't say that."

"Shut up, Tomi, just shut up."

She felt a lump in her throat and knew that it was stupid.

"I'm going out first. If it's Winston the fucker's gonna have tunnel vision and shoot before he knows who he's shooting at. If the coast is clear then I'll pull you out. You gotta be ready, sweets."

"I'll be ready."

"If he pops me I need you to promise me that you'll do everything in your power to get away."

"I promise." She nodded. She could still feel his sticky essence on her inner thighs, leaking out of her. She hadn't had time to clean herself.

He stood on a full dirty cardboard box and yanked the window open, paint chips littering the floor and scattering over the tops of his Toms. He pushed half his body out and froze. Tomi's heart dropped into her bowels and she took a step backwards, her fists to her lips. Ren's right hand very slowly moved to his hip, his finger jutting out toward the back windows. He jerked it twice to motion for her to leave that way. She shook her head but realized that Ren couldn't see her and took a few more shuffling steps backward. "No," she whispered. He jerked his hand again, this time more urgently. She turned around, jumping atop another cardboard box under one of the back windows, jerking the clasp with all the strength in her body.

"Move, Ren. Just fucking move. I dare you," whispered the detective. He knew that the grin on his face was twisted and maybe a little perverse.

Ren whispered too, "I did what you asked. You can see for yourself." His form through the dark was like a snake, half in and half out of his hide-out. "I shouldn't have trusted you, you scummy fuck."

Winston's stomach was squirming with fear. He knew it could be heard in his voice. The panic rose in his throat, "Where's Tomi? Where's the girl? You fucking let her die."

Avery was putting his shoulder and foot to the front door. It would be open soon. No doubt Ren had locked another. They had time.

He couldn't see Ren's face through the dark. He pushed the muzzle of his gun against the killer's head and Ren responded, "You thought I'd just give her away? Would you have given her to him? Winston? Would you have let him slide her panties down creamy white thighs and press his thumbs into her--"

"Where is she?"

"Getting away. In fact she's probably about a quarter mile from here at this point. She's an interesting girl, *detective*. If you're looking to get her you should probably start running."

"Fuck you."

"Fuck me? Fuck you, Winnie the Pooh."

He bit the inside of his cheek for just a moment.

"I did what you wanted," Ren's whisper was a little softer. "I did it how I needed to do it. He's dead. He's gone. Tomi's gone too. Safe from him. Safe from you." He paused for a moment before he continued, "Safe from me."

"When I find her, if she's had anything to do with you, I'll have her for aiding and abetting."

Ren's voice was a low desperate growl, "The *fuck you will*."

Winston grinned. "So there *was* something between you two? Does she know what you are, *pooch?*"

"She doesn't know anything. Leave her *alone*. She doesn't need to go home. Just let her *go*."

"Would you take a trade?"

"What?" Ren tilted his head, his eyes flashing in the dim light of the moon overhead.

"You or her. Can't have both. If I let you go, I take her. If I take you, I let her go."

Ren's lower lip twitched and his shoulders were trembling with barely-contained rage. He spoke louder now. Avery was inside the house, banging the basement door. "I did what you wanted. I get a ten day head start. I wanted to believe you. I'm so fucking stupid. *Fuck you.*"

He wasn't being fair. It was true. He wasn't being just. The other detectives would have told him that a promise to a killer was no promise at all. But it itched at the back of his mind. He had promised Ren a ten day head start. That had been before he had thought Tomi a victim of this game. He saw in Ren's eyes and heard in Ren's voice something he'd never recognized in a killer before. Something that sounded a little bit like attachment. Something that sounded like loyalty. Something that sounded like a promise made.

He sighed and held the gun with one hand while he put the other palm to his cheek. "Ren."

"What?" He sounded miserable.

"You or her."

"God...why are you doing this to me?" He sounded on the verge of tears.

"Because I need her. I need something to show for this wild goose chase. And that means you or her. I've got a cop on my ass and I need to give him something for his trouble. You wanna share a cell with me?"

Ren paused only a second before he stated clearly, "Her."

"When and where?"

"There's a little cafe in the next town to the west. She'll be there in three days. You can stake out the place if you want. But you're not going to catch her tonight."

"I'm going to follow you, Ren."

"You do that all you want. But if you know what's good for all of us, you won't approach. And I want my ten days goddamnit."

"Once I have her," Winston nodded, "you can have your ten days. Fifteen even."

Avery almost had the basement door cracked open. Ren was fidgeting. "Fine. She'll be there. Three days. Let me out, Winston."

He very slowly holstered his gun and offered Ren a hand, pulling him through the window. The young killer found Winston's eyes and leaned forward a little, taking Winston's hand and putting it palm up. Pressing something into his hand before nodding slightly and pushing

181

past him, disappearing into the dark forest.

His fingers curled around the paper pack of Marlboros. He smiled a little and knelt down by the window, picking out one of the cigarettes and popping it into his mouth. The basement door slammed open and cracked against the earthen wall before Avery hit it on the recoil and rushed down the steps.

"Hey buddy," Winston lit his cigarette and squinted into Avery's flashlight. "Looks like we missed something."

Patten's eyes shined in the dark behind his partner, examining the remains with a keen eye. His expression made Winston's gut squirm.

Her eyes strained through the dark as she ran. Her feet crashed through the forest, snapping over roots and dead leaves. Branches whipped at her face but she continued to run. She would do this for him. She would run as far and and fast as she could. Her bag snagged on a branch but she yanked it free, tripping a little before regaining her pace. The forest was thick. She didn't know what direction she was headed. She tried to not think about him but it was hard. When she was too tired to run anymore and a stitch burned her side, she fell to her knees, her hands clumping the duff in tight fists. She was sobbing but they were dry sobs that convulsed her body and forced her to wheeze hard at every breath in.

She didn't care if Winston was behind her. Or Avery. Or anybody. She didn't care if she never saw her brother again. She fell on the side without the stitch and curled into a ball, shaking and wheezing. She knew she was being foolish. She had made him a promise. That she would get away. That she would do everything to get away. But without him there seemed to be no reason for her to do so.

The leaves itched and debris scratched at her flesh but she couldn't get up. She didn't have the strength. It had been sapped by this darkness around her. When the convulsing sobs subsided she panted and rubbed at the stitch that had formed just under her ribcage on her left side.

Very slowly and with the grace of the elderly, Tomi rose. She trembled mightily but managed to come to her feet, the strap of her bag in one hand. She dragged it behind her as she walked, still panting, still suffering from that horrible pain in her side. Her hair fell into her eyes and swung as she walked, her ponytail loose and floppy against her back.

She threw up against a tree and put her forehead against the bark. Her cheeks tickled and she wiped them, finding blood seeping from several wounds that had been slashed into her face from pine boughs. She didn't know how long she walked but by the time she collapsed, the sun was peeking over the horizon. A soft patch of tall grass caught her. The blackness that surrounded her was total.

Patten was crouching on the floor beside the victim. Larkin Hensley, according to his driver's license, was 5'6", had hazel eyes, and was thirty-eight years old. Winston watched the detective examine the body without touching it, waiting for the crime scene squad to show up to take all their samples and keep things from getting too far out of hand in terms of crime scene contamination. But there was nothing here that Winston couldn't already process. There was nothing here that wouldn't tell him exactly what had happened.

There was a blonde hair on the back of the tall chair with the short back. It was laying on top of it. Just a single little breeze could whisk it away onto the floor. He took a subtle step forward. He would get there eventually. He had time.

"Ripped out," Patten mused. "And you said we were following Tomi?"

Winston shrugged. "I've got a theory."

"Pray tell." His voice was filled with a barely contained fury that was seeping out. Like smoke under a doorway. Winston could only hope he could avoid the backdraft.

"Well she obviously got taken up by our killer." He made a vague gesture toward Larkin, careful to not point as it might suggest he knew previously who Larkin was. "And that is saying if this Hensley character was in on it, then Ren might have had it in his mind that nobody touches his girl but him and gotten...well, jealous. I mean it's not everyday that a killer takes another killer's uh..." He frowned but said it anyway,

"Property?"

"Well there's plenty of evidence here to suggest that Larkin was our killer," Patten sighed, staring at the shoebox that had been left open on one of the cluttered countertops. "Those will have to be identified by parents or whomever." He scratched the side of his head. "Ironic that a killer should be murdered. Kinda fitting."

"And yet a little strange," piped up Avery who was leaning against the wall by the door and staring at Winston, "that there's a very different mark on his throat than just the single bite."

Patten frowned and examined the wound again. Winston could feel his heart beating harder in his chest. "You're right," he noted, "There's a cut. Through his carotid." The detective unconsciously put a hand to his throat and touched it gently with his fingers. It was a normal response. Winston had seen plenty of other cops do it and he was sure he'd done it himself when he first came across the victims of Ren Rockey. Nobody could really help it. It tugged at the idea that it was just too easy to kill someone. Even without a gun. "Why would he do that?"

"He isn't known for mercy," Avery pointed out. He was still looking at Winston so the investigator shot him a glance. A warning glace. He wasn't quite sure what Avery was getting at. That someone *else* had perhaps put the finishing touch on this kill? Tomi? He tried to imagine a right handed person cutting the carotid. It would have been easier to jerk a blade to the right with the thumb on it. That would cut the jugular. To go the other direction would be awkward.

But Ren. Ren was a southpaw. It would have been easy for him. His thumb on the back of the blade, just a quick slice to the left. He would have bled out. Quick. But not too quick. "It doesn't make sense any other way," Winston murmured. Patten was looking at him again. "Ren would have done it." He held out his left hand and made it into a loose fist with the thumb out. He jerked it to the left and gave Patten a questioning look. "Tomi's right handed." He put out his right hand in the same position. Patten looked down at his own right hand and he tried a few positions.

"You're right. It would have been awkward. She would have gone the other direction. Assuming he was down on the ground when it happened. Not to mention she was sitting in the chair."

"What?" Winston was almost breathless.

"There's a void in the pattern of blood. Larkin was standing in front of the chair when Ren bit his throat. There's blood around the chair and in a small segment on the front but nowhere else on the seat. Someone was sitting in that chair. And I'd give you anything it was her."

Fuck police detectives. He tapped his pocket, the Marlboro packet inside. There wasn't a chance in hell he'd be able to pull any amount of wool over Patten's eyes. He was too smart. He was too invested. Winston would lose this game. He watched as the too-smart detective continued to peruse the scene while sirens wailed in the distance. It wouldn't take them long now.

"Detective?" came an unfamiliar voice from upstairs.

Patten stood suddenly. "Kyler, don't touch anything. We need everything the way it was. Set up a perimeter around the structure and make sure the team knows they're dusting everything." He turned toward Winston, "They'll have to take a print of your shoes to exclude you two and if anybody asks, you're with me."

Winston grinned. "That's what I like to hear."

They got out of the way while the crime squad did their thing and watched them with eagle eyes. There wasn't much they could glean from the scene except what he and Patten had already gone over. There was no way of telling how fresh or old the scurry marks were when they had left, where Ren had gone in or gone out, there were plenty of theories tossed about as to the timing of it all and Winston was sure to supply at least one. But of course nobody could come close to guessing the truth. But Winston was sure that Avery was aware. Avery was thinking of a theory that just might have been true. But the P.I. couldn't say it. Winston grinned to himself while the medical examiner told Patten what she thought of the whole scene with the inevitable statement of, "We'll have to see after the autopsy."

When he and Avery managed to get away from the scene for a little while he was surprised that he hadn't actually noticed that Avery had been slowly herding him away from the bustle and activity to a secluded spot. It hadn't been hard. He'd needed a good smoke. Avery could have his moment.

"We could get both of them," Avery started. "But you're not going to let that happen are you? You know this all could end."

"I know." He lipped his cigarette.

"Have you ever been told that you're both very strange and a significant source of confusion?"

He chuckled, "I've been told more times that I'm the source of frustration."

Avery shrugged. "I don't get frustrated."

"We're the perfect match."

CHAPTER 9

Tomi awoke in the dapples of a tall tree. A warm wet cloth was sweeping across her forehead and cheek. She didn't open her eyes. She could smell tobacco. Her fingers found his shirt and gripped it in her fist. The familiar texture made her heart jump. He wasn't dead. He was with her. His brain wasn't spattered all over the ground outside that window. Winston hadn't won. Winston was probably dead.

She opened her eyes.

He held his hands over her shoulders and shushed her, preventing her from getting up. His blue eyes were warm and soft. So much unlike him.

"What--"

He whispered, brushing the cloth over her forehead. "You should be more careful, sweets."

"How did you get..."

He smiled at her and tilted his head. "They should have called me The Roanoke Rat. I'm a slippery little devil."

Something about the way he said it strummed a discordant note through her head and her stomach. She watched him from her position. The angle giving her a little better of a look at the way his mouth twitched a little with his smile. It wasn't real. Just a fake smile. Something was wrong.

"Am I awake?" she asked.

He was staring down at her and his smile faltered. "As far as I know, sweets. You're very much awake to me."

"I need to sit up," she stated clearly, forcing her way to a sitting position. "I also need a bath." His hand came around her, his palm resting a little below her navel. He pulled her backward into an embrace and held her there. "Ren, seriously. Where's the nearest stream?" She looked around for her bag and when she saw it she went to retrieve it. But he held her fast. She looked around her shoulder at him. "What are you doing?"

"I'm sorry," he whispered into the back of her neck, his hand pressing on her belly a little harder. Then he took it away and sat like a lifeless doll, his back slumped and his hands palms up at his sides.

She stood up and picked up her bag, looking around. "Come on, Ren. We have to find somewhere I can wash myself. I'm gross and sticky. Not to mention I really need to pee now." He didn't move. "Ren. What is wrong with you?"

"I'm sick."

A panicked flutter was starting in her chest while she watched him sitting there quiet. She approached him, looking down at him this time with her bag still clutched in her hand. He was with her. They had won something. Time perhaps. And yet Ren still seemed so...*off.*

One hand came up and gripped his hair and it jutted out between his fingers as he pulled. "I'm sick."

She knelt in front of him and tried a little humor. "And twisted and horribly sexy at the same time. It's horrifying. I should be committed for even liking you." She put her palms on his cheeks and forced him to look at her. His eyes were warm and sad. She pressed her lips to his and when she pulled away she asked in a murmur, "Is this Summer?" Her throat suddenly closed and she wondered if he was in fact in that rare season of summer. A season in which he might have a breakdown of awareness. Awareness of what he'd done, what he was, what had gone awry in his mind. She put her hand over his clenched fingers. "Ren," she said, "We're all a little sick."

He grabbed her hips and held her where she knelt. "You don't understand. You couldn't. You're so...different from me. You're not like

188

me at all. You never will be. I want you to stay that way. I want you to stay just the way you are. Cute and naïve. Adorable. Stubborn. Privileged. Please, Little Miss, you have to stay the way you are."

She stared at him while he held her hips for a long time until he looked up into her eyes, an unnamed burning inside him that she could see but not grasp.

"C'mon," she told him, pulling him up by his wrists and leading him off. It wasn't long before they found a stream and she bathed herself, watching him watch her. His eyes filling with something more than their deep sadness. A different kind of burning. A named one. He made love to her again at the edge of the stream and watched her with half-lidded eyes when she washed herself again. This time with a deeper pink in her cheeks that wouldn't scrub out.

When she was warm and cuddled into his arms under a large oak tree in the middle of a field, surrounded by swaying corn, she pressed her cheek against his chest and closed her eyes. "You knew," she stated in a soft voice, close to sleep. The sun was setting in the west.

"Hmm?"

She sighed against him, content. "You knew Larkin was following us."

"Don't say his name."

She smiled. Jealous bastard. "You knew he was there, didn't you?"

"Yes."

She whispered next, "Thanks for saving me. I wasn't very grateful at the time. I'm sorry."

He kissed the top of her head and played with her hair. "You were angry at me. You had every right to be. But it doesn't matter. He's gone."

The memory of his body sprawled on the floor came back to her mind's eye. A pool of blood surrounded him, quick to become sticky and congealed. A mess that would have to be cleaned up. She didn't know what Avery looked like but the man must have come upon a royal scene down in that godforsaken basement. She shivered a little but Ren held her tighter and she cuddled him a little harsher. "He's gone," she agreed. When she said it the briefest of images popped into her mind and no longer was she talking about Larkin.

Winston was gone too.

Winston was in fact sitting cross-legged on a hotel bed, papers strewn about in front of him. Lab reports, crime-scene crew reports, interviews, and other such items that Patten had been gracious enough to share. He tapped madly away on his laptop, attempting to formulate some kind of coherent report of his own for not only the agency but also for his clients. They had hired him to investigate the murder of their daughter and there he was with the alleged murderer dead. Was that enough for some kind of closure? Larkin was most definitely the killer. There was too much evidence to deny it. He got what was coming to him. There was no chance of some fluke in the justice system ever letting him escape. He was gone.

He'd heard of some families who would want to look into the killer's eyes, see what kind of man had killed their precious loved one. He hoped that the girls' families would accept Larkin's dark fate with open arms. His throat was gone. If they wanted to look at his cold body in the morgue—the wound that had taken him from this world—then that was their decision. But that particular killer wouldn't be looking into anyone's eyes anymore.

He bit his bottom lip and continued to type, shifting papers over the harsh bedspread to get more information from the autopsy report. Ren had killed a killer. But Winston had paid him to do it. Such things were not justice. He frowned while he typed. He wasn't a cop. He hadn't ever sworn to protect and serve. If anything a private eye's job was the opposite. Most of the time all they ever did was wreck relationships and arouse suspicions. Wasn't that why he and Avery had started going after the killers instead of the cheating husbands? Because they couldn't stand wasting their time? And yet here he was having hired a killer to kill a killer. Where was he in this game? Was he the player or the played? He stopped typing and put his forehead in his hand. He couldn't stop it now. He'd already rolled the ball down the lane. All that was left was for him to wait to see how many pins would end up on the floor in the end.

Avery watched him from the bathroom doorway, clad only in jeans and socks, he leaned against the door-frame with knitted brows as though he were some jilted lover. He crossed his arms and stared at his partner. Winston could feel his gaze creeping over his skin. He'd been watching Winston write this report for a long time—watching all of his telling expressions.

"Say it," Winston told him without looking up.

"If you know what I'm going to say then I don't have to say it."

"Say it."

Avery took in a deep breath and let it out. "Secrets don't make friends."

"That's...not exactly what I was expecting you to say. But fine then. Would you like to know all my deep, dark, fantastically insane secrets?" He finally looked up from his report and put a hand through his hair.

"No. I could go a lifetime without. But my powers of deduction aren't bad."

"So you know enough."

"I know enough to know that you're entirely out of your goddamn fucking mind." He'd said it with a straight face. Completely stoic. As if it were normal.

"Well then," was Winston's calm reply.

Avery continued, "You really did come to an understanding with him. I wasn't kidding when I said that you two were similar. But I wasn't aware that you two were *that* similar." Avery's eyes were burning into him. "You and he have some kind of deal. Now what I don't understand is what *he* got out of it. What did you *give* him?"

Winston sucked in his bottom lip and turned back to his report, the garish light from the Word document hurting his eyes. The black words suddenly blurred then came back into focus.

Avery crossed the room and sat on the other bed, watching Winston with a careful stare. "You're not the type to do something for nothing. Neither is he. Winston...goddamn it, *what did you give him?*" He was trying his hardest. He knew he was trying to squeeze blood from a turnip. Interrogating Winston would be like trying to interrogate Ren. Doable...but difficult. There was a long time where they didn't say anything, his partner's piercing eyes boring into his very soul. Finally Avery gave a frustrated huff, a very soft one. One he would never have given in a real interrogation. "We didn't even find Tomi. We set out to find Tomi and what did we get? Larkin Hensley, thirty-eight, possible murder suspect, dead in his basement with a good-sized chunk of his esophagus *ripped* out. By *teeth*, Winston, *fucking teeth*. Classic Ren." He put up his hands and then clapped them down on his thighs. "I know you had something to do with that, buddy. I know it. One hundred fucking percent."

Winston was still silent, staring at his unfinished report with glazed eyes.

"She's dead, isn't she?"

He was gone with those words. Avery had gotten him. He shook his head.

"Where is she?"

"Stop."

"Where?"

Winston put a hand over his eyes. "He's giving her to us."

"He's doing *more* for you?" Avery was leaning forward, incredulous. "How in the fuck are we managing this? What could you have that he could possibly want?"

He brought his palm down over his mouth and then down to his lap, dominated by his partner. Unable to keep from him these secrets. "A...a head start."

"You're..." Avery paused, his hands making odd gestures, as if he wanted to scratch his face or head but then decided halfway that it was a waste of time. "You're letting him *go*?"

"He did what I asked him to do. He's going to give her to me."

"How do you know?"

"I just do." He covered his eyes but it was easy to feel the weight of Avery's stare on his head and shoulders. "Just...let me type up this report."

"You're asking me to lie for you, you know."

"I'm asking for you to understand me. Please just understand me. You've been with me for years. You've been with me on my birthday,

Christmas, Thanksgiving. My family loves you. You're my brother. Please just understand that I'm killing two birds with one stone here. I can get what I need without getting what I want. He'll be out there for us to get later. He's not half as quick as The Strangler in his killings. He'd been dormant for months...I can get him. Later."

"He's your arch nemesis, he's the one score that you haven't gotten. He's the one that got away. You're going to just let him *go*? You really are out of your goddamn fucking mind."

He uncovered his eyes and found Avery to be smiling.

"I don't know if that smile is a good one or a sign that I'm about to get thrown into ten to twenty for being a total moron."

"If you hadn't done what you did," Avery was still grinning, "a killer who was slaughtering teenaged girls at a rate that could have far passed Ted Bundy might still be out there. Might still be strangling little girls and dumping their bodies in the woods. Heck we might have never caught him. And if we did catch him, he'd be living the high life in some state penitentiary with three square meals and a bed. I'm starting to think he got exactly what he deserved, ironic as it is that he was killed by another serial killer." His grin was ear to ear. "Now if you're right, and he gives you Tomi, we've got the other bird with your one stone. We get the girl, we give her to Nadine, all's right with the world. One less runaway Senator's daughter to worry about. Plus we'll be two rich motherfuckers at the end of it."

"You're not worried about Ren?"

Avery shook his head, "You're right about him. He's been dormant for months. If you give him a head start. Ten days, twenty days, whatever. He's not going to waste it. I know he won't. Because *you* wouldn't. He's going to get the fuck out of Dodge and stop killing. At least for a while. At least until he can't contain himself anymore. And by then you'll already know where he is, won't you Winston? Are you gonna just watch him a little? Play Clarice and Hannibal a little bit longer?"

He gazed down at the keyboard of the laptop in front of him. He sighed. He nodded just ever so slightly.

"Well then let's get to it. What's the plan, hotshot?"

The detective was pacing the floor. He'd sent everyone else out of the room. Except of course the sources of his ire—Winston and Avery. Winston blinked a few times to clear the sleep from his mind. It wasn't working. It was five in the morning and the two P.I.s hadn't gotten their full forty winks. They were too restless. As was to be expected when their pockets were full of secrets.

"He's in this radius most likely." He pointed to the bright red circle on the table.

Winston rolled his eyes. "Will you just give it a rest? If Avery and I couldn't find him the last time he disappeared then the chances of you finding him are slim to nil. Why aren't you focusing on Tomi? Just go pick her up and maybe he'll come after you the way he did with Hensley."

Patten's whole body stiffened, his face tense with something that was probably closer to fury than frustration. "I'm not letting him go."

"I'm not suggesting that," Winston sighed, "just don't expect that you'll find him just because you drew a circle on a map. If I were able to do that I'd have dozens of killers behind bars right now."

Avery cleared his throat but didn't say anything when the eyes in the room were trained on him. He merely shook his head at them with his brows raised.

Patten spoke again, "If you two aren't going to help me then you can just get out right now. I'll go myself."

"Then I echo what I said before. Don't go into those woods by yourself, Patten."

"Oh because I'll end up with my guts strung around the branches of trees, of course Winston, because that always happens to *everybody but you*." Patten's fist met the top of the table with a sharp bang. He went on in a sinister murmur, "How could anybody forget that those things just happen to people who work on this case? How could anybody forget that Ren Rockey is some kind of psychopathic sculptor with bodies as his medium? And how could anybody forget that Trent Winston, P.I., is his favorite play thing? His favorite *boyfriend*."

194

Winston could feel his upper lip twitch.

"Well I for one think there's something that smells about this whole situation. Something that smells bad. Maybe, if I sniffed really hard, it might smell a little like *fish*." He leaned over the table with both of his hands flat on it toward Winston as far as he could before his thighs stopped him. His sunken, tired green eyes bored into Winston's cold hazel ones and held them for a few moments. The two of them had their heels in the dirt. An unstoppable force had met the seemingly immovable object. "If I catch wind of anything remotely strange about this case that ties in any way back to you I'll have you locked up for the *rest of your fucking life.* Is that clear, Winston?"

Winston didn't hesitate in his response. "It is."

"Good." He retreated. "It doesn't matter. I'm going to send out an APB on the two of them to the surrounding jurisdictions. They can't stay out of the public eye forever." He snorted at Winston's eye-roll and turned around toward the window, looking out at the gray morning light that illuminated an empty side street with cracked pavement and overgrown sidewalks. The house across the street was dilapidated and marred with what looked like fire damage above the dark windows. Its mint green paint was chipping into nothing.

Winston tore his gaze from the window and forced himself to look at the red circle that was on the map. He could have put his finger on the place where he thought Ren would be. But there was no sport in that. There was something in his gut that told him to do so would be wrong. There was a piece of paper in his pocket. A message he had to deliver. There was a purpose to all of this. Wasn't there? Or was he just as mad as his killer? Was he just as burned out as that mint green monstrosity across the street? Was he losing his mind along with the rest of them?

He touched his forehead as the silence stretched out into an unbearable length. It was too long with his own thoughts. Left to his own devices there would be more chaos in his life than there was stability. Thank God for Avery. The one thing in his life that could temper him. As far as he could go toward feeling for Patten, there was nothing inside him. Just a deep pervading coldness that seeped from his bones. The man could take care of himself. Even if he didn't get what he wanted. Winston didn't care. Patten was just...

Background noise.

After Patten had let them go they didn't leave. They sat, tired and mute, in the Fusion. They ignored any calls to their cellphones. One from Nadine. One from Rayne Wilson. One from the lab. Winston slept for a little while the early morning sun, hidden in overcast, warmed the car a little, chasing away the dew and the chill of the gray. The car was facing the front of the precinct. The two of them took turns napping, silent and still. Their stomachs took turns growling but there wasn't enough hunger in the world for them to ignore the warning that had sounded in their collective minds when Patten didn't say he wasn't going out into the woods. Pride was the real killer here.

"Winston," Avery whispered, nudging his elbow to wake him from his little cat nap. He opened his eyes and focused first on the glass of the windshield and then through it to Patten dressed in a dark long-sleeved sweatshirt and jeans with tan work boots underneath. Hiking clothes.

"Son of a..."

"He's gonna get himself killed," Avery mumbled. "Where do we stop him?"

"Just follow him for now. I'm not going to ask you to do anything to stop him, Avery. I'll do it all. I don't want you hurt in this. Legally, physically, anything."

Avery licked his lips. "I might not agree with you on everything, buddy, but I trust your judgment. I don't know why, you're an emotionally devoid jackass most of the time. But there it is. I'm in this with you."

"'preciate it," he responded. He frowned and scratched his head. "Where the fuck is Patten's partner? Doesn't he have a partner? Or are they really that low-budget around this place?"

Avery chuckled, "I thought we were gonna be tussling with a sheriff in this town, not a detective. The fact that they have *one* is impressive to me. A small place like this?"

"Suppose you're right..." Winston nodded. "He probably doesn't have a lot of people on in this town. Maybe a dozen or so."

"How could he ever believe he could just walk into the woods and find a man?" Avery crossed his arms.

Winston was silent. Too silent it seemed. That was the moment for agreement. But he didn't so Avery looked at him suddenly with a sharp turn of his head and a question in his eyes.

"You could do that? You *did* do that. My god. How the hell had I thought you were communicating with him? I couldn't have thought letters. You actually *found* him and it was half luck wasn't it? It was half luck but it was half something else." He turned the car on and put it in gear, his eyes wide as he backed carefully out of the space and followed Patten out off the lot. "How?"

"I don't know. I just knew."

"You know where he is now."

"Not exactly. But I could make a good guess."

"And we're not rushing out there guns blazing for what reason now?"

Winston gave him a long drawn out sigh while he followed Patten at a distance. "Because he told me not to approach. If I knew what was good for me. He knows that I know where he his."

"And you trust him to give her to you?"

"He did what I asked before. He'll do it again. She's important to him."

The conversation had come to a natural pause so Winston closed his eyes and put his forehead against the cool window. The smooth ride of the Fusion lulled him not into sleep but into some kind of space in between sleep and consciousness. A gray world of blankness and the white noise from the engine and the wind around the car. He wondered if he should be feeling something. For other people. Even for Avery. As time went on there was less of him. He was almost unreal to himself. Perhaps this gray nothingness half-way to dreaming was the reality and the rest was simply fantasy. Was it too much to hope that maybe one day he could have his world tugged inside out and Ren could be nothing but a dream and this nothingness could be the real thing? A picture flashed into his mind. The bottle of Prozac sitting on the shitty little oak bedside table at the motel. Had he remembered to take it today? Not that this would happen if he missed just one pill but he would have to take it later.

Did he take it this morning? Or had he been too zombie-like to remember?

Avery's voice was calm and low but it interrupted a useless thought pattern and jarred Winston back into the real world. The jolt was enough to make a tiny bubble of anger pop in his chest and he breathed evenly to balance his emotions. "Are you doing this for yourself? Is this what you really want?"

"Have you ever..." Winston started and then stopped. He was trying to put his thought together correctly. "Have you ever wondered why Ren never killed me? Why he plays with me? Why he's, as Patten would call him, my boyfriend?"

Avery laughed. "Are you kidding? I know exactly why he treats you the way he treats you."

"You do?" He looked at his partner with brows knitted by confusion. Was that possible? That Avery knew and he was still in the dark?

"Of course I do. Because you're a total head-case. He could probably sniff out the crazy in you from twenty miles away. Everyone else is boring. But you're different, Trent. You're different and you know you're different and that's what he likes about you. I always had my suspicions that he didn't ruin your proposal as some weird act of revenge."

"What?" he felt himself becoming breathless.

Avery shrugged one shoulder as he turned the car down a winding back road. A sign for a state park marked the way. "I think he was just trying to get you to focus more. On him. On yourself. I think he thought he was doing you a favor. And being a dick at the same time of course. But as you remember quite clearly, he did not kill you. He could have. Very easily. In one stroke. Like he did to Larkin. But he didn't. Because he wanted you to remember him."

Was that what it was all about? A legacy? A struggle to become a vivid memory? A story to tell the grandchildren? As if there could be any, now that Winston was ten thousand miles from being able to create emotional bonds. He put his forehead to his palm and sighed again loudly. "You know what the sad part about all this madness is?"

"Don't tell me. I already know."

Winston looked over at his partner's wide smile.

"You don't even care."

There was nothing else to say to him. Avery was as close as anyone had ever been. The man knew everything. He was good at that and he relished that skill more than any other. To read Winston was to have the ability to read anyone else in the world. Why he was a tracker and not a profiler was baffling at best.

"Well here we are," Avery stated, pulling up behind an old brick building that was possibly once a factory building of some kind. "Patten parked a little way over there. He's getting out of his car. I dunno what he's doing. Is he on some kind of track?"

Winston looked around. "Meh. I lost my sense of direction a while back. Lemme get my bearings and I'll let you know." He got out of the car and stretched out his arms and tried to flex his butt muscles to wake them up. He hated car-ass. They watched Patten moving and Winston nodded very slightly. "I see what he's doing." He could recall this point on the map that was still spread out on the table at the precinct. There was a East-West rail line that was becoming overgrown from disuse. Tall pillars of steel stood as silent specters every mile or so, void of their precious wire that they used to hold diligently. They were relics of not so long ago. Patten was going to wander the tracks in an attempt to find a trail. It was a clever idea. To follow an easy path that could lead him where he needed to go.

Trick was: it might.

Winston spat in the dirt and wanted a cigarette. "He could end up where he wants to be. The idiot."

Avery scratched his foot into the gravel on the cracked pavement. "Will you feel responsible if he ends up dead?"

"A little bit maybe. I mean after all, he's an idiot."

"Did you feel responsible for Maldeen?"

The immediate answer he wanted to say was "of course." But that wasn't entirely true. Maldeen's demise had been a simple matter of time. A brushing off of Winston at every turn that had finally just pissed the killer off enough to give him forty whacks so to speak. The guy hadn't exactly been walking in the woods on a hunt for the killer like the moron, Patten. He'd actually only been walking beside them. On a sidewalk with a chainlink fence beside it that held in the wooded area where he was killed. He never made it home that night. Despite the fact that he'd been at his girlfriend's house and was walking back to his marital home, the wife was never even considered a suspect. Perhaps because of the way he was found.

A teenager had been walking to his school bus stop when he'd smelled something rather peculiar. There was something that looked like a slimy sock stuck to the top of the fence. When examined closer he found that "sock" was in fact not a sock at all. And it was very long. A string of bowel that was pulled taut, stretching back into the woods and disappearing. The boy had wisely gone back into his home and told his mother to call 911. He thought there had been a murder. "Thought" was the most ironic word to Winston since generally speaking there was no other reason for a network of bowel to be webbed through tree branches about ten feet off the ground. They'd found his head and torso hanged by a length of small intestine from a birch and his legs a mile away discarded in a creek. Unnecessary for artistic purposes.

He'd seen Maldeen's remains as they were. He'd been called by Maldeen's partner, Blake Clarell—who did *not* relish picking up the case where Maldeen had left it. He was well-aware of the warning Avery had left with the former police detective. The letter that had warned him of giving Winston the cold shoulder. Clarell was a reasonable man. He allowed Winston to inspect the crime scene, be present at the morgue when the coroner presented his findings, and further allowed him to all the evidence dealing with the case. An ironic but fitting way for Maldeen's investigation career to close: with a P.I. doing most of the legwork.

Avery and he crept closer to the brick building and then behind a broken down bus where they could keep track of Patten, who was looking at the ground and moving slowly, and not be seen. His partner whispered to him while still staring at the detective. "She really was there. That's a no-brainer. Or else Ren would have strung Hensley out. Just like the rest."

He was somehow glad that Avery's thought process was much like his and his partner had also been reflecting on the method of Maldeen's death. Not to mention the others. But Maldeen's had truly been Ren's magnum opus up until this point. Not once before had Winston even heard of a killer being so dedicated to a kill that he was willing to spend the time to connect point upon point of bowel, cut with discarded old kitchen scissors, to tree branches to make a spider web. The term "premeditation" would be considered a mild way to put it.

"When it comes down to it," Winston conceded, "I may have felt a minute prick of guilt."

"At least there's that," Avery breathed. "Now what's the plan?"

"We could always hit him with the car." Winston scratched at one of the bandages covering a wound on his arm. "Or...we could just watch."

"Watch what?"

"Ren's little doggie ears will prick up. He'll hear him coming. He'll sense it. He'll *smell* him. His brows will raise. He'll tuck away his little sweetie and he'll start to stalk. He'll start to really crave that blood and give in to that thirst."

Avery looked at him with a strange expression. "You're suggesting we observe a murder."

"Not quite."

Her head was resting against his chest, his back on the trunk of the oak tree. She was drifting in and out of consciousness, the birds chirping around them. The breeze rustled the leaves in the oak and the grasses in the meadow. There were no other sounds. She could feel the beat of his heart and the heat of his body through his T-shirt. His breathing was even. She knew he was asleep. She could see his hands. She touched the back of one of them and waited for his breathing to differ. For any sign that he might be awake. None came. She picked up his hand and pulled it toward her face. He did not stir. Ren's fingers were limp and she stared at them. His hand was warm and she contemplated it.

He had killed with this hand. He had killed with his teeth. He had killed with his body. A dog slept under her. A rottweiler. His fingernails were short, as though he chewed them when he was nervous. She wondered if he was nervous a lot. The lines etched on his palm caught her attention. They said that one was your life line, another your heart, another your head, and the last your fate. She traced the one she thought was his lifeline with her thumb. It was deep and long. She hoped that meant he had strength. The others she wasn't so sure about. She brought his palm to her lips and held it there against her mouth. His hand smelled like tobacco and dirt.

She felt his fingers curl a little and touch her cheek.

"What are you doing?" was his sleepy whisper. She shook her head and took his hand away. He settled it cupped over her breast and tightened his hold a little before relaxing. His voice was husky. "I can't stay with you." Cicadas started to whirr in the distance. An ominous summer sound.

She tried to breathe normally. It was hard.

"Little Miss, I told you a long time ago that it was time to go home." A flutter filled her chest.

"You've been out here too long. You're tough enough. You can wait a little longer to see your brother, wherever he is. What is it? Just two years and then you can do whatever it is that you want. Just two years. Not even. One and a half now?"

Her chest started heaving and a burning sensation stung at the backs of her eyes.

"Summer's almost over. It's getting nippy at night. You can't stay with me. It's time for you to go home, Little Miss." The hand on her breast squeezed softly and his other hand moved to her belly. "Calm down, silly goose."

She tried.

"It's time to buy that puppy. It's time to go back to being spoiled. Summer days on the beach. Make some actual friends this time, okay? And for fuck's sake take the bus and don't talk to any more strangers." He chuckled.

She turned in his arms and pressed her cheek against him. She couldn't make the tears come. "You can't make me."

He petted her hair. "No. I can't make you do anything. If you would like to try to find your brother, I won't stop you."

They were silent for a little while. She felt him move and knew he was tilting his head the way he was wont to do every so often as if he were listening to someone speak. She wondered if he *was*. She traced small designs on his T-shirt and knew that he was watching her. She wouldn't go home. He knew that. She watched the grass in the meadow sway in the breeze. She could almost smell the change in season. Late summer was all around them. It was in the deep greens of the leaves, the dry crunch of grass under their feet. The low monotone of the cicadas roamed across the countryside.

"There's no such thing as home," she said to Summer.

"I know," he replied.

She fell asleep on him again as dusk approached and he held her until the sun was gone but the sky was just a dusty orange. When he left he was silent and she was curled under his heavy sweatshirt on a soft patch of warm grass.

The sun was casting long shadows across the railroad tracks as Winston and Avery crept back toward their car. The whole world had taken on a faded, old fashioned hue as though reality had somehow been cast into a sepia-toned movie. Somewhere in the distance a murder of crows squawked into flight and a broken black cloud filled the sky to the west. A point behind Winston's eyes hurt. They'd followed Patten into the woods and along the edges of the cornfield on the other side of them. But it was time to retreat. Patten had decided on investigating the forest more with his pocket flashlight. He was scanning the duff with a curious eye but seemed to be getting tired of it. He would retire tonight like every other night and go home empty-handed.

Of course that's how it was supposed to happen. But as soon as the two private eyes got back to the car they knew that this night was not going to end very well at all. Crumbles of brown dirt were strewn over the top of the formerly pristine black Fusion and down the hood. Halves of footprints made by someone who walked primarily on their toes.

Ren's prints.

"Trent...?" was Avery's wavering question.

"Don't worry. We're supposed to be here. He's just letting me know that he knows where I am and acknowledging that I know where he is." He hoped he wasn't lying. The thought that he could be lying was weighing at him, making his bowels squirm in his belly as if a thousand small snakes had been let loose in there. "But this means he also knows that Patten's here."

The two of them didn't need to say anything to each other. They turned around and walked toward Patten's Chevy Cobalt, white in color and still as clean as it came. A loud bang startled both of them and Winston immediately drew his gun while he turned sharply. The rusted out school bus was behind them. They shared glances before making their way over to it. He examined it a little more, his heart pounding even harder against his chest. It felt like it might escape before he could possibly get closer to the entrance of this bus. Weeds grew up under it and around it, some of them reaching all the way to the tops of the dirty glass windows.

"Careful," Avery whispered when they rounded the front of the bus. There was no sound other than the faraway cries of birds and the consistent whirring of cicadas. He felt as if every hair on his body was poised to feel something. That his ears couldn't miss a single sound. That everywhere was dangerous. The inside of this bus. An unbearable stifling raw heat was radiating out of the cracked open door. "Winston," Avery whispered again, motioning to the ground. Sharp marks scuffed the grass and gravel in front of the bus's door. A struggle. A fierce one. Dragging. Fighting. *Fucking Patten couldn't just give it a goddamn rest.* The sharp scent of cigarette smoke met his nose and he took the first step onto the bus.

He held his gun tight as he moved up the stairs, fighting the urge to back down into the cooler night air. To back away from that lit Camel and escape. The scene was laid out before him in an instant but Ren gave him much more time to contemplate it. Patten had been stripped of his sweatshirt. Underneath he'd been wearing his normal work shirt and his tie—a rather nice-looking dark red tie that his wife might have bought him for Christmas one year from J.C. Penney. As it was now, he was dangling in the middle of the bus, his tie shut tight in the fire escape that lead to the roof of the vehicle. He was struggling, his feet just maybe two inches from touching the floor. His hands were bound behind him and as he struggled he spun a little back and forth allowing Winston a glance or two. Strips of the sweatshirt were binding his hands and feet. He was missing one of his hiking boots. Odd gurgling and gagging sounds were escaping him and his face was red from his attempts at breathing.

Smoke coiled up from behind one of the seats in the back.

"Ren," Winston pointed his gun at the seat. "Stand up, Ren."

He did more than stand. He leaped upward and balanced on the back of a rickety old seat, the rusted thing crunching and creaking under his weight. He put a hand against the metal wall beside him while he crouched there next to his prey. A spider guarding his fly. His took a quick drag off his Camel and then plucked it from his mouth, throwing the still glowing butt at Winston without taking his eyes from the P.I.'s. His animal-like movements were unnerving. Disturbing to the eye. The smoke that had gathered in the back of the bus gave them all a hazy unreal look, as if Winston were simply watching a play on a stage. The gun was trained on him. The sound would be deafening in such a cramped space. It would distort his senses if he fired. If he missed, he'd be a sitting duck. He couldn't unload the barrel if his senses were shot. Patten. He had to think of Patten.

"What are you waiting for?" Ren asked. His face was confused. No. Not confused. Sad. His brows were pulled together in a soft manner. A pleading one. "Aren't you...?" Ren leaned forward a little on the seat, rust falling in crumbles under his feet. He tilted his head back a little while watching the gun. "I'll kill him. I will."

Winston blinked. He was lying. Ren was lying. There was something in the way he said it. The inflection. There was something in the way he begged for what he thought would be Winston's inevitable reaction. "You're too close to him for me to shoot you."

"Don't bullshit me." This time he was genuinely irritated, the frown turning his expression darker.

"Let him go."

"No."

"Ren, just let him go."

"Over my dead body."

"Not an option."

Ren scoffed and sidled closer to Patten whose face had taken on a light purple hue. He was getting breaths every so often. He pulled a cigarette from his pocket and lit it with a match, shaking the little thing out and throwing it again at Winston. He blew the initial drag into Patten's face and studied him a little before taking the cigarette and putting it in Patten's gaze.

"Ren," Winston warned. He glance to his left. Avery was still at the bottom of the stairs. There was nowhere else for him to be.

"I bet you're wondering how I got him like this." Ren grinned, "It was easy. Too easy. You see this little boy right here just kinda fell right into me. Of course it wasn't as hard as pulling that fat-ass Maldeen over that chain fence. You know he lost a lot of weight when I cut off his legs. I suggest that as a weight-loss option if you or Avery ever get to be fat fuckers."

"Ren," Winston said again. Again a warning.

Patten made a pathetic little gurgle and Ren sucked in his bottom lip before he met Winston's gaze and pressed the tip of the lit cigarette onto the exposed flesh of Patten's throat. The detective made a stifled groaning sound and wriggled hard until Ren pulled it away and re-lit it, taking a drag deeply into his lungs and blowing it again into his face.

"Mmm," Ren smiled, "You smell delicious."

"Cut him down."

Ren's eyes flashed in the darkness of the bus. Sunset was almost finished, gray light flooding the inside of the bus with a gray hue that made Ren look even less human than usual. "Cut him...?"

"Down," Winston cursed his word choice.

"Haven't you heard the golden rule, Winnie the Pooh? You never *ever* pull out a gun unless you're prepared to pull the trigger. Didn't you know that, Winnie? Didn't they ever teach you that at gun school? Because you know what the secret is? I bet Patten knows it. What's the secret, Olive? What's the secret about guns? Come on, you can tell me." He put his ear close to Patten's mouth and his toothy grin grew wider at a pained gag on behalf of his victim. "That's *right* my sweet little po-po. The secret is too wonderful not to share with our friend Winnie, isn't it? Well here goes. He repositioned himself on the seat and kicked out his leg, his foot connecting hard with one of the dirty windows, shattering it without much effort. "A gun only gives you more power if you're *prepared to use it.*" His movement was so quick that Winston wouldn't have had time to pull the trigger if he'd wanted to. He'd already sunk his teeth into Patten's throat.

He didn't have time to think. He simply pulled the trigger. In his heart he knew he'd missed. The bullet had gone wild, Ren was gone, and Patten's front was very quickly getting soaked in blood. Winston's ears were ringing and he took a step backward. The entire world was silent save for a loud ringing. A terrible high-pitched warble that deprived him of everything that made him who he was at that singular moment in time. He stumbled sideways, dropping his gun on the stairs on his way down. He fell into the gravel at the bottom and struggled in vain to get up. His balance was gone and he fell again while he watched Avery running at his top speed toward the railroad tracks. He could feel. He could feel everything. The scrapes on his elbows and hands stinging. The cooler night that had descended around the heat of the bus. He could smell the fresh air of the world outside that horror.

With a sharp movement he pulled his cell phone out of his pants pocket, scraping his knuckles hard against the gravel ground. It hurt badly and he was sure he drew blood.

He couldn't hear them but he knew what they would say. *9-1-1, what is your location?*

"Dirt road off of Alamack. There's a factory and an old bus by the tracks. Ambulance. Medics. Emergency. I can't hear you. Don't ask questions I can't hear anything. Please just send someone. Detective Patten is dying. I can't get up. Send someone. Send anyone." It was enough. He put his face down into the dirt and tried to breathe normally but found it exceedingly difficult. His wounds ached and itched, the maddening ringing in his ears overtaking his mind and flickering it toward that gray darkness of which he was so fond.

He'd forgotten his Prozac that morning. Hadn't he?

CHAPTER 10

And there will come a time, you'll see, with no more tears.
And love will not break your heart, but dismiss your fears.
Get over your hill and see what you find there,
With grace in your heart and flowers in your hair.

-Mumford and Sons, "After the Storm"

She vaguely remembered him picking her up in the middle of the night. Carrying her on his back, her arms entwined around his neck. The scent of cigarettes and blood forced her to cling to him harder, pressing her body into his back as he walked with her before she drifted back to her dreams, peaceful despite the swaying of his movements under her.

Morning came too soon. The brightness of the sun was what eventually woke her. She could feel him playing with her hair idly, as if he'd been awake for hours and stayed put just to allow her to sleep a bit more. She shivered despite the sweatshirt he'd draped over her back. The warmth of his body was incredible. He was practically a human heater. She tried to press herself into him. To take some of that heat with her.

"Mornin' sweets."

She didn't answer him. It was pointless. She just propped herself up and stared at him, his lazy half-lidded eyes looking back at her with empathy. He touched her chin with one finger and smiled at her.

"I'll miss you," he said.

She didn't reply to that either. She didn't even bother to comment that this wasn't the same corn field or tree she'd fallen asleep under. She just continued to stare at him. After all the times he'd left her, there was a deeper sense of finality. She thought it might have been because he was telling her beforehand. Because it was a plan. Because he had thought it all out. He couldn't make her go home, but he could leave her. She got up, pushing her arms into the sleeves of the hoodie and zipping it. Her sneakers squished into the impression she'd made in the grass while she slept. Ren didn't move. He just looked up at her.

"Hungry?" he asked. "I have bagels in my bag."

She nodded and he sat up, rooting through his backpack and pulling out two plain bagels. She nibbled hers still standing until he tugged the bottoms of her shorts and she sat cross-legged in front of him, uncomfortable in his stare. She looked at the grass in front of her.

"Do you think," he started in a soft tone. A voice that was unfamiliar to her. God, he even sounded like Summer. "That someone...if they tried hard enough...could change the fabric of their being?"

"Like...genetics?"

He nodded. "Yes. What if someone was predisposed to say...alcoholism. Do you think they could...you know...after having been an alcoholic...do you think they could stop?"

Tomi thought for a few moments, "Even if you're not drinking anymore, you're still an alcoholic."

Ren's shoulders drooped and his eyes lost some of their shine and focus. "It is our past that defines us then. I...am a victim of myself. But if I hadn't been myself...I would have never met you. Little Miss Tomi. I suppose I shouldn't be mad at fate for what I am. Or mad at myself. That won't get me anywhere, will it? I haven't blown up a classroom full of children or...shot up a campus. The devil takes many forms I guess. And here he is." He opened up his arms and shrugged. "I was just too weak to get rid of him."

Tomi watched emotions ripple through his expressions.

"I still am. God. I told you that I'd never hurt you. I told you that I'd kill anyone who did." He turned his head and stared off toward the meadow and stopped talking for a little, swallowing convulsively.

Tomi's eyes widened and cold fear gripped her heart. She whispered, "Don't you dare."

He didn't look at her but his eyes dropped a little. A sign that he'd heard her. That he had acknowledged her opinion on the option of suicide. The definite "no" vote probably wouldn't do much in the long run but it was something for now. Winter would come back and put a stop to all of that nonsense. It was funny how she was starting to gain an appreciation for his darker side once she'd fully seen the light. Summer couldn't be happy. He would exist in a realm of self-loathing for the rest of his life if Summer was permanent. No wonder there had to be a Winter. To keep what was left of his sanity. To keep him from feeling.

"You're not evil."

"Aren't I?" He still wouldn't look at her.

"There's no such thing as evil. Just people. There's no such thing as the Big Bad Wolf or the boogeyman. People make up things like 'evil' because they can remove themselves from it. But we're all the same in the end. I'm guilty of defining you by the actions I chose to see. Everyone does it. But when I opened my eyes I saw things that you've done that weren't anything close to something a wolf might do. You're human after all, Ren. We all are. That's all we'll ever be."

Tomi rubbed the sleep out of her eyes and ate the rest of her bagel. She watched him. He was still strong with sleek muscles that slid easily under his tanned and freckled skin. His lips were soft and pink. His eyes held within them both experience and naivety. His body language was different from his wintery self. A vulnerability. A shyness.

"I guess..." she stated, "that this is goodbye then."

It made him look at her with wide shining eyes. He was almost unable to say anything at all. She could see his jaw sticking together as if locked in place. He was hurt and lost and she knew he felt useless and abandoned. It would have been easier to leave Winter. "I..." he tried.

"This is where you tell me that you're terrible with goodbyes and you just leave..." she supplied, but she knew he was unable to do such a thing. "Isn't that how it happens in all the new movies out now?" Even though she was trying to think of the newer movies, all she could think of were the old ones. The ones where John Wayne says his goodbyes to the would-be lovers who had fallen in love with his rough-and-tumble self along the trail or through hard times. "It's better this way." She stood up and he leaned forward as if he wanted to stop her. She slung her bag over her shoulder.

"Wait," was his feeble response. He had to think for a few moments, listening to that voice that made him tilt his head. What he heard must have been painful because his expression was pinched. "There's a....there's a town. Just west of here. There's a cafe. You should..." He stood up and appeared flustered, swinging his backpack onto his back and checking all of his pockets before he met her eyes. "There's a cafe. You should have some coffee there. You know. Put yourself together a little."

She made a tiny smile. "I don't look like the one falling to pieces."

"Just..." He took some deep breaths. "Just go there. Okay? They've got a fantastic house special mocha."

"Mocha?" She giggled.

"Yes. I promise."

The two of them stood awkwardly for a little while before he took her into a rough embrace, holding the back of her head and burying his face into the curve of her neck. He took in a deep inhale, as if he were attempting to memorize her very scent. "Be careful," he whispered into her ear, his warm breath forcing goosebumps to rise over her arms.

Patten lay in the hospital bed with what seemed like a permanent scowl on his face. Winston was leaning forward, his hands on the end rail of the bed and his head tilted slightly sideways. Patten's wife was in the chair to the detective's left. Every so often her emotions would boil over and she would leak a few tears or a sob or two. Martha Patten was a very pretty woman with dark auburn hair and a soft demeanor that reminded Winston very much of Grace. Not a very good way to be when married to a cop, he thought.

"Mar...tha," Patten said, pretty good for a guy who had a hole in his trachea. Ren had bitten him in a very specific spot. That small spot under everything important—where doctors shoved a tube when they had to bypass the mouth. Winston knew Ren had done it on purpose. "Go," he motioned with a hand to the door and Martha nodded, getting up with her purse and walking toward the door, looking once backward before leaving her husband with the P.I. Patten's attention shifted to Winston. "You chased...him."

"Avery did. If you remember correctly I fired a shot and pretty much destroyed my senses. I couldn't walk much less chase him. He got away."

"Of...course he...did." Patten was taking deep breaths through his mouth. "He was," Patten's face distorted into confusion and recollection, "very strong. Very clever. Very fast. I under...stand now. Why you have...such a difficult time." He tapped his thigh with one finger. "He knew...I was there. He...found me."

"And he's gone now. You don't have to worry about him. Chances are he's probably way out of your jurisdiction by now. We'll take it from here. Us and probably some team from the F.B.I. or something. Not like they're much help." He gave Patten a crooked grin.

"Thank you for rescuing me."

Winston shrugged. "Hardly rescued. Kinda just stood there with my thumb up my ass."

"He wanted you to...shoot him."

"What can I say? I'm not really into giving killers what they want. We're just lucky we were there when we were. We're lucky he was feeling generous. You could have ended up all over the inside of that bus." It would have looked like a bomb had gone off in his gut. It would have made Winston throw up.

The hospital room's light shifted when a cloud moved over the sun, moving the shadows of things around drastically in a short span of time. The blinds were open, displaying a garden of sorts that was lush and green and unlike anything Winston was used to. He was so enamored by the colors of summer that they seemed unreal. As if his whole life was nothing but the blunted colors of winter and here before him lay the ethereal intangible life and sound and vibrant being of summer. It was almost too much. As if someone had taken a photograph and enhanced the colors to a state of surrealism. He wished for winter when everything could take on a dreary muted set of tones that brought it back to an earthy, natural state. He longed in that moment to feel the nip of frost on his cheeks and to retreat back into a bland state of being and living and seeing. Summer was almost over anyway. He could wait a little longer for the first frosts of November.

Patten was looking out the window as well. He murmured in an odd tone, "You'll get him one day. You think like him."

His response was silence.

"I'd like to be alone."

Avery nodded, sliding his sunglasses on top of his head. His hands were still on the steering wheel, as if he were just going to drop off his partner and make a get-away as opposed to wait for at least a few hours for a miracle.

"I don't want her to think that we're going to hurt her. So I'd like to be alone." He didn't need to explain. Avery knew the plan. Avery knew Winston.

After this they did not say much to each other. Avery relaxed a little and sipped his Chai tea from Starbucks, watching the door to the cafe while Winston tried to breathe evenly, tapping his fingers against the door handle as if she were going to show up at any given moment. The inside of Avery's Ford Fusion still had that scent of new car. Winston desperately wanted to smoke a cigarette but knew it was out of the question. The car was off so as to not seem suspicious but the black exterior and the leather interior had the uncomfortable effect of heating up quickly in the August sun. They'd gone back to suits. He was beginning to regret that decision. He looked at his watch. It was just about noon. His stomach growled. Breakfast had been large but hours before. He wished he were better at stake-outs. He wished he had some beer. He wished he was on the beach instead of waiting in some podunk town watching the only cafe on Main Street for some girl who probably wouldn't even turn up.

He sighed and started to fidget.

"Calm down," Avery smiled. "You said that you just knew that she'd show up. Trust yourself. I trust you," His partner looked at him and nodded before turning his attention back to the sidewalk in front of the coffee shop. "You're not waiting for the wolf. You're waiting for the lamb."

Winston tried to laugh but all that came out was a choked-off giggle. "You mean she should be less frightening? She's probably the one that almost knocked my brains out of my ears."

Avery chuckled. "She might have been. But you won't know anything about her until you meet her. Face to face. Eye to eye. She's probably adorable all covered in dirt."

"He fucked her."

"Does that make her disgusting?" Avery's dark eyebrow lifted.

Winston pouted then conceded. "No."

His partner nodded. "I've never thought of you as the jealous type before. Interesting. You've always been kinda stand-offish with all your amorous pursuits. That's why Grace left you, you know."

He shrugged one shoulder. "You know perfectly well why Grace left me," he snapped.

"Maybe Tomi would be more to your liking."

"Jailbait," he replied, touching the pack of Marlboros that Ren had returned to him through the fabric of his suit pants.

"Ren didn't seem to mind." Avery sipped his tea calmly.

Winston's mouth felt like it was zipped shut. He knew what his partner was trying to hint at. That he was just as guilty of horrible crimes as Ren. That it shouldn't matter if he committed one more. That he *might as well*. The jab was well-aimed and Winston sat sulking in the passengers seat for at least another half hour without talking to his partner again. His partner would be the first to speak.

"Well, well, well, there's your lamb, Trent. Sic her."

He didn't respond. He simply opened the door and left.

She felt like a ninnymuggen sitting at some stupid table by the window and sipping a mocha that wasn't even all that good. It even had some kind of syrup in it that had been called "Toasted Marshmallow." It had looked promising. But the thought came to her that it probably wasn't the mocha that lacked body and flavor. It was probably her. Her taste might never recover. The empty raw space that was in her chest might never be filled. She would get used to it. The feeling that she'd been punched in the gut. That her heart had somehow been removed with a saw through her sternum. She was alive. Barely. He was certainly a murderer. He took from her more than her life.

She sipped the mocha delicately as if she might will some more flavor to come from it. The heat was a comfort at least. He'd told her that she might collect herself here. What was he busy doing? Was Summer forcing himself to look down some precipice and contemplate putting an end to whatever demon was inside him? She suddenly didn't feel so confident in Winter's ability to stop it before it destroyed him. What if he did it? What if he killed himself? She put her finger to her lips and watched the world move on outside. Her dirty shoes squeaked against the smooth floor under her chair.

The thought of him dying was almost uniquely pleasant. Almost as if a band broke up on stage at the end of a show she'd just attended. She had been the last to hear his music. She smiled at the way the light played on the sidewalk through the clouds as people walked by. She wondered what day it was. She should be going back to school in September. This part of her life was over. But would she? Would she give up and go back?

Back to icy blue disapproval. To hollow, meaningless existence on some vast gray expanse of beach. A rich prison. She had been free. Her toes on dirt and grass, the moon her night light, the rain her shower, a lawless boy her only companion.

The chair across from her skidded backward and she started, her mocha coming down hard on the table's surface. The small paper thud was unimpressive and did nothing to voice her heart's cry of injustice.

Winston quickly sat. "I didn't mean to startle you."

She was well aware that her breath was coming in short pants.

Panic made her fingers numb. "You're..." she breathed. "This is..." She couldn't control herself. "Imposs...Im..."

"I'm sure I know what you thought." From up close he looked perfectly dapper in his black suit and tie. He was well put together, that was for certain. His back was straight and his shoulders squared. The slight discoloration under his eyes suggested a lack of sleep and she noted the gray in his hair that Ren had mentioned. He seemed much too young for so much gray. There was a rather large band-aid on the side of one of his hands. She tried to not look at it.

Tomi was quiet, she narrowed her eyes at him and moped. He was alive. Tired and maybe a little annoyed, but alive. Her mind was racing with the possibilities. They had been too close for both of them to walk away. Something was amiss. There was something wrong. She must have been a red three. And here he was. Winston had her.

"You're a hard girl to find, Miss Balekowski." One side of his mouth was tilting upward just ever so slightly.

This she decided to answer in a very soft voice. "I can't imagine why."

His grin deepened. "Right. Of course you can't. Of course *I* happen to be a hard man to kill. Wouldn't you say?"

She pressed her lips tight together.

"Never mind, don't answer that. The fact that I'm here is answer enough."

She contemplated bolting for the door but he probably had someone out there. His partner most likely. Waiting for her so he could catch her about her middle and shove her kicking and screaming into some ominous black car. She scanned the outside and picked out which car she thought it was. Black. Sleek. Perfect for men in suits. "Am I going to jail?"

"For running away?"

She looked at him again, studying him hard.

"I can't think of a reason for you to go to jail, can you?" He was doing it on purpose. He was going to let her get away with knocking him unconscious. Attempted murder. At *least* battery. He was going to let her get away with aiding and abetting. Accomplice to murder. Charges

217

kept piling in her head and he was going to just take her home? He was still grinning. "Your parents have been worried."

She rolled her eyes and leaned back in her chair.

"Well." His grin morphed into something warmer. "I don't think they need to have worried. You seemed to do very well by yourself."

"I..." She wanted to say that she hadn't been by herself. But Winston knew that. He was pretending that Ren hadn't existed. He was pretending in order to protect her. A surge of sudden appreciation crippled her voicebox and broke her off. Her empty chest tightened.

"Don't you think it might be time to go home, Tomi?"

She could feel her face pinch and tears start to gather in her eyes.

Winston reached into his jacket and pulled out a small folded piece of paper which he unfolded and flattened on the table, sliding it over to her. She peered at it while she sniffled, trying to hold back the tears. It was just an address in Buffalo, New York. A simple street address with no name on the top written in bold black Sharpie. The detective noted her puzzled expression.

"Your brother has offered for custody of you until you turn eighteen. Would you like to go home, Tomi?"

She looked up at him through the blur and nodded, letting a few of her sobs escape her. He offered his hand, palm up, across the table and she took it. It was warm and dry and reminded her of Ren. He held her hand until she'd collected herself and then offered her a tissue from his jacket pocket.

"Do you think you can handle the winters up there?"

"Yes," she whispered. "Oh yes."

His smile was warm. "I know you can. Do you have enough money for the bus, little lady? Because you're *definitely* not walking."

She giggled. "I have enough money, Detective..."

"Winston," he supplied. "But I think you already know my name. Is there anything I can do for you before you scamper off into happily-ever-after?"

"Yes." She looked at the table instead of into his eyes. Her words couldn't come. She knew what she wanted to ask but her mouth was stuck open. Her eyes on her hands. "Actually. No. I...thought I did.

But...I don't."

Winston appeared to breathe a sigh of relief. "Will you listen to any advice I give you?"

"You've probably got a lot you could tell me."

He nodded. "I want you to be happy. That's why I'm doing this. You're curious, you're clever, and you're empathetic. I don't want you to stop talking to strangers. I don't want you to not trust people. I want you to reach out. I want you to move forward and smile like I know you can. I want you to love again. Passionately. Deeply. Desperately. I want you to find yourself in a place with stability, loyalty, and understanding. More than loving I want you to *be* loved. Honestly."

She couldn't help but watch him say this and nod her head. Of course he did. And of course she would.

"So talk to strangers, Tomi." He met her gaze. "Make friends. Lots of them. Make enemies even. Lots of them too. Sometimes they're all the friends you have."

She was free. Winston had left her with her cold mocha and the slip of paper with Bo's address on it. The letters were blocky and thick and in all capitals. Easy to read. She folded it back up and put it in her bag in the little make-shift pocket along with her cash. She wouldn't lose it. She slipped herself off the chair and threw the rest of her mocha away in the trashcan by the door when she left. The bus stop was only about a mile up Main Street. She looked around for the ominous black car that she was sure the detectives had arrived in but found it nowhere in sight.

The bench was empty when she sat on it. Empty save for a small used-to-be-white envelope that looked to have seen better days. It was crinkled and folded and creased. But it had her name on it in ballpoint pen. Blue. Scrawled as if in haste. Her heartbeat increased and she held it in her lap for a little while, just letting the paper lay under her fingers. In a few minutes the bus would be there. In a few minutes she would begin her journey to a set destination. In a few minutes the world would be open to her. But for now. Now she had this.

Her finger slipped underneath the edge and she very slowly ripped through it along the crease. When she pulled it out of its sheath it made a very distinctive sound, a sound that she would remember for the rest of her life.

She unfolded it.

Tomi,

She took a deep breath in and then out.

I love you, I love you, I love you, a hundred thousand times, I love you.

She crumpled it into a ball in her hands, tight against her palms as if she could absorb those sloppy blue ballpoint letters into her very flesh. She breathed through her teeth a little and closed her eyes. She tried to imagine him. With a pen he found on the ground. With stationary he stole from some hotel. With an envelope he probably had in that stupid bag of his forever. She brought the ball up to her nose. It smelled different. Interesting. Not quite like him. She wasn't sure what she'd expected. She looked at it in her hand. Crumpled. She shoved it into her bag and then looked around. There was no one. Not even a passerby. What had she expected? That he would watch her? That anyone would?

She crossed her ankles and closed her eyes. She kept them closed until the bus came.

They were packing all their things to go home. Avery was folding shirts. Winston was collecting their toothbrushes. Nadine was out by the car, cross as usual. She had been completely averse to allowing Tomi to travel alone. Winston had calmed her with his usual banter but she was still angry. Something about how they had just found her and now they were just going to "let her go."

A familiar voice sounded by the door, "Gentlemen."

Winston popped his head out of the bathroom and Avery looked up from his suitcase. The suave and collected Nathan Balekowski was wearing a slick gray suit with a dark navy blue tie. Slightly blue-tinted glasses sat upon his nose and his arms were crossed in front of him, his back straight. He almost looked angry.

Winston held up his hands, palms out. "We did what we thought was right, sir."

Mr. Balekowski's mouth stretched and curled into a grin. "You did very well, Detectives. I'm actually rather impressed by how well you did. And I'm willing to give you both your rewards."

"Sir," Avery smiled, "we don't need any of your rewards. This isn't meant to be offensive but we've gotten all the rewards and punishment out of this assignment that we can possibly handle."

The politician's face warmed—which Winston thought might have been just by two degrees. He leaned against the doorframe, the sun shining in around him. "You don't want anything for finding my daughter then?"

Winston shook his head. "The idea that she's okay seems reward enough to me. That much money would ruin me anyway. Why don't you send it to her? I'm sure she could use a little bit of start-up cash to get whatever she needs. It might be a good way to get back into her life." He cocked a brow.

His grin didn't waver. "You're a good detective, but you're awful with people, aren't you?"

Avery snorted laughter and Winston threw him a dirty look.

"Tomi would see any money I sent her as a bribe. She'd see it as some kind of sad attempt to get her back to me. She's better off being a little girl for a little while. Having her adventures, smoking a little pot and just being a teenager. She couldn't do that with me. She can do that with her brother. I'll set up a trust fund for her. When she's twenty-one she'll have access to it and she can get everything she needs." He nodded to himself as if congratulating himself on his own genius. "But I'll be sure to include a little note saying that you guys donated it to her. Then it won't be on my hands but yours. I think she'll appreciate that."

Winston's brow remained cocked when the old Senator disappeared out of the doorway as suddenly as he had showed up. Winston went back to the bathroom and shrugged to himself, wiping down the counters with the small motel towel in an effort to be courteous to the clean-up crew. "He's a strange man."

Avery let loose a laugh. "No, *you're* a strange man. He's normal. He's probably the most normal person we've had contact with for a long,

long time." Avery cleared his throat a little, an action he only did purposefully, and Winston looked out of the tiny hotel bathroom so he could see why. The dark-haired agent stared back with a lop-sided grin. "You know, Winston."

"What do I know?"

"You're right handed."

He meandered out with their toiletry bag and plopped it down on the bed next to his suitcase. "Point being?"

Avery paused to zip up his bag and get everything else settled by the door. Nadine was on her way in so he answered in a low tone. "Your handwriting doesn't look anything like Ren's."

EPILOGUE

ANOTHER THREE YEARS

Cold blue eyes scanned the brick main street. Brightly colored shop windows announcing that there were used books available, pet supplies, shoes and colorful silk scarves. He was especially amused by the two shops that sold nothing but olive oil and spices to season bread. Who in the world would need two shops that sold the same thing *on the same side of the street?* It was an odd little place. He liked it. The single screened theater's marquee displayed that morning's matinee show in big block letters and that night's retro showing of the Wizard of Oz below it. The fancy Bistro buzzed with activity. He imagined the waiters moving about easily behind closed doors, waiting on society's cream. Maybe the owner of a sports team or two. Their cloth napkins in their laps.

Their smiles painted on.

He blinked.

There was something you were looking for.

Right. There was. He shook his head and blinked a few times again, adjusting his sunglasses on his nose. He watched for a little longer. He continued even when he felt a presence on his right. He tried not to prickle but heat burned in his chest.

"Hide and seek champion of the world. Autograph?"

His lips thinned and he felt the bottom lid of his left eye twitch once. Twice.

Autograph. Sure. Something small. Want to give him one? Want to give him one? Want to give him one? Want to--

"Hello, Winnie."

The figure at his right shifted a little. "I liked your natural hair color better."

He smiled. It had taken a very long time to bleach his hair to make it completely white. He'd managed. "I rather like how this came out. Where's Avery?"

"Hospital."

There was a long strange pause in which Winston didn't shift or fidget at all. He wasn't even smoking. He hadn't quit. There was no way. Ren crossed his arms in front of him and continued to watch the sidewalk on the other side of the street. He licked his lips. It was at least a minute before he responded verbally. "Why aren't you there?"

"It won't change anything." The edge in his voice was sharp enough to cut.

Ren watched the detective out of the corner of his eye and murmured, "What *will* change something, Winnie? What do you *want*? Is there something...that I can *do* for you?" He tried to suppress his grin. He heard the agent sigh but blessed the silence that came after when he saw her. Her blonde hair was longer, flowing freely about her shoulders. She had a daisy perched behind one ear. She was smiling. A coffee in one hand and her other arm linked to a rather tall classy-looking fellow. Tanned, long dark hair, he had a smug little smirk. Or was that just his imagination? His heart beat faster and he could feel a scowl starting to push his brows together.

Winston spoke again in a low tone. "His name's Jay. He's nothing like you."

Ren ground out, "Better for it."

"Have you been a good boy, Ren?"

"You tell me." *Been good. If you don't count the late Kent Newman. Poor guy. What a loss to the world. Whore-kicker extraordinaire. Could have been famous. Could have made something of himself. Could have kicked more tits in.*

Winston didn't speak again until Tomi and Jay had disappeared into a cheerful florist shop. "There *is* something you could do for me. Since you mentioned it."

Ren turned to watch Winston's face and perched his shades on his head in order to see emotion more clearly. "Have a taste for vengeance, do you?"

His face tightened into silent cold fury and his eyes were unfocused, staring off at the fancy Bistro across the street, glazed with hate. "He cut him." Winston swallowed. "He cut him. He tied him down to a chair. What a great prize he was. A detective. He cut his face. Like a...like a Cheshire Cat. So yes, Ren. There is something you can do for me. There are a few things you could do for me. I don't care how long it takes. I don't care what you want. I just want my partner to be okay. And I just want this man dead. Not just dead." He was shaking. He was looking for a word.

"There's a reason you found me, Winnie. You don't just want this one dead. You want him *eviscerated.*" His grin was ear to ear.

ABOUT THE AUTHOR

A. Sleeper lives in the small Western New York town of East Aurora with her African Lovebird, Beebs, and a plethora of incredible friends.

Send all questions or feedback to asleep19@mail.com

SNEAK PEAK INTO *A DOG IN SHEEP'S CLOTHING*

CHAPTER 1

The hospital room was dry and sterile. The countless flowers that sat in their pathetic bouquets which were supposed to be cheery and filled with goodwill were crisped around the edges as if they had been burned by a cruel kid who'd found his first lighter. The walls were a pale shade of salmon and the only redeeming feature happened to be the large picture window that took up almost the entirety of the south-facing wall. It opened up to a world of rooftops and a river not too far away, glittering in the early summer sun as it had for hundreds of years before. Trees lined its edges, filled with the light greens of young leaves, shuffling in the breeze.

The harsh texture of the hospital chair's fabric annoyed him. The way the room smelled annoyed him. The fly sitting peacefully outside the glass of the window annoyed him. Tension built. Not in the room. Only in him. Everything went through his mind at once as if it were impossible for them to be separated. Colors melted into sounds. The hum of the radiator, the salmon on the walls, the blip of the heart monitor, the black of Avery's hair. It felt as though he were a balloon waiting to pop. As if all it would take was a needle and his entire body would simply burst with blood, intestines, brains, and bone. He tried to breathe evenly but it was impossible. He tried to still his shaking but found that to be impossible too. He needed to scream. He needed to pick up this stupid fucking chair and smash it out that window and watch it crash down onto the sidewalk and splinter into a hundred thousand little pieces of wood and tufts of stuffing. It wouldn't be enough. It would never be enough.

"Trent?"

His eyes lifted to the plastic and fabric of the hospital bed. The wires and tubes. Avery, his partner. "I'm here, bud." He couldn't tell if he was shaking from unreleased tension or trembling in fear. The idea filled him with rage. Another cause for shaking. Avery sighed through his nose past those annoying little plastic things that gave him oxygen. "Bad shape" was what Bentley, their boss, had called it. "Bad shape" was, in Winston's opinion, a mild way to put it.

He'd been stabbed in the abdomen three times with what looked to be a switchblade. While bleeding he'd been tied to a chair and the bottoms of his feet had been cut cross-ways five times each to make it nearly impossible for him to run away if he did manage to escape. His blood had made a pool on the floor under him. He had burns on his neck and shoulders and down one arm from scalding water that had been poured onto him. Worst of it all... Winston took in a deep breath and then let it out when Avery put his hand out and he took it in his, squeezing gently. Worst of it all his cheeks had been mutilated. What Detective Wilson had termed a "Glasgow Smile." The corners of his mouth now reached the edge of his jaw.

The damage was extensive. Permanent scarring was unavoidable. His partner would be different for the rest of his life. Physically. Mentally.

"Trent," Avery said again. He had his eyes closed. His speech was slurred from muscle damage and pain. "Dunn. Don...t. Go. Alone." The warning was a simple one. It had been given to him many times in the past and most of those times he had listened. Waiting for Avery to come with him.

"I won't be going alone."

Avery opened his eyes and his brows knitted when he looked over. "Who?" There were only a few options on the table. Either take Rayne Wilson or the newb rookie Ned Carter. Wilson was too nosy and Carter would get himself killed. Winston couldn't have either of them. He wouldn't be going alone.

"Don't worry about it, Avery."

That was an impossibility. If there was one thing that Avery could do and could do well it was worry about whatever hare-brained scheme his partner was up to. This time was a little different. This time there was vengeance on the table. This time Winston had taken out all the stops. There would be no jail-time for this killer. There would be nothing for this killer but suffering. More suffering than he could possibly imagine.

TRENT WINSTON TITLES:

DOG DAYS OF WINTER

A DOG IN SHEEP'S CLOTHING

THREE DOG DAYS